WHERE DID YOU, COME FROM?

WHERE DID YOU, COME FROM?

DOUGLAS HARVEY

authorHOUSE®

AuthorHouse™ UK
1663 Liberty Drive
Bloomington, IN 47403 USA
www.authorhouse.co.uk
Phone: 0800.197.4150

Published by AuthorHouse   11/28/2014

ISBN: 978-1-4969-9787-6 (sc)
ISBN: 978-1-4969-9786-9 (hc)
ISBN: 978-1-4969-9788-3 (e)

Where did you, come from?

His ship, now having dropped her pilot, leaving Galveston, Texas, USA and heading for Coatzacoalcos, Mexico, building up to full sea speed, the captain being rather tired following a hectic five weeks handed the con over to the Chief Mate by saying, "You know Blackie, I hate long pilotages, there must be a quicker way of getting from Houston to Galveston, and then to sea."

Briefly interruptedly with, "Thanks Abner," as the captain was handed back the keys to the Bond Locker with "I hope that you helped yourself to a case of beer. Now when he isn't looking, get these 2 bottles into his bag, and chuck in whatever is in the gash bucket as well."

Both being performed simultaneously, but un-observed by the Chief Mate, or the pilot, thankfully, Americans not always in tune with other English speaking nation's sense of humour, despite the common language, well roughly common, if you ignore some or most of the spelling, and the arrogant superior slang.

"Is it this bag that you want taken down to the top of the pilot ladder, pilot?" asked Doug, the ship's captain.

"It is, and why can't any of you do as you are told?" With that superior arrogant air.

The bag launched from the bridge-wing, roughly finding its' right spot, much to the horror of the pilot.

"My crew, and myself, DO NOT DO AS YOU SEEM TO THINK DO, AS WE ARE TOLD, because YOU, do not command this ship, whereas I DO, and you are only here to give advice. Which we can or cannot ignore, should we consider it to be wrong, and the law regarding American pilots having authority over the master in The Panama Canal was changed a long time ago. Next time you come

1

to a ships' bridge, try having some respect for those you are going to, give advice, to."

"Second mate, escort this man to the pilot ladder, he is leaving. Good-bye pilot."

"Now hold on a minute……….."

"Do you want to go the same way as your bag?"

He left. The muttering inaudible behind steel doors.

"You have something to say Blackie?"

"I agree captain, but that was a rather obnoxious pilot, who I don't think liked just what you said to him, when we emergency anchored. And made even worse when he dictated, or shall I say bullied the second mate to take his bag down to the top of the pilot ladder, despite being told that he wasn't getting off for another 15 minutes, and he could have taken it down with him then. Did you think it wise, throwing his bag down the express way? From the bridge wing! There did seem to be an awful lot of breaking glass as it landed, and possibly a few radios that he has to explain away. Did you perchance add a few bottles of that rather cheap brandy that came on board in Corpus Christi?"

Proof then, from a few minutes earlier.

"Have you, captain, met this pilot before?"

The smug smile and a wink following. "Off course, only when his bag was let fly from the bridge wing, I actually missed the deck. But I was only Chief Mate then."

Concerned heads swung towards him, but no answer was forthcoming. (Until several weeks later.)

"Acht weel, he's away now. Right I'll have a quick shower, before I send the outbound telexes. You okay with the con Blackie?"

"Perfectly captain."

"Right keep winding her up and join me for a beer when you finish your watch," he said as he left the ship's bridge.

Closing his cabin door and stripping off on his way to his bedroom, was absolutely astonished to find a female sitting cross legged on his bunk, on his way to the shower.

"Hi Doug," she said, "but after you sailed from Corpus Christi, I knew that my love for you was more than I had for my husband, and couldn't bear not being with you."

"So you are now, a stowaway!" said in a rather shocked manner, leaving a pause, before, "come here you dope," as she jumped up and fell into his arms. "I hope you've brought your passport."

They both falling into a very loving and tight embrace. "Off course," whispered almost silently, as she nibbled his ear lobe, "and enough clothes, I hope you don't mind, but I've already unpacked." She then kissing him very passionately, with the odd stop for more air.

"Oh, an organised stowaway then, why not stowaway as most others do, in a lifeboat?"

"Because your bed is more comfortable, and I couldn't get the lifeboats door open."

Seemed reasonable, the logic would catch up later, hopefully. But at the same time, not being overly honest, she not overly sure how he would react to that to which she was with-holding from him.

Previously, some weeks before!

8 o'clock on a fine US, Texas morning, Christine sat at her desk, and opening the mail.

As she did every morning, she being the secretary to a firm of Shipping Agents, where life was pretty dull, but it paid for her and her husband any ways. She German, her husband, Australian, and trapped in an unhappy relationship. Where love, may not have been there from the start.

"Good morning Romero," as her fellow colleague walked in. He was the one who dealt with the ships captains, and all of the other requests demanded from the ships in port. He fell into a chair, legs extended and gasped, "any chance of a coffee Christine, I've been up all night."

"Yes off course," she said, as she got him his coffee, "what's up?"

"We got a call last night, after you left, we are appointed as agents for a gas tanker, the mv Norgas Challenger, and from our database she doesn't exist!"

"So where have you been all night?" asked Christine.

"On board the damn thing, mostly, even the Port Officials and pilots are as confused as to how she got here, never mind the US Coast Guard!"

"So how did she get here," asked Christine?

"Seemingly, she broke down at sea, after leaving Port Arthur, Louisiana and our partner agents were dealing with her, and has diverted here for repairs."

"So what's the problem?" asked Christine.

"You my friend have not as yet met the captain, but you will, as I made the mistake of asking him if he was English, he being British, only to be told that he was not. He was from Scotland. His accent did confuse me, as he did not sound as being from Scotland. His calm voice had a lovely lilt to it that I've never heard before, and was really quite distinct."

Christine asked "what is wrong with the ship, that they have come here?"

"They aren't sure yet, but they think that they may have bent the main engine crankshaft. And the new owners just bought the ship 7 days ago, and wait for it, $23 million."

Christine asked "is that serious?"

"Very," said Romero, "we might just have our work cut-out here, as they are already having trouble with communications to Oslo, but I gave them our satellite signal 'phone and explained how to use it. Now that I've cleared the ship in, and paid the $USD fine of $250 as the captain didn't give the USCG 24 hours' notice of arrival, which as he pointed out was a bit tricky to do, seeing as they were only 10 hours away and on passage to Mexico at the time. We agreed it was cheaper to pay the fine, than to argue. But Christine, I'm bushed, so have a good day, I'm going to bed. I think though that you might rather like this captain, there is something with that glint in his lovely blue eyes that tells me that you might just get on rather well. Oh! And by the way, he is the same age as you. 34. What is very unusual is that he has been captain in another company, and for the past 3 years, then to be transferred from one company into another company and still as captain, probably unique, but he certainly knows what he is doing."

Christine was intrigued, as she buried herself to the day, when her boss walked in.

"Richard, how are you?" He was having marital problems, and sometimes confided with his secretary, a sort of shoulder to cry on with her Religious Faith, knowing that she would be most discreet. As he plunked himself into his chair, and groaned, "why, did I, get, married?" a question to which he already knew the answer to.

"Christine!" Came, a loud shout from next door, "we've got a gas tanker coming in, have you told Romero?"

Christine grimaced, why did he have to shout? "Richard, we are already on to it. Romero spent most of last night handling it and the ship is now nicely berthed at Cargo Dock 12, and might just be there for quite a long time. Would you like an Aspirin?" She needn't have bothered, as the reply was not polite.

A few hours later, Christine looked up from her desk, as this stranger walked in, sweat pouring from just about everywhere and asked "is this Been & Company, shipping agents?"

"Yes" she replied, "who are you?"

"I'm the captain of the Norgas Challenger."

At once he spotted this delightful fair haired blonde, with gorgeous green eyes, including the twinkle that did suggest, fun. He couldn't take his eyes off her, and she responded in the same way, the eye contact never breaking. He thought about 5 foot 4, and very trim. What a beautiful woman Doug thought.

"Why are you so hot? And how did you get here?" as she passed him a bottle of water.

Richard also came from his office, and introduced himself. "Gee captain, you look as you are about to melt."

"This, as he held up their satellite signal 'phone is about as much use as 10 men missing," he said. "But nowhere close to my company in Oslo. And why I am sweating, because I walked here!"

Richard exclaimed "but that is 4 miles!"

"Yes I know, I couldn't even get a taxi on that useless 'phoney thing, and so far, me and my officers have spoken with a hotel in Hong Kong, a French restaurant in Spain, even London Zoo! Getting directions from the odd pedestrians I came across is nigh on impossible. So far, showing Romero's business card for directions has led me to 3 Baptist Churches, a petrol station, which doesn't sell petrol, but this dumb thing called gas, to which my gas tanker could load masses of it, but can't, and when I did get directions, damn near got me killed. Do Americans, who drive on the wrong side of the road not understand, that when a traffic light is red, that means STOP until it goes green? And why are they called sidewalks? When hardly anyone ever walks on them?"

"Captain, if there is nothing coming, then it is okay to turn right on a red."

"Now what can I do for you?" asked Richard.

"First off, I need to hire a car, then I need 2 'phone lines run into my ship, as that little 'phone box at the bottom of the gangway is already full and we've run out of these funny little coins, who the pilot told me were dimes. Then I need to go to The US Coast Guard, and get a few permits."

Christine looked up, eyebrows raised, as nobody had ever spoken to Richard like that before.

"Captain, you need to slow down, how about joining me for lunch?"

"Nope, haven't got time. My ship is losing $23,000 a day, and lunch can wait for another day. Now where is the nearest car rental place?"

"You can't get 2 'phone lines run in, that could take a month," explained Richard.

Christine again looked up as she suspected what was coming.

"If I don't get 2 'phone lines run in by this time tomorrow, then I will take a hacksaw and remove that little 'phone box, with its wiring, splice in our own wires and move it to the ships office. Now stop telling me what you can't do, and start getting on with what you can. We'll start with the car hire company, so I can get wheels."

"But I can't leave the office."

Is this man about as slow as American traffic? The captain mused.

"Your secretary can, so I'll take her."

Christine jumped up from her desk. "No problem guys, Thrifty car rental are just up the road."

"You know captain," she said as they headed out, "he'll take ages to settle down. Do you always move at that speed?"

"I haven't even started yet. We are about to get a whole lot faster. So why are we waiting for a lift, sorry elevator, when we are only 1 floor up? Couldn't we use the stairs?" The lift arrived so they got in. And ended up, going up. 5 minutes later, they got out on the ground floor, after deciphering that the ground floor was actually the 1st floor.

"Okay captain, this way," as they walked out into the baking sun, my car is over here. She opened the door, started the engine and put the air-conditioning on full blast. "It'll only take a minute," she said, as they sweltered in the heat. "Right, let's go" as they strapped themselves in. "Christine, let's drop the captain bit, my name is Doug."

"Here we are Doug, Thrifty car rental." He looked a bit mystified. "Christine, all up it has taken us 10 minutes to go from your office to here, and we have covered a total distance of 200 metres. We could have walked here faster."

"Yes, I know, but 10 minutes in your company is better than sitting behind a desk, and I want to see your ship."

"Well in that case, after I have rented a car, you can show me the way back to my ship, I'll follow as my Superintendent is flying in tonight, and I have to pick him up at the airport, and any chance of a map?"

"The car rental people will give you one."

Sometime later, with the hired car being explained to the captain, most of which was lost on him, they set off, at a snail's pace which seems to be the speed that Americans drive at, and got back to where his ship was berthed.

"Well there she is Christine, 6500 tonnes of Norwegian Gas Tanker, only 5 years old, neglected, and I've got the job of putting her all back together, which is why I need 2 'phone lines run in, so when you get back to your office, lean on Richard, as we are going to be on the 'phone an awful lot, and I don't move at his speed. Drop by anytime, you will always be welcome. It's a sort of Scots Tradition. Oh wait please, I need to get the ship's certification, then you can take me to the US Coast Guard. The hire car can wait here, until I figure out the Corpus Christi traffic sign system."

"Why?" Christine asked.

"Because Interstate Highway 37 directs you North to South, when the road actually goes East to West."

"Now wait for me, I'll be back."

Christine looked up as he ran the steps, and thought, he is just my kind of man, decisive, thoughtful, efficient, but at the same time, caring. She had never experienced that before. Not even from her own husband, who she thought, didn't really love her. And she had only known this Scot, for less than an hour.

Gosh, she thought, that didn't take long as he came clattering back down, arms full of files.

"I've left the car keys with the Chief Engineer and the map, so he and the crew can play with it, and find out how to get around town, now take us to the US Coast Guard office."

"Who's us Doug?" asked Christine.

"Oh, you're coming into the US Coast Guard office with me, as their rules are so complex that even they don't understand them. So we'll need to use the Triple B system, and you making a reservation, is just what I need for a diversion. My superintendent is arriving tonight as I have already said, so on that bloody useless 'phone, book him into The Best Western hotel for 28 days, plus a further 14 days, if we need it. That's the one we passed just along from the ship a bit."

"Eh, Doug?" why do we need a diversion, and just exactly what is the Triple B system?

"Just drive, I'll explain later."

Christine drove with a bit of apprehension, but also incredible wonder, as nobody has ever taken on the US Coast Guard before, at least in this somewhat aggressive way.

"Doug, have you already had a run-in with the USCG before?" as they crossed Corpus Christi Harbour Bridge, akin to The Sydney Harbour Bridge in Australia, on their way.

"Yes. In Houston, they just haven't puzzled it out yet how it was done and most probably never will."

"Without going into this, what did you do?" her anxiety slightly increasing.

"I was on a gas tanker, as chief officer and the gas analyser didn't work on automatic, nobody could get it to work. It is an important thing that has to work. Even the company that made it couldn't get it to work. And The US Coast Guard were hot on this, and were amazed when we got into Houston with it working. Even my captain was amazed. But we cleared in and the US Coast Guard remarked that this was the first time they had seen one working. They even took photos of it on automatic."

"This Christine is strictly confidential between you and me, it goes no further, and I hope that I can trust you on this. If the USCG were ever to find out what I did, then I will not get the certificates that I need, that we are going together to get."

"Will you tell me later?"

"Off course, if you will let me to take you to lunch."

Intrigue, prompted the reply, "you get the certificates, and we'll have lunch together."

Now in the USCG offices, and Christine with a degree of trepidation, having now replaced anxiety, as she was rather out of her depth.

"Good afternoon, I am the captain of the mv Norgas Challenger, currently alongside Cargo Dock 12, and I have a problem. This is Christine, from my agents, and I need certificates which will allow me to discharge my main engine bilges to a shore receiving unit, plus certification to use my cranes in port."

Christine stood back amazed, he's only 34 and how does he know about this? This law only came in a month ago.

"When I receive them, Christine will get them laminated, and we'll attach them to the crane base at the top of the accommodation ladder, and we can get on with the repairs to my ship. How long will it take, as I have a lot of work still to do, so we can get started? Here is my ships documentation."

Lieutenant Commander Doug Cameron, an American, stood back amazed. "Are you from Scotland Sir?"

"Isn't that obvious?"

"Give me 10 minutes sir, and I'll see what I can do."

Christine stood back in further awe. "Doug, you can't talk to the USCG like that."

"Watch me." Ten minutes passed

"Okay captain, here are your documents, if you will just sign here, and here, and thank-you sir."

"Anytime you are passing Lt. Commander (USCG), pop on board, and join us for dinner," said the captain.

Christine looked up, as they left, "how the hell did you do that?" whispered as an aside.

"Because he and I know, something that you don't, and something that The USCG & Det Norske Veritas don't want anyone else to know. Now let's get back to my ship, because tomorrow, you are all going to be very busy."

"I trust you 'phoned the hotel Christine." A slight nod indicated so.

"Doug, I am curious," as they drove back, "just what did you do when you were in Houston on that other gas tanker?"

"Only if you promise not to tell another living soul?"

"Okay, I promise." Said Christine, the curiosity now really rankling her.

"Put less pressure on the accelerator pedal, we're now doing 65 in a 55 mph zone."

Gosh, he doesn't miss much, as Christine realised her mistake.

"We took the back off the gas analyser, and put the 3rd officer inside it, he was the smallest on board, with a bit of wire and a stopwatch, and a list of where to short out various circuits to make it look like it was operating automatically, then screwed the back, back on, with him still inside it."

"And you got away with it?" asked Christine incredulously.

"You, Christine just have no idea, just how many things we can do, to pull the wool over other people's eyes."

"And the Triple B System?" she asked.

"Bullshit Baffles Brains."

Christine smiled inwardly, not yet realising that she was starting to fall in love. I like this man. I wonder what will happen tomorrow.

Next day.

"Good morning Christine," as she walked into her office, not expecting to meet the captain at 8 o'clock in the morning.

"Doug, how did you get in?"

"I came up the stairs, the elevator didn't work, and your door wasn't locked, and seeing as your company share your office with a bank, thought it a bit unusual, that the doorman had no sense of security, until he explained that this bank has no money in it. So what is the point of having a bank with no money in it? Don't bother to answer, as Texas logic is nothing like British logic."

"When did you get up Doug?" asked Christine, as she moved past and round to her desk.

"I didn't get up," he replied, "I haven't been to bed yet. As you know, my superintendent flew in last night and my Chief Engineer and I drove to the airport to meet him. That was the easy bit, getting him to his hotel was the tricky bit. We got lost, several times, and then ran out of petrol, but the Corpus Christi Police helped us, and after finding a 'gas station' refilled the petrol tank, sorry, gas tank, and then showed us how to find his hotel. Then I, after decanting Einar, my superintendent, and my chief engineer, went to park the car, whereupon, I promptly fell asleep."

"So why is your neck at a funny angle?" asked Christine.

"Have you ever tried to sleep in an American car, where the steering wheel is on the wrong side? Okay, for you being German, it is the correct side, but not for me."

"But enough, the first thing is to get my engine room bilges discharged to shore, now that I have the required permit. Is there a company that can receive it?" asked Doug.

"Yes, I think so, but Richard isn't here yet. He'll need to clear it first."

Suddenly! "Good morning all," as Richard walked in, "captain, what are you doing here?"

"Does that require an answer Richard?" asked the captain, "I'm trying to get Texans up to speed and it is proving somewhat tricky."

"Captain, I spoke with AT &T yesterday, and they are going to run in 2 'phone lines into your ship this morning, probably as we speak."

"Good, thank-you Richard, now I need a reliable ship chandler, who can deliver what my ship needs, like yesterday, and I mean it."

The reply taking just a little of time to sink in, followed by.

"Now for today, I need a 50 ton crane, with an extendable arm. By midday if you can manage it."

"What do you need that for?" asked Richard, who had as yet not even found his chair in his own office, far less his brain cells.

"Because, we can use the time until the engineers find out what is wrong with the main engine, to put on the spare anchor replacing the bent one, on the port side. Might also need rather a lot of acetylene too! The spare hasn't moved for 5 years.

11

Oh, and later this afternoon, I'll need Christine's help, as we need a lot of stationery, and a table."

"What do you need a table for?" asked Richard.

"Because we are also having an Inmarsat A system installed, and we need a table to put it on. Now is there a local company that can make the mast, for the Radome?"

"Yes, we can call in Coastal Iron. Do you want me to send them down to you?" asked Richard?

"And like yesterday Richard?"

"We're onto it, give them a call Christine," he said as the captain left the office.

Christine quietly mused to herself, this is going to be one heck of an interesting day. Like how is he going to get a desk, from an office supplier, back to his ship, in a hire car? It won't fit. This she had to see.

"What do you make of him Christine?" asked Richard.

"Different, oh so different, and after upsetting the port authorities, like a breath of fresh air, and I have a feeling that he is going to upset them even more."

"I agree," said Richard, "we need to back him 100%."

It didn't take long before the 'phone rang.

"Is that Becn & Co? Captain of the Norgas Challenger here, is that you Christine?"

"Yes it is, where are you 'phoning from?" as if she didn't know.

"Got 2 'phone lines run in, here are the numbers, and bang off a fax to Norway confirming them. Now after 30 hours on my feet, I'm going to sleep on a beach, as that is the only place where I can get some peace."

"I thought that you needed some stationary and a table?" asked Christine.

"Damn, forgot about that. Okay. The Chief Engineer will drive, and my superintendent will be coming too, see you in about 10 minutes, and bring a receipt note."

Arriving at the stationery store, the 3 did not take long to select what they had come for, but now had a small discussion as to a table.

"What exactly goes onto this table?" asked Christine.

Doug replied, "The screen unit and the receiver, both about 60 centimetres wide. No real weight as such, but because ships bounce about a bit, we need to bolt them down and secure the table to the bulkhead, or in as I am now fast learning in American, a wall. I'd like to meet the joker who taught Americans, English, as none of it makes much sense. Even to me, and I'm Scottish."

"How about this one?" asked Christine?

Einar and Mike, the Chief Engineer were having a little quiet word together, both with faint smiles on their faces. One said to the other "we didn't bring any tools with us, not even a screwdriver, so how are we going to get that table into the car."

The answer coming almost immediately and apparently stupid to boot, although rhetorical might just explain it.

"Right, let's go, Einar you help Christine chuck the loose stuff in the boot, sorry, trunk. Mike, give me a hand with the table," from their shipmaster.

"Now stop," said all three in unison, "where is the table going to go?"

"Oh yea of little faith," said Doug, "on the roof-rack off course, but upside down."

"But we haven't got a roof rack!" said all three in unison.

"That's because we haven't made it yet. Einar you drive, Mike, open the sunroof, and Christine, you can hold my legs and sit in the back, sorry, rear."

Christine stood amazed as the captain climbed onto the cars roof, dropped his legs through the open sunroof, laid back and said. "Now hand me up the table, and upside down mind!"

To which Mike and Einar did. "Now don't drive too fast as we don't want to draw attention to ourselves."

"THAT! Is, going to be very difficult," said Mike as he got in.

"And no low bridges!" hailed from above.

After about a mile, the blue's and two's came on from a police car behind, to which Einar pulled over.

The policeman got out, and said, "oh no, not you lot again. You're not lost again are you? And where is your driver from last night?"

"Em, look up," was the reply.

"Good afternoon sir, I'm not lost, unless these down below me are, and if you don't mind, my neck is getting its 2nd crick today, and

I'd rather like to get this table back to my ship, as I've got an awful lot to do yet."

"I'll give you an escort, as long as any of my fellow officers can drop by for a beer, and have a look around your ship, as I have the strangest feeling, that we are going to meet up again. This is one tale that I can't wait to tell my pals about."

"Deal done, anytime." said Doug, to the departing policeman.

"So much for not drawing attention to ourselves, both of you!" hailed from above. "Now pay attention, as we might find our way through these mazes of streets, the police way. Christine, when you get back to your office, we need a high pressure washer and a lance. Tip pressure of at least 250 bar, and a portable generator to match, our ship is 220 volts, 60 Hz, and America is 110 volts, 50 Hz, and tonight."

"Anything else?" coming from the leg holder below.

"Yep, I have to send a daily report on the main engine repair to my managers in Oslo, for forwarding to the new owners, and it will go out by fax sometime after 6pm each night. I need someone to come down to the ship, collect the report, and fax it off, so they have it in the morning, they are 5 hours ahead of us, and seven days a week."

Christine thought, I'll do that, and then I can spend some quality time with Doug, my husband doesn't treat me like a lady, but this considerate man does.

"Anything else?" she asked.

"Yes, take my left foot trainer off, my leg is starting to go numb!"

Arriving back at the ship, "you did that deliberately, Einar, you swerved into every pothole you could find, now get this bloody table off me!"

"It was your idea in the first place, so stop griping," as 2 engineers laughingly walked away and up the gangway.

Revenge would be sweet.

"Okay Christine, let's get you back to your office."

"Doug, it has been a great day, and it is Saturday tomorrow, my husband is in Houston, and I'd really like to see all of your ship, not just the bridge bit, but the rest, the bits that you don't normally show to such as Agents secretaries as me."

"Okay," he said, "but I warn you, you are going to get very hot, and very dirty. Bring an old pair of trainers, sorry sneakers; I'll attend to the rest. And you will get, very hot."

Christine couldn't wait, as he dropped her off at her office, she with a little skip in her jaunt, not felt for years and an inward smile that only she could see and feel. Developing love perhaps?

Saturday.

"Good morning Mike, What have you done with your ship," as Christine walked into the ships offices.

"What do you mean?" as he turned from his desk.

"Well last night, one end looked like the other, sort of flat, but now the front bit is higher than the back bit." The nautical terminology would come later, hopefully.

"That Christine, is called trim, sorry in, American, drag, and early this morning, the captain started moving ballast around, to lift the bow out of the water, which at the same time, moved all of the engine room bilges back also, as we high pressurised washed the bilges under the main engine. Off which, we have and are now doing. We need clean bilges as when we take the main engine apart, anything that drains there, can be accounted for. Which our captain foresaw, with the USCG, and that we already have the necessary permits."

"So where is he?" asked Christine of the Chief Engineer? "He doesn't look like he is in his office."

"Christine, go up to the masters cabin, and you'll find in his dayroom a boiler suit, safety helmet, working gloves, then get into them, and minimum underwear underneath, because, where you are going is rather hot. He's changing the bearings and seals on the emergency fire pump, which over the life of this ship, has only been run for 8 minutes in 5 years. And that is why the bow is out of the water, as that is where we keep it. He does have amazing foresight."

"Is the door locked?"

"No, he has a code. If his cabin door is open, then anyone can go and see him. When it is closed, he is either asleep, or wants some peace and quiet. For you this morning, it is closed, but not locked. You know where it is, don't you?"

15

"Yes, 3 decks up and opposite yours. I passed it the other day on my way to the bridge. Mike, are captains also engineers?" she ventured.

"No. But this one is, and expect to get involved this morning, as where you are going is rather cramped."

Christine smiled inwardly to herself, as she set off to climb all of these stairs, not only would she see her new friends private cabin, but could work alongside him as well. How unexpected. Christine opened the door gently and slipped through, closing the door quietly behind her. What she saw rather surprised her. A neat and rather luxurious room with a suite around a coffee table, to one side, a desk, bookshelves and a refrigerator, or in American parlance, a cooler! As she looked around, there was a little note on the 'fridge. 'Help your-self Christine.'

How thoughtful she thought, as she moved from his dayroom into his bedroom, and restroom. (This in British parlance is shower and toilet, or bog, depending on which part of the country one is associated from.)

Christine locked the door, stripped off and climbed into her sweetly smelling new boiler suit, zipped up, and with her working gloves and safety helmet in hand, moved rather reluctantly from his private space, reluctant, as there was a smell here that she was not familiar with, but enticing, his after shave perhaps?

"Okay Mike," said Christine, as she got back to the ship's offices, "where is Doug?"

"Well, ordinarily, we would show you, but everyone is really busy just now, as we are going to have to cut a hole in the hull, and everyone not free are dismantling the other equipment that's in the way. Go out from here, walk up the 'flying bridge' that's the walkway above the deck in the middle, and you'll find an open door. Go in, go down the steps and go to the starboard corner, and give him a shout from the hole in the corner. When you get a shout back, then go down the ladder, but take your time, it's a long way down. And remember, there is not a lot of room at the bottom. Now fill up your pockets with water bottles, and keep drinking it, as you are going to sweat like you have never sweated before."

"Okay, thanks Mike," as she set off. This getting more exciting by the second, and saying to herself, I've never done anything like this before as her heart pounded. She wondered just how much room there was down there, would she feel him close to her?

"Hello down there!" after finding the right corner, and now realising why she was going to get very dirty, and hadn't even started to descend into the bowels of what looked like a place that foreboding. But her new friend was down there, and she wanted to get close, come what may.

"That you Christine, Come on down, but take your time, especially near the bottom," the voice echoing around her.

With her heart pounding even more, she rather timidly took to the ladder, and started on down. After leaving the clear area of the fo'c'sle, claustrophobia set in, but she fought it, stealing to herself with the thought that safety was at the bottom in her new friend.

"Only a few more rungs Christine," as she neared the bottom, only lit by a few torches.

Made it, as her feet landed on what felt like steel. Now she knew what Mike had told her that it was a bit cramped.

"Good morning Christine, I see that you've already started on the getting dirty bit. Well not to worry, you'll soon end up like me."

"But where are you?" she asked, "underneath you, in the bilge!" came the reply.

Christine marvelled in the torch light, as her eyes adjusted to the darkness, he looks like a reversed panda.

"Good morning Doug, is this what you call going out on a date?"

"Champagne Christine?" he replied, offering her a paper cup, before wrestling the top off the bottle with a controlled sigh, "can't pop it as usual, down here there's no telling where the cork could go or who could get hurt." He smiled as their cups met in a toast, "welcome to the life of a ship's captain. Now shall we finish the bottle first, or finish fixing this pump and drink the rest as we do it?"

"You are the most incredible man that I have ever met, is there room for 2 down there?" hopefully hoping that he would say yes.

"Only if you don't bring the bottle with you, but I warn you, it's mighty dirty down here, and we'll leave the cups topped up within reach."

After a bit of clambering down into the abyss, their bodies touched, warmly from within their clothing, albeit now very wet clothing, but their heads were now side by side.

"I must be mad Doug, when I wanted to see your ship; this is NOT quite what I had in mind! So what are you doing?"

"I'm changing the bearings and seals, which I have just finished doing, so you can help me by putting the end covers back on. Here are the nuts and bolts, and here are the spanners. I'll just re-connect the motor while you do so, their bodies moving gently against each other. Christine thought that in her un-happy marriage, she had never experienced anything as sensitive as this before, and didn't now, want it to end.

"Right," he said, "all done, now let's get out of this hole. I didn't think that you could get anything dirtier than The Black Hole of Calcutta, but I was wrong. Christine, do you have a bottle of water with you, I've used mine up."

To which he poured some of the offered bottle onto a cloth and gently wiped clean her face. "Not a good idea to wipe the sweat off your forehead with the back of a dirty arm."

Christine felt a tremor passing through her tummy and with a glint of a smile at the same time, as she climbed out and back to the plate above, breathing somewhat heavily, he following, also breathing as heavily, it being hard to decipher, just who was sweating most.

"Might just as well finish these Champers, less weight to carry out," as they snuggled up close to each other. He with his arm around her shoulders in this confined dirty space. Not exactly what Christine had in mind, a bit less comfortable than his cabin, but there was a chemistry building between them.

"Right, we've run out of champagne, so it is now time to go topside. You go up the ladder first, and when you get topside, shout down and I'll follow with this bucket of tools."

A few minutes later he arrived and into the fo'c'sle, sweat not obviously showing, he being so dirty, that was hard to comprehend.

"Right, we'll re-trim the ship, and when the bow is back in the water, we'll test the pump. Let's go aft hopefully Mike will have a cold beer ready. Coming? as this isn't over yet."

"What do you mean Doug?"

"You'll see. Now we are going to clean the bit we've just been into. And the mess we are dragging behind us on the deck."

Christine looked forlorn, as they wandered aft towards the ships office. A tapping on the window, and a hoi! Come out here sign, brought the Chief Engineer out on deck.

"Mike, do we still have the high pressure washer, and the suction tanker?"

"Got the high pressure washer, but the suction tanker was full. Why?

"Need to clean the emergency fire pump space, it's full of, well let's say, things that aren't supposed to be there."

"Most of which, is on you and Christine," said with a somewhat smug grin.

"Mike, get the crew to move the high pressure washer up to the bow, dockside, and run the lance inside. The mate can re-trim the ship, which will take about 2 hours, during which Christine and I will get cleaned up. Then after the crew high pressures wash the whole thing from top to bottom, we'll pump out the residue into the dock.

"What about the pollution?" said Mike, somewhat concerned?

"We'll take the water supply from the dock, and then we'll neutralise whatever comes out of the discharge side, with the best oil dispersant known to man, which I need to go and buy, after I get cleaned up, as we haven't got enough on board."

"What's that?" asked Mike.

"Dhobi dust!"

Christine's curiosity in the heat made her ask, "What's Dhobi dust?"

"You'll see," was the only response she got. "Now we'll go up the outside way, and take these boiler suits off, before we go inside. You can use my cabin and I'll use the spare cabin."

The look on Christine's face already asked the question.

"Don't worry, I'll go in first, and I won't look, nor will anyone else see you in your underwear, as they are all still in the engine room."

A relieved Christine smiled back, falling just a wee bit more in love, just wondering what was going to happen next. But one thing was certain; it was going to be unusual.

An hour later.

"Had a nice shower, and cooled down a bit Christine, after getting all of the grime off," as he arrived back into his own cabin, with a towel wrapped around him. She also wrapped in the same way, and to their mutual embarrassment, had to concede, that going into the shower, neither had given any thought as to what they would wear, when they came out, and dried off.

"Doug, my underwear, was absolutely soaked in sweat, I tried to wash it in the shower, and all that I have managed is to get it clean but still wet, and I can't think of any way to dry it, as climbing into wet underwear is not very comfortable. What do I do?" she said a little distressed.

"Use mine and you still have your top clothes, which should cover you as your bra dries out, bottom drawer in the bedroom for, knickers. Oh, they may be a little on the big side, but I'm sure we can find some safety pins, to, sort of, contract the waist a bit, anyway it is only going to be an hour or so, till we can get you new one's"

She gave him that look that said, 'you are not serious.'

"If you and I are going to get along, then you'll need a sense of humour, as I was only joking, give me your bra and knickers, and I'll bung them into the tumble drier, back in about 10 minutes", as he left with his own top clothes also, and "help yourself from the fridge, I'll get dressed in the laundry."

Christine felt at peace as the door closed, but her heart thought otherwise, as she slid into one his cabin chairs, not completely relaxed, but pretty close to it, just that lingering doubt as to what might come next.

'I wonder just what is in that fridge', she mused and opened the door.

Strange, no beer, just soft drinks to which she took one. There was something strange here, as her Australian husband didn't seem able to survive without beer.

Christine relaxed within her towel, as she felt somewhat elevated, almost as if she was drifting in to a place she had never been to before, but this private thought was not to last as there came a knock on the door, which changed into alarm, 'Who knows that I am here, wrapped only in a towel?'

But not to worry, as the captain's head, ventured in. "Are you decent Christine?"

"I don't very often have to knock on my own door you know!"

"Right Christine, here is your underwear, all nice and dry, and there is some talc in my restroom cabinet if you want," as Doug arrived back. "Get dressed in my bedroom, as we need to get a move on."

Christine closed the bedroom door gently behind her, and then found that her bra didn't fit, or at least as it did this morning. Nor did her knickers, both seemed to have shrunk.

"Doug" emanated from this voice from the bedroom, "my underwear has shrunk what did you do to it?"

"Well you needed it back in a hurry, so I wound the heat up in the tumble drier to 14 kilowatts, how badly has it shrunk?"

"Let's just say that, you are very lucky that you are a complete wall away from me, so I'll borrow a few of your shirts for now."

"Christine, walls on ships are called, bulkheads."

Christine emerged from his bedroom, not exactly dressed in the way that she had gone in, and before she set off for work that morning.

"Well, I think you look great," stifling a smile to his best efforts, which was not in the least convincing, as the look of daggers said otherwise.

"Now we need to go and buy some Dhobi Dust, so I'll drive as I've..."

"Oh no you won't", said Christine, "I'll drive as you are still full of Champagne from that hole we were in this morning. Now where are we going?"

"Nearest supermarket, or whatever Americans call them, preferably with one that sells ladies underwear."

Another daggers look suggested that this comment was probably not wise.

"Right Christine, here's $50, you get yourself some underwear, I'll get the Dhobi Dust, and a bottle of Champagne."

"What do we need another bottle of Champagne for?" a little exasperatedly, said Christine.

"Because the one we had this morning, wasn't. It was just a bottle of bubbly that I got from a ship chandler in Port Arthur, non-alcoholic!"

Christine looked perplexed.

"Well you didn't think that I'd take a bottle of REAL Champagne down there did you? We'll drink this one after the crew clean out the hole, only this time from the dock."

"No! You and I are going together, and never be apart, because I do not know what else you have up your sleeve," she said, somewhat huffily.

"Okay, lead on McDuff!" he mused, a challenge he was always up for. Losing her for 15 to 20 minutes, just the start.

Later.

"Feel better Christine?" It, being only 20 minutes to select a bra and a pair of knickers to which she replied suspiciously, "yes, and what have you being doing in the meantime?"

"Oh the usual things when I get bored in a supermarket. I've wound up all of the alarm clocks, and set them all to go off in about 45 minutes, and put them back in their boxes ready to ring, done the same with the egg timers, they'll go off in about 15 minutes, and whenever anyone with a trolley wasn't looking, just added a few more things into their trolley."

"Such as?" asked Christine.

"Well, Americans are not the most vigilant of people, they just at the check-out, pass everything through, bag it up, and take it home, only when they get home do they realise, that they have bought something that they do not need, or even want."

"Such as?" asked Christine with an air of suspicion.

"Well........if you have a cat, what do you need dog food for? And if you have a dog, what do you need cat food for? And if you haven't got either, then they get both."

"I think we'll get this Dhobi Dust, and the Champagne, and get out of here as fast as we can," said Christine, "Doug, what else have you done?"

He just smiled, but that glint said otherwise.

At the check-out, Christine explained to the check-out girl, "A bottle of Champagne, and 2 big boxes of automatic washing machine powder, a huge tub of butter, and 2 cases of chilled beer?"

"Christine, let me just pay for it, and then let's get out of here, before these alarm clocks go off."

"Done" she said, as they left together, heading to the car.

On the way back to the ship, Christine ventured, "Just exactly what is Dhobi Dust?"

"Christine, if you go back to the time, when there was the Raj system in India, then the man who did the washing of clothes, was known as the 'Dhobi Wallah', the word derives from the Hindi, of, 'he who does the washing.'

Unfortunately, this term was picked up by merchant seamen, and expanded. Years ago when I came to sea, it was not uncommon for British ships, to carry British Officers and Indian Crew, and in mutual respect for each other, one of the apprentices jobs was to learn to communicate in Hindi.

And in one unfortunate way, Hindi, and seamen's parlance took over, so 'Dhobi-ing' was doing your washing, the washing machine was known as the 'Dhobi-engine', and the washing powder was known as 'Dhobi dust.

And it is the best oil dispersant known to man, especially when mixed with butter and beer!"

Just then they arrived back alongside the ship.

"Mike is the high pressure washer ready to go, up front?" asked the master getting out of the car.

"It is, but the crew aren't too pleased."

"Why?"

"It's a Filipino thing, they think that they are going to get the blame, for this, and all want to leave the ship, so they don't lose face."

"Where are they Mike?"

"In the dayroom."

"Right Mike, get me a case of beer, we'll sort this out right now."

"Okeydokey, you lot, now what's the problem," as the captain entered the dayroom. I've seen the note on my desk, that you all want to go home, even although you are contracted for another 5 months.

"Why?"

To which, there was no response.

"There is no point staying silent here, as if I don't get an answer, then you will all be going home, minus your certification."

That shook them up.

"Sir," ventured the 2nd Engineer, you have only been with us for 2 weeks, and you have found so much wrong that we are going to get the blame for, as we should have done much better in the past."

"Who is blaming you for anything?" asked the captain.

"But sir, we feel that with you fixing the emergency fire pump, and getting so dirty doing so, along with your new girlfriend, that we should have done all of this before, and but sir, we all feel responsible for the mess that this ship is now in, and want to go home."

The captain smiled, "Nobody is blaming anyone about anything. This gas tanker was previously owned by a company who ran container ships, and knew precious little about gas tankers, which are not the easiest of ships to operate. The only difference between you and I are, is that I do know how to run a gas tanker. Now put your fears behind you, sort out your fears, have a beer, and then let's get wet together."

"Do you think that will work Doug?" asked the Chief Engineer.

"It better had, as I'm running out of ideas, especially as our Chief Officer, caused the 3rd mate to lose face yesterday, and that German Chief Officer is on a very fine line, as it is easier to replace him, than the whole crew."

"Eh, captain," came the voice of the crew representative, "Where do we start," as he slinked into the ship's office.

"Where we start is to where we all were 2 weeks ago. I am the captain. And we all operate together. Any grievance from anyone, and they come and see me first. And make sure everyone understands this. There are 5 different nationalities on board this ship, and we all have to work together, and there will be no more crew meetings. Are we clear?"

"Yes captain. So where do we start?"

"Until we find out exactly what is wrong with the main engine, we might just as well, get this ship cleaned up, so get the boys into swimming trunks, as they are all going to get very wet, because on the way to the emergency fire pump space, we might as well clean out the fo'c'sle space at the same time. Chief mate, put on a 3 degree starboard list. I've already set up the eductor in the emergency fire pump space to pump the bilges overboard, and Christine & I will deal with discharged contents."

It only took a few minutes, for the crew to be seen scurrying forwards, all eager to help, as this was a captain, not to cross.

Christine, watched all of this in amazement, she had never seen people more motivated in Texas, far less Germany, than this Scot could do.

"Okay, Christine bring the Dhobi dust, the beer and the butter up to the edge of the dock, and take a seat. It will take a few minutes before anything comes out of that hole, just above the waterline, before we throw, effectively, snow balls, or Dhobi dust balls at it."

"Is this a wind up?" she asked.

"No, came the reply, you smother your hands in butter, dip them into the beer, and then take a handful of Dhobi dust and form it into a ball. See, like this" as he demonstrated.

"Better move fast, as the eductor is now discharging. See any oil, and throw a Dhobi ball at it Christine, and make another one, you never know what comes out next."

"Doug, just what is an eductor?" asked Christine.

"Think of it as a pump with no moving parts, I'll explain in more detail later."

A few minutes passed.

"I don't believe this! It works," she exclaimed. "Where did you find out about this?"

"On another gas tanker, when the engineers spilt rather a lot of heavy oil, in off all places, Norway. We spent the entire night painting one side of the ship covering it up, while the oil drifted away and this Greek bulk carrier got the blame for as the spilt stuff got stuck to its hull."

Over the next hour, they playfully threw more balls at the discharge outlet, and there was not the merest hint of pollution.

"Hey captain, we've finished" came the voice from above.

Reluctantly, they ended their fun, before Doug told her.

"Christine, to avoid the crew losing face, we need to go and inspect their work, and you have to do it with me."

The smile said it all. She was going to get wet, very wet, again.

"Nice move captain," from the crew representative, he being the bosun, "you certainly have the crews respect now sir. Oh, and sorry as the switch, for the lights, well sir, when we went in, the guy with the lance slipped a bit, and that is why there is no switch left, or at least the plastic bit that makes the actual switch turn. But we, sort of made it work, with an adjustable spanner, or as Americans call them, a monkey wrench."

"Just tell me or any of my officers the truth every time, no matter what you break, and don't cover anything up as I will find out eventually, and if I am told at the time, will most probably laugh, and then we will sort it out together. Okay? But if I have to find out later, will get me angry, and you don't want to see me angry."

The bosun replied, "I've never sailed with a Scottish captain before, but I think we are all going to get along pretty well. Eh, sir, what do you require the crew to do next?"

"You'll find a very cold case of beer in the chill room. Knock off for today, as on this ship, you never know just what is going to happen next. But don't head off ashore just yet."

Eight Filipino's, and One Indian AB departed, but not until, Mullah, the Indian AB said, "But I don't drink beer, could I have it in Rupees instead?"

The daggers look from the captain was conveyed to the bosun, who grabbed him, and despite protests from Mullah, was told in no uncertain terms, that he and they would get more out of this captain, if he just kept his mouth shut.

"Is this the same place we were in earlier?" as she arrived on the bottom plates, it now being completely clean. It looked totally different, as it was now lit.

"We've now got to get the rest of the ship the same way, and we are going to need your help, as there is a massive amount of help that we are going to need, so expect the 'phone to be ringing rather a lot in your office.

"Now let's get a shower, before we open that Champagne, and relax properly, before you go home."

"I can't, my underwear is soaking wet."

"Eh, not quite, because when I said I had to go to the restroom, that was just a diversion, and when you were away from your trolley in the supermarket, I slipped another spare set in, same style, for you, a new dry set."

After changing, Christine arrived back in the ship's office, to be met with, Blackie, the Chief Officer, who said, "Captain, we have a problem, a big one."

"Which is?" asked the captain.

"The gas analyser has alarmed, in Number 4 void space."

"Oh!" said the captain, "well seeing as we have not as yet loaded any liquid gas, that can only mean one thing, we are going to have to go in, and change the detector head."

Christine ventured, "Is this serious Doug?"

"Very, as the hold space is full of dry air."

"Right, as I've not seen a spare one anywhere in the last 2 weeks since I have been here, search the entire ship, and if you don't know what you are looking for, there is one in the engine room. Let's get started, and leave no drawer unopened, as there might just be one underneath it."

Those on board, decided not to argue.

Eh! "Why the rush," asked Christine, "we've only just climbed out of one hole, why do we need to go down into another one?"

"We, Christine won't be going into this one together, but if we cannot get the Gas Analyser up and working, then we won't get clearance from this port, far less load any liquid gas, anywhere."

"Eh; why?"

"Because this, is the United States of America and probably the most convoluted country in the world, where logic makes no sense to anyone who wasn't born here."

The crew had gathered outside, as the captain addressed them, "this is what we are looking for," as he held it up, what looked like the inner part of a toilet roll, with a few indents and brown in colour.

"Now I have a lot of experience in just what can be hidden in a ship, from stores orders that got cocked up, and others who cocked up, and chose the same hiding places as me. So I know where to look.

Don't be embarrassed, no-one is blaming anyone for anything, but we do need one of these.

We'll start in the cabins, not the obvious places, but underneath all of the drawers, which you take out completely, and bring whatever you find down to my office, and I can assure you, you will find some amazing things."

"But captain? How do you know about this?" asked the 3rd mate.

"Because I worked for this Scottish gas tanker company, and we could hide cargo in cargo! And just about everything else. And as you questioned me, I'll bet that you haven't taken your drawers out, in your bunks since you arrived."

"Right, you guys, get busy, because after this, we are going into the dirty bits, where I know we will find, shall we say "interesting things."

It only took a few minutes.

"Captain," I found this, underneath the bottom of my wardrobe. What is it?"

"Thanks Jesus, (pronounced yehsous) said the captain, "but whatever it is, it looks expensive, and I've never seen one before. Keep on searching."

"You still here Christine?" good, then you can find out what this is!"

"How do I do that?" She replied.

"Well it's got its makers name on it, try there for starters, and I did say you would be on the 'phone a lot. So, get busy."

"Doug," "yes Mike," the Chief engineer, "what have you found?"

"A complete set of the most precision micrometres ever made. I'm stunned, these things cost thousands."

"So why hide them Mike?"

"I haven't a clue," said Mike.

"Excuse me captain," as 2 AB's walked in, "we found these, laden down with sea boots, or in English parlance, Wellington boots."

"How many?" he asked.

"It depends upon how you define pairs."

"Go on."

"We've found 13 sea boots, and as long as you can find 6 people with 2 left feet, and 1 with a right foot, but in a different size from any of the left."

"So where did you find them?" asked the captain.

28

"Eh, in the lazarette, underneath some old mooring rope, plus a few other things," was the reply.

"Well, put them to one side for now, and carry on searching, and as you have been down there, try the steering gear flat next."

"Doug," said Christine, who had just come off the 'phone, "I've found something out about that box, but I have to leave. It's nearly 8 o'clock and my husband will be wondering where I have been. He should be back from Houston by now. What should I tell him?"

"Try telling him the truth that this ship is putting more demands on you than normal, and your secretarial role now includes working overtime and on this ship with the time difference to Norway."

"Okay, I'll be in the office tomorrow morning, just give me a call if you need anything."

Christine smiled inwardly, as she got into her car and thought, now that's clever, I don't have to lie to my husband, but I can also spend rather a lot of time with Doug, as she drove home.

"Captain," said Mike, "what do you make of this? I found them underneath the gas engineer's wardrobe cupboard floor. And for some reason, he is just a wee bit apprehensive, as to explaining just why they were in there in the first place.

"Well Mike, let's just say that, when this ship was built, there were an awful lot of very good salesmen, who talked the owners into buying an awful lot of things that they were never going to need.

And I have just found something very unusual. For a gas tanker at least, which is never going to be used. Something we can trade with."

"I agree." Not believing just what was in front of his eyes.

"Now that's enough for today, we'll think better with a clear head tomorrow, let's grab Einar, and we'll have a few beers in his hotel."

This after half an hour or so, the three arrived in the hotel bar.

"Have you got something on your mind Doug?" asked Einar, as the 3 sat together along this bar looking at a formidable array of bottles opposite and 3 freshly cold beers placed in front of them.

"Yes, when we first arrived on board, and up until the time I took command from Captain Olsen, he was very defensive, as if he knew that there was something, that he did not want me to know such as why he wouldn't let us into the void spaces, far less into the cargo tanks. But even more puzzling is that climbing up the stairwell from the office going up to the bridge, there are 3 flights of stairs with 13 stairs to each, but at the last set, there are only 6. There must be a half deck somewhere, but I can't find the door."

"That thought also occurred to me, but we've all been so busy, that I also put it onto the back burner for now. Let's check it out in the morning," said Mike.

A diversion presented itself.

"Gentlemen, can I interest you in perhaps having a cocktail, as you can see, I have the most interesting selection of bottles and I, Romero, your cocktail waiter, can make anything that you may choose, from anywhere in the world."

A fleeting glance of eye contact between Mike and Einar was enough to confirm that their rather friendly captain was already thinking ahead of them.

"Romero, what is, Galliano?"

"Oh Signor, it goes into a Harvey Wall-banger." He not realising the captain's surname, it not being Wall-banger.

"Yes, but what does it taste like?"

"For you Signor, I give you a little sample, as he poured a miniscule amount into a small glass."

"What do think signor," asked Romero.

"Damn awful, let's try the next bottle to it."

Which for the next 20 minutes, Romero obligingly did provide before catching on, that all 3 were sampling rather a lot of alcohol, without actually paying for it.

Einar nudged Mike, "restroom time."

To which both left, and upon arriving in the restroom, asked the same question, "how does he get away with it? It's damn clever, or brave, or both."

"Beats me," said Mike as they walked back to the bar to be confronted by Romero. "Signor Roos, here is zee bill, for your drinks."

"Where has my captain gone Romero?"

"So very sorry Signor, but your friend, he give me $20 and told me not to tell you. Goodnight Signor."

"So where the hell has he gone Mike?" asked Einar.

"I have a funny feeling that he knows where the missing half deck is, but how he is going to get there, puzzle's even me."

As they both left the hotel entrance, one going to his room, the other heading for a taxi, back to his ship, they both failed to notice another in the background. And her new friend, with Doug, the captain!

"We'll give them a 10 minute head start Julie, and we'll then sneak on board, quietly. Hope your boyfriend doesn't mind you doing this," somewhat clandestinely.

"Don't worry Doug, he's on nightshift tonight. I met him going in as I was going out, and he is not in the least suspicious about anything.

Are you going to exact your revenge for the other day, for them driving into potholes, with you with that table on top of you?"

"Oh, we are not going to wait that long, revenge starts tonight, and concludes tomorrow night. I just hope that the girls are up for it Julie."

"They are Doug, they most certainly are. Now where are we going?"

"Do you know how to swim Julie? And climb a rope, albeit a steel one?"

"Off course, why?"

"Seamen are very superstitious by nature, although I am not, so to get past the guy at the top of the gangway, we need to sneak aboard, and then become 'ghosts'. Then start setting off alarms, and some other things, such as, why we changed the spare anchor today, and the windlass suddenly comes on, walking the anchor cable out. And when they are all investigating that, we'll be at the other end, in the missing half deck. I found out how to get in this afternoon, but I've kept it a secret until now. There is going to be awful lot of head scratching going on tonight, especially after one of the generators runs out of fuel, in about 3 hours' time."

"But I haven't brought my bikini Doug!"

He gave her that odd look reserved for Americans, "what the hell do you need a bikini for, in the middle of the night, Julie?"

"Come on, we've 3 miles to walk first."

An hour later, as they approached the stern of the ship, "right put your purse with my wallet into this plastic bag, and we'll pick them up in the morning. Nobody will look for them under a mooring rope eye. Now it is swimming time, a slow and quiet breaststroke, round the stern and up to the fire wire on the port side of the bow, and no talking. Okay."

As they both slipped silently into the warm waters of the harbour on this quiet and very still night she, swimming more gracefully than he.

When they arrived, Doug spoke softly, "use the tails of your blouse to protect your hands from the wire, and climb gently upwards, it is only about 10 feet, and then gently crawl through the bottom of the rails, but stay low. I'll be right behind you."

"Well done," as they lay together in the shadows, "day after tomorrow I will take you shopping for a new blouse, and judging by your middle, I think that you may need a new pair of shorts also. You okay for the next bit?"

Julie thought to herself, this is not what she expected in the least as she followed her slithering new friend up onto another deck, but willingly helped.

"Now come on, all I have to do, is release the brake on the windlass, it is still in gear, nip down below, and start the pump. Then we go aft under the flying bridge, as everyone else on board comes legging it up the other way."

A few seconds later, all hell broke loose.

"I thought you were only going to start a pump!" said Julie, in alarm. "I did, but I suddenly remembered that there were a few other alarms that I could set off at the same time. Well, this is a gas tanker after all, now come on."

As all of the crew ran forwards, they sneaked aft beneath them.

Once aft, they descended backwards through an Emergency Exit, and into the ships engine room.

"Right, I'll just close this valve here," as Julie stood back in the ships' engine room, amazed at the masses of pipelines, wondering how any brain could sort this lot out, far less operate it.

"Come on Julie, missing half deck time now, this way," as she was rushed out of this hot space, her companion managing to set off more alarms on the way.

She was dragged into a broom cupboard with a sink to one side, a curtain was drawn back, a door of half size opened, and guided into a space about four feet high, and remarkably well lit, as the entry system closed behind her, or put another way, the door.

By way of explanation, Doug said "I got this out of one of my crew today, this is where they hide the girls, when the Brazilian Police come on board, as under Brazilian Law, girls are not allowed on foreign ships, and the penalty for each one caught is to the owners a fine of $10 000."

"I should think that by now Julie that you might be a tad thirsty, there's a cold case of beer, and a cold case of soft drinks, and some food in the corner, help yourself, as we are going to be in here for the rest of the night. I could only get 1 single mattress in through the door, so you use it. I'll just be playing around with all of these switches, for all of the equipment on the bridge, which we need to overhaul anyway, and that will be enough to drive everyone demented for hours, especially when that generator runs out of fuel."

To which it duly did, as all the lights went out, and more alarms went off.

"How many alarms are there on a gas tanker Doug?" asked Julie.

"Not just a few, but hundreds, and we are now on emergency lighting. That's it for tonight it is going to take them hours to unravel that lot, and even more hours to get it all going again."

"Well, there is enough space on this mattress for 2 you know!"

"There certainly is Julie, but I do believe that we might just have the better part of a case of beer to finish first. I trust that you like beer Julie?"

"I do," she replied, "but not half as much as to what you are setting up between us," with a twinkle in her eye.

"Forget it Julie, let's leave that for another day, maybe tomorrow. Sunday, "would you like to go sailing?"

"Never tried it Doug, but where are you going to get a sailboat from?"

"Oh yeah of little faith, we have one on board, its' just now not quite been out of the box yet."

"So we have to assemble it, before we go sailing on it."

"Oh no, it is already assembled, it's just the instructions for rigging it are in another language."

"Is nothing ever easy with you? What language?"

"Greek."

Monday, but it could be any day, the ridiculous hours that those connected with this ship had been working.

"Good morning Christine," as Richard strolled into his office at 7:45 am, "what time did you finish up on Saturday night?"

"I left the ship just after 8pm, and got home at 8:30," came this rather tired German reply.

"Oh something went wrong with their gas analyser, and everyone was frantically searching the ship for a spare part, so they could get it fixed, me included, and now this morning, I have to find out just what this is? It was found, in of all places, underneath a drawer in one of the crews cabins."

"Hi Christine," in a lighter air, as Romero also breezed into the office, "What's that?"

"That my friend is what we have to find out, and I have a feeling that we are going to be rather busy today, that captain on that gas tanker goes at one hellava speed."

The 'phone rang, and was switched straight over to the speaker.

"Morning Christine, we found a spare part last night, so I need you to buy me a one piece chemical suit with a respirator face mask linked to a breathing apparatus unit as well. This ship is metric, and nothing fits American sizes, so it will be quicker if we just buy an American suit. For a 6 foot male. And a tub of barrier cream! Got that?"

"Yes Doug, anything else?"

Silly question!

"Yep, get Romero onto why the harbourmaster promised me to take care of my ships garbage, and now doesn't want to return my calls."

"Yes Doug, anything else?

"Find a company of riggers, and send them down to the ship. Tell them that I need all of the ships rigging changed, and it has to be done in stainless steel."

"Yes Doug, anything else?

"Get me a service engineer who can overhaul a Sperry Mark 7 gyro compass. I switched it off last night."

"Yes Doug, anything else?"

"Find me a compass adjuster, for my magnetic compass, we found all of the soft iron and hard iron correctors last night, and we need his advice on how to install them. And then when we ever get around to actually sailing out of port, for him to adjust the compass."

"Yes Doug, anything else?"

"Get onto the US Coast Guard, and tell them I want a permit to run my lifeboats in the water."

"Yes Doug, anything else?"

"Find a service engineer who can check out a Krupp Atlas ARPA and my secondary radar at the same time."

"What's an ARPA Doug?"

"Automatic Radar Plotting Aid, Christine."

"Yes Doug, anything else?"

"Yes, book a table for 4, at 6pm tonight in Einar's hotel, and if you can find the time, find something to wear tonight, as you are coming with us, husband not included off course, smart, but casual."

"Delighted Doug, I know the very thing, I'll get on with all of this and let you know."

"Good Christine, but I might not be on the end of a 'phone, as something else has cropped up. If you can't contact me, you might have to pop down to the ship. In any case, Mike will know where I am. Good luck."

As Christine smiled inwardly to herself, "Right Romero, and Richard, get on with it, you heard the man."

Richard and Romero exchanged glances, is this man for real?

"Why buy a one piece chemical suit, when the space they are going into is full of dry air, mused Richard and Romero, and with breathing apparatus? It doesn't make sense. I think I'll give him a call back."

"Captain, glad I've caught you, it's Richard, Romero and I have been having a discussion, it's about this one piece chemical suit and breathing apparatus. Why do you need this, if you are going into a space full of dry air? Surely, you just go in and breathe air, no need for any of this extra equipment, can you explain?"

"Richard, in this heat, and it is over 100 degrees Fahrenheit every day, although we use degrees Celsius, you sweat, and any exposed part of your skin with sweat on it, will immediately be absorbed by the dry air, as the sweat boils. It is like getting seriously burnt, but in reverse."

"It takes us ages to get dry air around our cargo tanks, as this combats corrosion, so just go and get me a suit as asked. Unless off course your local fire service, might like to use this as a training exercise, which we off course, will pay for."

"Now why didn't I think of that? "mused Richard, "Okay cap, you're on."

"So it's bent, by how much?" Asked the captain.

"Well, in Hardness Vickers terms, way off the scale."

"David, don't bullshit me, it is either bent or it isn't, which?"

"In your rather rough and direct Scottish way of using words, we are going to have to put a new one in."

"And where is the new replacement one?"

"It is currently in Helsinki, Finland."

"Then you, David, get on the 'phone, and get it onto a 'plane, today, and don't send it through Schiphol, Amsterdam or Dallas, Texas as that 6.5 tonne piece of crankshaft could easily get lost, and most probably will be, if it goes through any of these airports."

Shortly later, one of the two ships 'phones rang.

"Mike, chief engineer here," he said.

"Is the captain there?" asked the voice on the other end of the 'phone.

"Sorry, you just missed him, he's away to buy something but didn't say what it was. Is that you Christine?"

"Yes it is Mike, we spoke to the fire service and they are dead keen into getting involved as they don't often get the chance to go on-board ships. The fire chief wants to know when it would be convenient to come down and see Doug, he suggested this afternoon at about 1."

"Christine, by now you should know just what Doug's like, tell him 12, and to come for lunch, but limit the number to 8."

"Okay Mike, I'll get onto it."

A few hours later, Christine arrived on board the ship, and as she entered the ships offices, was met by the Chief Engineer Mike, and 6 rather burly Americans, of various different skin patinas, and

2 of the female variety, who were somewhat odd, and suggesting to all, that their slender frames, might just be holding a secret, as to their abilities. Their ring fingers devoid of any embellishments, but the skin clearly showing otherwise. Engagement and wedding rings had been taken off. Not something noticed by normally married men, but those not yet caught in the loop of infidelity most interestedly were.

"Mike," said Christine "is Doug's cabin open so I can drop these off?"

"Should be, and when you get back down, do me a favour and join us all for lunch, you take Doug's chair in the ships restaurant, and we'll split these guys among other tables. Hopefully, our captain won't be too long."

A minute or two later, Christine re-joined the group.

"Now come this way gentlemen, you were invited for lunch, so let's all go, for lunch, our captain being represented by his new girlfriend, Christine, who has already been into some of the more or the lesser parts of this, shall we say, rather complex gas tanker. Oh and before you ask, he is not married, so please relax."

He, very briefly having overheard a whispered conversation between the 2 females of the Fire Department, who did not like being addressed to as 'gentlemen.' Gentle persons not as yet being within the politically correct American version of the English language, and probably never would be. Because they can't spell.

Let's see the captain talk himself out of this one.

Mike starting to set up a rather cunning plan, which unfortunately would have to reveal that Christine, was in fact, married.

Duly seated, lunch arrived, served by the Filipino steward with a glittering array of dishes, some being seafood based, the others being meat based, and presented in front of them, along with various types of rice.

"Enjoy ladies and gentlemen," as he placed hot plates in front of each one.

The glittering array of food, rather took these Americans somewhat aback, they expecting something like a burger and a few French Fries, or for British readers, chips. Well, why describe sticks of potatoes as French as they could have come from any field, in any country. Ever heard of Mongolian Fries?

"Is this lunch Christine?" asked the boss of the fire department, as he somewhat timidly scooped some rice onto his plate, his friends beside him already realising that this was just more than better being good, it being excellent.

"Well, if you don't sample some of this pretty soon, then there might not be much left," replied Christine. As a few very surprised mouths had to agree with, and for the next few minutes were silent. That being strange for Texans, as they could still talk with the upper and lower lips super glued together and chew at the same time. How the food actually got in there was anybody's guess. But this was Texas. Where everything was possible to a point, only many days later finding out that Texans go rattle snake racing.

"If this is lunch, what is dinner like?" he asked, as the captain walked in.

"Ah Christine," as he kissed the back of her head, his arms sliding down from her shoulders, to her elbows, "looking after our guests I see. Thank-you, not much food left I see, not to worry, we do have a table booked for tonight I trust."

"Doug, this is head of the Fire Department, and his colleagues. You weren't here, so Mike asked me to step in, I hope you don't mind?"

"Goodness no, I was delayed. I trust gentlemen," speaking to all concerned, "that you have had an agreeable lunch. Doggy bags are available, although I rather get the impression that we are not going to need any of them. Or even Doggy pups bags."

"Captain, delighted to meet with you, my name is John Standish, head of Corpus Christi Fire Department, and on behalf of my colleagues, we thank you for a most delightful lunch. Now I believe that you have a problem that you require our help with."

"Finish your lunch first, then come through to my office John and I'll explain."

The finishing their lunch bit, ensured that there was nothing left.

Just after leaving, Mike took the captain aside. "Where have you been mate?"

"Oh, to a place where some idiot tried to steal the wheels off our hired car, but it solves our next problem. Tell you later."

An inward groan suggested that this was going to involve something else, probably border line legal, or just plain, illegal.

"Okay Mike, here are the car keys, it's in the boot, or as Americans say, the trunk. Now if you don't mind, we have other guests to consider."

"Now John, here is what I need," as the captain explained their predicament in his office.

"When do you want us to do this?"

"Only one of our void spaces is under dry air, so you can practise inside the other three, and I'll take you around them first. The void spaces are where we keep the liquid gas cargo tanks."

"Doug, we don't often get the chance to board ships, they tend to be alongside jetties, and our access is limited, could we use your ship as a training facility. Like, could I bring my fire crews and use your ship as a training model?"

"John, the only bits of my ship that I need just now, are Number 4 void space and the engine room, so as long as you keep away from the back bit, you can do as you please with the rest of it. Just don't operate any of the valves, we need to keep our cargo tanks as they currently are."

To which agreed by John.

"Oh, and you may need to include a female with a very inquisitive nature, who has this desire of getting wet, who you may know as Christine, who works for our shipping agents."

"Brilliant! And I don't mean Christine, but can we use your ship, for say the next 2 to 3 weeks?"

"Well, we aren't going anywhere, with our main engine in bits, the cargo tanks are under nitrogen, the gas plant will not be used until we start loading cargo, so you can configure in your own mind as if this ship construed as to being anything, because a fire on anything, might just help you to work out just how to put the fire out on a ship where a lot of water is not always best."

"Do you require us to give you any notice of our arrival?"

"Give Christine a call first, and then she'll 'phone me, I'll warn my crew, and then you can do as you please. Realism adds to the adrenal rush, and from the previous crew, who did not dispose of all the out of date pyrotechnics, which I found in a wardrobe, at the very least, should make a pretty good simulation for your boys to tackle. It'll be yellow smoke. I will need you to sign a 'Letter of Indemnity,' but that's just a formality."

"Void spaces tomorrow, early afternoon, so I can brief my boys up first?"

"Off course John and we could also do with running up our deck spray system. Not got around to seriously testing it yet, ten minutes is not really enough, when we can get it on for 2-3 hours."

"I can't wait," as he and most of the others departed, recognising that this was not an opportunity to be missed.

Christine looked at her new found love, why does this highly educated and caring man push himself like this? She failing to notice the two female guests from the fire department passing little bits of paper over to The Chief Engineer, or the little private conversation between all three.

"Well. That, Christine, is enough for now. I'm going up to my cabin, and I am going to lay back for an hour or so. Sort of chill out on my sofa, probably with a cold beer, I trust that we are still on for tonight, for dinner."

"Yes we are," replied Christine, "but there is only one difference."

"Which is?" he asked.

"We are going to chill out together, here and now."

"Eh, no, because you are heading back to your office, relaxing in my arms will be between when you finish work, and before we set off for dinner. Who knows afterwards, but that might be a day or so away yet."

"I still need a company of riggers, and others that I asked you for this morning, so the sooner you get it all set up, the sooner you can get back here."

A somewhat sad Christine had to agree, as that smiling look suggested that this was not a time to disagree, so rather reluctantly set off back to her office.

It was a melancholy afternoon, where time seemed to drag although with the 'phone constantly going, she and her 2 office pals getting nowhere close to what her new friend expected of them, Christine caught up indecisively, between her desire to be back on board his ship, and for what he had planned for this evening.

There was an air of mystery about it all, which only heightened her intrigue. But the time still dragged.

The clock slowly dragged its hands round, before the hour hand eventually getting close to the number 5, when Richard exploded, after answering the 'phone. Yet again!

"Why can't that Scottish captain just be like every other captain? Now he wants me to contact the Norwegian Consul, and ask him to be on board his ship whenever he is free tomorrow morning. Right! That's it for tonight. I'll see you all in the morning." He not knowing that The Norwegian Consul, was in fact female.

Romero and Christine exchanged glances, to which Romero said, "I'll finish up here, you go and don't drive too fast."

Christine was out of the office like a rocket, not bothering with the lift, to which her boss was still waiting for, into her rather hot car, to which the air conditioning still had to catch up with, and arrived in record time at the bottom of her friends ships gangway, only to be met with rather more than just, a few, fire engines!

"They weren't supposed to start until tomorrow," thought Christine, as she ran up the aluminium steps, and into the ships' offices to find no one there.

"Well, you took your time," as she ventured into the masters cabin, "I thought that Germans were supposed to be efficient."

"Come here," as she fell into his arms, at last relaxed, "take a seat, and start off by cooling down."

"Going to be pretty difficult, snuggling up close to you Doug."

So, she has a sense of humour, akin to a Scottish one, he thought.

"So what devilment are you up to tonight Doug?" relaxing and nestling into his warm arms. "Getting your own back on the potholes, table and roof rack bit?"

"Absolutely, and it is all arranged, although, you haven't met Julie yet. Just when we go in, try to avoid eye contact. This will hopefully embarrass Mike and Einar to hell and back."

There was a knock on the door, to which came the request, the door opening just enough for it to be heard.

"Doug, I've got the impact spanner and an air hose already run down to our hire car, are you coming to give us a hand, or are you going to lie in with Christine?"

"See Christine, no privacy on ships."

"Be right out Mike," shouted in return.

"Christine, I'll be about 10, maybe 15 minutes, so if you want to, grab a shower and get changed, because when I get back, I'll be going into the shower, and in this heat, it will be for a colder one."

He left, but only after grabbing something from his cabin desk on his way out.

Christine smiled inwardly, with that air of suspicion already arising within her, just what is he up to now? And to her puzzlement, just how exactly do you 'grab a shower', when it is a lot of water in little droplets, and impossible to catch them all when they arrive at speed. German logic having the same logic as Texans.

That would have to wait, as she undressed and entered into the shower, completely forgetting that she was already married, her intrigue blocking out that fairly major factor, thinking not of her husband, but as she hoped, her new found friend.

On dockside, below her, things were going in a different direction.

"Right, get the wheel covers off," as the Chief Engineer, Master, and most curiously, all of the Filipino crew duly did."

"Doug," asked Mike, "what are we doing?" Emulated also by the bosun, and his crew, minus Mullah who was nowhere in sight.

"I found out something today about The United States that they are not complying with International Maritime Law regarding Marpol 3, regarding how we get to dispose of our ships garbage, and I'm laying out a few precautions, just in case."

"What has this got to do with wheel nuts on a cars wheel?"

"Because, where I was today was in one of the less salubrious parts of town, where they will steal almost anything, and seeing as this is a rental car, can't afford for us to be without wheels. So we are going to glue them on."

Mike stood back amazed. And including the Filipinos, "how is that going to work?" asked all in various different levels of chorus.

"What we do, is put a plastic bag of ships garbage into the inside bottom of a brown shopping paper bag, that all Americans use, and add a few cheap things on top, place one or two on the front passenger seat, leave the windows down, and wait until someone comes along and steals it. But we can't afford to lose the cars wheels, so stop arguing while I start mixing up this 2 part epoxy resin."

"Right bosun, start taking off the wheel nuts, spray the threads with Electrolyte, which dissolves the grease and after we have coated the threads with a liberal amount of this epoxy mixed resin, put the nuts back on, but don't stop as the impact gun stops, keep it on until it is tight as it can go. Even, if we have to stretch the studs."

"You do realise Doug, that they will have considerable trouble getting them off again after we, or shall I say you, return the hire car to them," said Mike.

"A minor detail Mike, think of it as a Crime Prevention Issue. Anyway, we'll be long gone by then."

"They might have to use a gas axe to get them off again you know Doug."

"That's their problem. Providing that they know what a gas axe actually is!"

There was a 10 minute or so pause in conversation, due to the frenetic activity from all, before it being asked? "Just where did these nuts come from?" Not an overly wise thing to admit to in the confusion, as they had 4 wheel nuts left over in the bucket being used to stop anything rolling away. And to which none did which didn't really explain why they now had 4 left over.

"Right, get the wheel covers off again, and check to see if any wheel hasn't got all of its nuts," said Doug.

To which there being none missing, rather than being logically thought out, was dismissed with "right, chuck them in the dock."

It was only some hours later that the car being parked next to, upon driving away, was suddenly short of a front wheel. The wheel heading in the direction of the dock, the car not, the wheel cover, no-where in sight, not that that really mattered! Much.

Unless, you just happened to be the driver, who now in total darkness, apart from the sparks flying off the hub slightly illuminating the area as he didn't make that good an attempt of stopping, or even managing to control his car, found himself stuck on the middle and side of the road at the same time, unfortunately with the only other front good wheel, in a ditch, or as Americans call them, drain a-ways.

Going to be interesting seeing how they were going to drain away this 3 wheeled car. Its back wheels no longer in touch with the road.

And observed from the ships side by one very embarrassed Filipino, now having realised that when he was given the impact spanner, had actually gotten the wrong car.

Knock Knock on his own cabin door, "safe to come in Christine?"

To be met gently with 2 outstretched arms protruding from a towel wrapped around a beautiful blonde female who answered with a very soft kiss.

"Come on, we haven't got much time, I just hope that that cold water is cold enough."

It was as he emerged a few minutes later, and dressed in other clothes not full of sweat, to be met in his dayroom by a beautifully dressed German blonde, a rather ageing English Chief Engineer, and a Norwegian Superintendent, with a puzzled face akin to a troll.

"All ready, then, let's go, as I've ordered in some very special king sized prawns, to which we all in the past are very likened to."

Einar nudged Mike, "what is he up to?"

"If you haven't puzzled out yet what that very complex mind is up to by now, then neither have I, but I'll tell you one thing, he is without doubt, one of the very best captains that I have ever sailed with. There seems to be no end to his knowledge, and how to manipulate it."

"Good evening ladies and gentlemen, a table for 4 is it? Come this way," as they arrived in the hotel's restaurant.

"Excuse me," asked the captain, "but where is Julie?"

"Oh sir, she went sailing yesterday afternoon in the bay, and got seriously sunburnt and somehow also burnt her hands, something to do with a Greek ship-owner? She won't be back for a few days, but I'll be your hostess partly for this evening, now come this way, I'll show you to your table. My name is Suzy." With a delightful, white toothed and totally false American smile.

The plan was already unravelling, but where there is a will, then there was also, another way.

"Now what would you all like to drink?" as Suzy handed out the menu's.

"I'll have a beer," said Einar, "me too," said Mike, "I'll have a Coke," said Christine."

"And you sir," asked Suzy with yet another phoney smile, "I'll have a glass of iced water," replied the captain.

Amazement frowns emitted from three of the four puzzled faces.

"Iced water?" asked all three in unison, "why?"

"Because, if I spill it, it will be less trouble cleaning it up, seems eminently sensible to me. Now shall we decide what to order, before Suzy gets back?"

Suspicion had been aroused in two of the three, Christine being the exception, as they could already see where this was going.

Christine's only problem being just where, it was all going to end up, but it was sure to be fun.

The drinks arrived, were duly served, which was where the argument began.

"What is the difference between a number 12 prawn, and a number 15 prawn Suzy?" asked Mike.

"That is the number of prawns you get per pound, a number 12 prawn is bigger than a number 15 prawn."

"How can you tell the difference? Is it stencilled on the prawns back?" asked Mike.

"It goes by weight and length at the market." said Suzy.

"But we are in a restaurant! do you have any scales so that we can check?"

"What for?" asked Suzy, as other customers and diners, were starting to look on with varying degrees of interest. The peculiar accents being different from that from which they been accustomed to hearing.

"Just in case the chef has gotten the prawns all mixed up off course, we could be paying for number 12 prawns, and getting number 15's instead." Suzy looking a bit perplexed.

The captain jumped in, "Julie told me that she was going to serve up tonight some very special King Sized prawns, but she didn't mention anything about numbers."

"Oh sir, we have them, but they are reserved for this Greek ship-owner," replied Suzy.

"Suzy, I'll let you into a little secret, the Greek ship-owner is a friend of mine, although that is not strictly true, I work for him and his luxury yacht is parked, sorry berthed, just a little way from here, although he this afternoon, flew out of town. Now, take this $10 bill, and bring us the BIG prawns."

"Off course sir," and with a gracious nod, left, although her next movements were not lost on the captain, as she instructed another waitress to look to the table, accept the order, and proceeded into the kitchen.

"Since when did a 6500 tonne Norwegian gas tanker with a broken engine look like a luxury yacht?" asked Einar.

"Well if you squint with one eye closed under your left armpit, angle your head at another angle, then look at the floodlights, and it off course being dark, then anything could look like a luxury yacht. Come on you lot, time to change tables, and bring your drinks."

Christine smiled inwardly as she got up, thinking now that she knew just what he, Doug was up to. The other 2 with puzzled looks followed, eye contact between each making no sense whatsoever as they moved to another part of the restaurant.

As they arrived at a completely new table, beautifully laid out as before.

"Good evening lady, and gentlemen, my name is Rose, can I get you anything?"

"Do you have a very dry Californian White wine and four glasses, we'll order later thank-you, but we are rather thirsty, so the wine first if you please," offered Doug.

"Certainly Sir," and with a gracious bow left to get the reserved bottle of wine, she also noticing the wink that no-one else had seen having been previously advised by Suzy.

Another waiter offered a basket of rolls, to which all but one of the four graciously took one.

The two engineers, Mike and Einar prising theirs apart causing, a huge amount of crumbs before spreading on the butter, as each being somewhat hungry. Christine noticing the wink left hers alone.

"Okay guys, time to move tables again," said Doug.

"Why?" asked two of the three, "we've only just sat down."

"Have you not noticed the looks we are getting from these guys over there?"

"No," as they all looked around, with dozens of faces looking at them, all mostly female.

"We seem to have strayed into the non-musical part of this restaurant."

"Come on, bring your rolls and drinks, there's a rather nice looking table beside the band."

Chaos ensued, with several waitresses, some with food, and some with wine, who now couldn't find just which table their guests actually were at. And not in the least assisted by the others, who had not cottoned on to the wink from the captain that they could also join in the fun. Not all residents of Corpus Christi, they from the non-shipping fraternity, now enjoying dishes that they had not ordered, and started moving tables as well. Each waitress, arriving from the kitchen laden with food, to find just where it was intended to go, were 2 or so more diners greater than what they were carrying, and in a different place.

"We didn't order prawns," was the common response, although those who had did not refuse the fillet steak!

"It's going to be hell sorting out the bills" commented one waitress to another.

"Mike, what's that under your arm?" asked the captain, as he raised his arm.

A loud hail went up, "Who ordered crayfish?"

Ah, as he was spotted, with his arm raised.

"Do you think that you have enough space for this?"

"Off course, from the 4th member, newly arrived, I'll have it." John Standish amazed as to what he was seeing; now having the answer to Mike's problem.

"Christine," in a low voice, "time to go," said Doug "but do so discreetly."

To which they both did, with the same reason that each had to go to the 'restroom.'

"Doug, shouldn't we pay for our share of the bill?" asked Christine, as they arrived in the hotel car park.

"How do you figure to that? You didn't eat anything, you didn't drink anything, and neither did I, apart from a roll, which I left and according to the menu was complementary."

"I think we'll just leave my 2 engineering friends to sort it all out, although I'd love to be a flea on the wall tonight, listening. See you in the morning Christine."

"Not until you kiss me goodnight," dragging him into the darkness, where he suddenly recognised, the smell of her perfume.

This lady has class, he thought, although it did smell somewhat identical to the rather expensive one he bought at Heathrow, on his way out to join this ship, a few weeks before, didn't recollect it though being in his restroom cabinet, more like as being in his desk drawer, destined eventually for his daughter.

Next day.

"Good morning John," said the captain, as the Corpus Christi fire chief arrived in the ships offices, to be met with several reporters and 3 TV film crews.

"Doug, after last night, I had kind of figured out, that you were not a typical ships' captain, but why bring in the press and the media?"

"Because my friend, this is a gas tanker. It's a bit of a give-away with LPG painted on both sides of the hull, and an even bigger 'No Smoking' on the bridge front in bright orange. Not also including the big hut above the main deck, with NGC painted also in big letters, which translates into Norwegian Gas Carriers.

And with your boys arriving in their fire engines, with all horns blasting, and flashing lights on, that this might just scare a few of the locals into thinking that there was a real emergency."

"Now why didn't I think of that?" said somewhat rhetorically before the captain went on.

"You can use any part of the ship you like, to take these nosey reporters and film crews around to make their copy, and ensure the reading and viewing public are perfectly safe. Except the engine room and number 3 & 4 void spaces only, and I won't explain why. The Press reporters after you finish will be away like a rocket, to get their story into copy, but if any of the TV crews linger, invite them to stay for coffee, while we get changed."

A puzzled look emanated from John's face, as he continued.

"I've had the big fan on all night, so No's 1, and 2 void spaces might just be of interest to these TV guys, and as I am highly educated in the gas tanker world, and know for a fact, that a TV camera has never been inside a gas tankers inner workings, so they are going to get a scoop, or whatever name Americans call it."

"But will there be enough light Doug?"

"Oh yes, the lights are on as well, they might need to open the aperture of their camera lens up a bit, but it should be okay. If there isn't enough light, then they can bring their own lights with them tomorrow."

John smiled inwardly to himself, as after the previous evening, had already worked out that what was said did not actually mean what a logical American brain at first thought.

He was interrupted.

"Ladies and gentlemen, if you would like to bring your equipment next door into my ships' conference room, we can brief you and answer your questions accordingly."

Twenty minutes passed, before the newspaper hacks departed, all eager to run copy, while the 3 TV crews relaxed with coffee. Or so he thought, as they had not actually, left. A smell and taste of coffee not indicating anything un-toward.

A few minutes later, in the master's office, John asked. "Just what are you up to? And don't try to run another stunt past me like last night. That one I still haven't fully worked out yet. There was absolute chaos when you sneaked out with Christine."

Who just happened to arrive at that moment, with a gentle, 'knock?'

"Oh hello, what are you doing here Christine?" asked the captain, she just arriving in the nick of time.

"I've got the riggers you wanted, I've brought them with me, and I had to get out of the office, Richard is going demented with that box you wanted investigated."

"Good, keep him at it, as I already know what it is, but don't tell him. The Chief Officer will show the riggers what we need."

Who just showed up at the door even although his desk was just 10 feet away, the door frame conveniently at times holding a door in the closed position, but now, not.

"Blackie, make sure the riggers understand that we want everything in stainless steel, and not only the wires, but every joint and coupling as well, and all of the spliced eyes with Talaurits, then also to replace the lifeboat falls, as they are over 5 years old, and should have been replaced by last survey. You'll find the new one's in the fo'c'sle."

"No problem Doug, but can I get all of the blocks freed up as well?"

"Off course, anything to do with safety equipment, get it fixed."

"That is going to be a lot of work!"

"What better way to spend 3 weeks then, and get that dozy Norwegian Gas Engineer to give you a hand. He is after all, earning twice what you earn, just by sitting on his fat arse, and if he disagrees, tell him that I have an open airline ticket for him in my office, which he is welcome to collect at any time."

"Right, I'm onto it."

"Oh, and get 4 new pilot ladders made," the captain suddenly remembering as he left his Teutonic Chief Officer to get on with it.

"But captain, can we afford this in the ship's budget?"

"To hell with the budget, safety comes first, and I'll easily find a way of getting all of these costs into the Insurance Claim, which I can tell you now, will be very complex."

He left and now delighted that his Norwegian beer drinking friend was now actually going to be doing something useful!

"Now Christine, John and I are just about to go into the 2 void spaces, to show him what cargo tanks look like, with not only local firemen, but 3 TV crews to boot, and before you ask, you are not coming. Okay?"

"I've got a free hour," she ventured.

"No," was the distinct reply, but not received at all well.

"Okay Doug, I've waited long enough, just what are you up to?" from John.

A similar question emanated from Christine very quietly, not quickly ignored, but received anyway.

"What I cannot stand, is when reporters, being press or TV, push microphones into your face, including TV cameras with questions that you do not have time to answer, and are then quoted with what they have already decided to print or broadcast, whether it is true or not. So, it's payback time, only the answers to their questions will be done at my speed, not theirs," as he left his office, and went up to his cabin to change.

John and Christine exchanged glances. "The Chief Engineers cabin is opposite, you change in there, I'll change in my fire engine, but keep out of sight until we get into these, void spaces, whatever they are," emanated from John.

It only took 4 minutes.

"John, where is Christine?" asked the captain, as he arrived back.

"Well Doug, if truth be told, she was rather upset at you brushing her off like that, so stormed off with a rather angry face, which was mostly bright red. And some comment about falling in love with someone who was not her husband, but it was in German, so I didn't get the whole translation, although I rather got the impression, that it might take rather more than a dozen red roses to get her back."

"Well, I'll deal with that later, come on, and let's brief these TV crews," as he headed off to the ship's conference room he, not noticing now that he was on his own.

A few decks above, and away from these nosey reporters, a new scenario was beginning to un-fold.

"How did I do John?" asked Christine, as he entered the Chief Engineers cabin, and was stunned. "Christine, you look totally different, what have you found?"

"Mike, it appears doesn't get time to wash his coveralls, but this was the least smelly but dirtiest that I could find, and the cap, I can fold my hair into. A bit of a smudge from the grease, and I could pass for the Chief Engineer. What do you think?"

"I can't wait to see Doug's face when he eventually spots you."

Later, with all assembled a motley bunch of note but still with an arrogant expression akin of those who thought that they knew everything, were just about to find out, that they were somewhat slightly misguided in their own opinions of themselves.

"Ladies and gentlemen, where we are going is to a place where we keep the cargo tanks. On any other sort of tanker, the cargo tanks are an integral part of the ship and contribute to the structure of the ship, but not on this semi-refrigerated gas tanker. We are going to show you just what a cargo tank actually looks like, only what you are seeing, is the covering of several inches of insulation. It has to be this way, as when we cool the tank down; it has to be able to contract. That's enough of the technical information for now, any other questions, ask me when we are inside, or when we get back out. Now, follow me in, take your time, and look where you put your feet, before moving onwards."

"Christine," asked Mike quietly, a few seconds later, "where did you get that boiler suit from, it looks like one of mine."

"Is it Mike? Oops, well, I sort of, found it, didn't think anyone would mind, seeing as it is so dirty."

"Here take this," giving her 2 bottles of water, "the TV crews are going in with none, and if I know this captain, they are seriously going to need it.

After a tortuous descent into the partly illuminated gloom, involving several ladders and walkways, all 3 TV crews arrived at the bottom behind one cargo tank, along with The Chief of The Corpus Christi Fire Department, and 7 of his officers. With very little room to spare as some females, came into rather close contact with males, who not to put it lightly, probably hadn't actually showered that morning, with sweat pouring out everywhere, and now didn't need to, a sort of washing from the inside to the outside.

"This is what is termed a Siamese cargo tank. Think of it as 2 sausages pushed up against each other lengthwise," as he pointed this out.

"Now the reason that we are down here, is that in another part of this ship, we need to change a gas analyser detection head, so follow me, as these things are in the most convoluted of places, the reasoning of which I will explain later, when we get back on deck."

A spell of foreboding abounded the others, as the captain started off up the centreline of the tanks supports slithering in a very cramped way of gloved hands, elbows and knees, to which each duly followed. It not being long before many bangs and curses in various accents and languages, before swearing followed. With no choice, to go backwards they had to follow his lead, as the only way out of this hell-hole, was to follow him. One of the best being from a TV camera operator who got his shoulders stuck, not able to go forwards, or even backwards, and had to be pushed through, from those following behind, and not too graciously at that. His female camera assistant found another use for his manhood, to which he shot through, his highly expensive TV camera, being the loser, but he was, through!

A smile emanated from John, The Fire Chief, as he emerged at the other end, some 2 pints of sweat lighter, or so it felt, than he was 20 minutes before, this being tried in his and his officer's full fire gear, each arriving in desperate need of water.

"See this bit John, this is what we need to change in No 4 void space, so now you all know where it goes. Right, let's get topside."

Somewhat breathlessly, prompted the question, "Doug do you expect me to go through all of that again, only this time in a full chemical suit, with breathing apparatus on my back, just to change a poxy little thing no bigger than the inside of a toilet roll?"

"No!" came the somewhat lying innocent reply, as he started up the ladder to climb out.

Many bottles of water later, as each emerged, to the men and woman declaring that they would probably never do anything as stupid as this ever again.

"Doug?" asked John, he also now topside, "why not?"

"Because the one head to be changed is at the bottom of a ladder underneath a deck hatch, I'll be in and out in less than 30 seconds."

"So why has everyone crawled underneath a cargo tank, including 3 TV teams and their back-up people?" asked John.

"Well my friend, if you haven't worked that out as yet, then I'll get Christine to explain why later," as he went aft, leaving John more than just a little perplexed.

Christine just surfacing back onto the main deck, wishing that she was back in her Agents office, and not knowing how to get out of this filthy, sweaty boiler suit, where her real clothes were in a cabin opposite her new love, who she had hoped didn't actually know where she had just been.

"Christine," said John, "I think that this captain will find out later that you were in there with us, if he hasn't already done so."

Sneaking in silently in to the ship's accommodation block, even more sneakily into the Chief Engineers cabin, retrieving her clothes, and even more sneakily, getting out again, plus also getting successfully down the accommodation ladder to her car, jumped in and drove a short distance, with a huge wave of relief.

'I love this man,' she thought, and I can't afford to lose his trust. Plus I need to get clean before going home.

Upon which, and only after driving another further short distance, pulled to the left, put her head back, and promptly fell asleep, the long hours she had been working, eventually taking its' toll. And it was only early afternoon. In a car which was rapidly warming up.

Meanwhile, back on board ship, "Okay ladies and gentlemen, now that you have been

Re-watered, and have had a chance to catch your breath, we can try No 2 void space, only this tank is different from No 1. This one is a cylinder and transverse and to the best of my knowledge, this is the only ship built like this."

"Are we going to bang our heads, or crawl around again?" asked a few.

"Absolutely not, we'll do this one from above, apart from upwards backwards crawling, where I can show you that the cargo tank you are lying on isn't part of the ships structure."

"Where has everyone gone?" as 2 TV crews were no longer in evidence. No one else venturing an opinion.

"Eh Doug," from John Standish, "this little female and her crew work for a very small, and struggling TV station who can't compete with the other stations, and are prepared to go in again, but only if when they, and you are all in there, that you conduct an interview, explaining not only the cargo tanks themselves, but also the structure of the ship. They've got their own lights. This will go 'on air' tonight, in a few hours from now."

"Follow me Alison," to which she and her team did, gaining rare footage, her team delighting in the unusual crawling upwards and backwards technique using a rope, with their noses getting alarmingly close to the actual hull of the ship, or put another way, under the bottom side of the main deck.

"See that bit there Alison," as she and her crew looked upwards, all lying on their backs, that is where the cargo tank meets the ship. Go on, press it," to which she did, and found it to be rubber.

"Do you mean captain that as the tank contracts that little bit of rubber takes up the difference between the tank and the ship?"

"It isn't just a little bit of rubber Alison, it's rather a big bit of rubber, and goes all around the top of the cargo tank, and one of the most difficult things to fit, when the cargo tanks go in, and after the deck above us, is welded on top, when a ship such as this is built. And you are the first film crew in The United States to have ever filmed it. From, the inside that is! In fact, you might be the only TV crew in the world to see this, in situ."

"Let's go boys, this we have to get this on air, tonight," forgetting off course that the only way back down involved only one rope, shared on the way up, with now two others realising that lying on their backs on top a cylindrical tank, that gravity, tends to work no matter just wherever you are.

Fortunately, their downwards progress was temporarily halted by the walkway surrounding the top of the cargo tank to which now, three pairs of legs were firmly stuck. Their language not being suitable to put into print, but the camera recorded it all, much to their later embarrassment. Yet another case of the record button being stuck, and in the wrong position, of he, who held the camera.

"John, give me a hand, and pull these 3 idiots out and back topside."

Extrication language not improving one iota, as all fell onto the deck above after scaling a 15 foot ladder each vowing never to do such a stupid thing ever again.

"Care for a cold beer John?" as they both together watched a film crew leaving his ship.

"Sorry Doug, but no. When I get home, I'm going to see what these TV stations broadcast tonight, but I might drop by, if you are in that hotel tonight, and might bring my wife with me."

"Are you expecting me to get up to something tonight, with my boys in tow?"

"Absolutely, see you later Doug."

Later, being 7 at night, the daily report having been written and ready to be faxed off, but no sign of Christine.

"Nothing for it Mike, we'll fax it out from Einar's Hotel, let's go, as I am not only a bit thirsty, but could do with something to eat."

The journey passing in the usual way, being an argument, as to just which side of the road they were meant to drive on, it making little difference avoiding the potholes, and these little markers which said 'Left, or Right,' which some little bugger had in fact changed pointed them in the wrong direction, and no prizes for guessing who that was on his way back with a confused female in tow, to his own ship no-one noticing the adjustable spanner that he always went out with. Before going for a swim, the "Keep Left" arrow, intending to get drivers going round in circles, sort of fell off, it being damn hard trying to swim and keep this sign afloat at the same time. Not that that made much difference as they took the short-cut over the grass anyway, with the cars suspension appreciating that it was not long before it was abused in any other way like this again. Well, at least there was no possible chance of losing a wheel.

Little did it know!

"Now I have only known you for a few weeks Doug," said Einar, as he and Mike entered his hotel, "so no more stunts like last night. Mind you, in the end, for a reason that I am not going to begin to un-ravel, the hotel might like you to try it again, as they made a whopping great profit last night, and they also, cannot understand why."

"Which might account for this rather crowded bar tonight then, eh?" when a huge cheer went up, as they made their way to the bar.

Mike and Einar exchanged glances, as a tea bag on a string was pulled from Doug's shirt pocket, and laid on the bars top.

They being, by now somewhat wise, into not, asking why.

"A beer for you sir?" asked Romero, "great night last night eh. I eventually got home at 4 o'clock this morning."

"Yes Romero, eh 3 beers please, and see if you can find a table for me to hide under."

It started immediately, and from the leader of the band, a loud mouthed Texan, trying to play an electro guitar coupled to an electric organ, from which only one tune seemed to emanate from, with off course many variations, depending upon the level of alcohol most graciously received from many of the listeners, it not permeating the grey matter of his brain, that they were trying to shut him up. Preferably before he started on telling jokes, to which he duly did.

"Hey everybody, we've got Captain Doug with us tonight, he's the captain of the Norwegian Gas tanker parked just up the road, and after last night, one hell of a swell guy."

To which a huge round of applause broke out.

"Romero, where is that table? The one I want to crawl under?"

Appreciating the furore, a few gracious hand swings, smiles in response, and a grateful smile, did not lessen the enthusiasm of the crowd, bolstered now by the band leader, whose wife playing the drum-kit in accompaniment was trying in vain to curb his enthusiasm, and failing terribly.

"Hey captain, have you ever been to Texas before?"

Any answer was pointless, as he had the microphone, the amplifier and the speakers, and apparently had the crowd on his side. But he meekly tried anyway.

"Yes, I've been to Texas, a couple of years ago in fact."

For some unusual reason, the tumult quietened down, probably out of curiosity.

"So what do you think of Texas then?"

"Well I can safely say that the end of the pipeline in Antwerp, Belgium, looks exactly the same as the one we connected to in Houston, about 8 inch and 300 ASA, with 12 bolts coupling us together. Then we pumped 3000 tonnes of liquid gas through it. And Texas doesn't look that big, the Stetsons in Baton Rouge in Louisiana, where I have also been to, are a lot bigger than the ones you guys wear. And actually, this is the 1st time that I have been on these shores, apart from the ports, of The USA and it doesn't look that great."

This did not go down well. At all!

But a few were noticing, that little glint in his eye, the little change of posture, that he was now baiting the leader of the band, and couldn't wait to hear what came next.

"Captain Doug, or can I just call you Doug?"

"Off Course, Fire away!"

"Texas is so big, that if I was to get up at 6 o'clock tomorrow morning, get into my car and drive all day, then all night, then all the next day, then I would still be in Texas!"

"Well, I had a car like that once." Doug replied.

In his inebriated state, this was lost on him, but not on the others, who erupted into huge guffaws of laughter, even his wife struggling to contain her composure.

The hotel manager approached and asked, "Captain Harvey, could we have a quiet discussion in my office, if you don't mind?"

"I've just been watching the news," as he settled the captain into a chair, "care for a cold beer perhaps?" which was politely declined, "and I have an idea that I would like to discuss with you."

"Which is?"

"Could we set up a barbecue on the foredeck of your ship, after the emergency services have finished for the day?"

"It is bound to draw crowds of onlookers. We'll supply everything."

"And any profits?"

"We are having a new seamen's centre built, it's all going to go there."

"Sorry, but no, what you are suggesting falls under the auspices of barratry, but I have no objections to you setting up on the dockside, but not on-board my ship."

"What is barratry?"

"That my friend is something that you are going to find out for yourself. I thank you for your hospitality, but now, I am, after collecting my two friends, going to have something to eat, and probably a few beers, and then going back to my ship. Providing that there is no hostility between us that we might be able to return here tomorrow night and then you might all find out just, the more amicable way as to why there is a tea bag on a string on your bar top.

Think of it, as an intelligence test."

The puzzled Hotel Manager sought out a dictionary, and slowly beginning to appreciate just what barratry actually was.

Hmmm he mused, there is more to this man than he initially thought.

However, his two friends decided not to leave with him, keen on keeping the evening going, so he found his own way back to his ship, in a rather dubious taxi, with little in the way of braking, this being found out, when it hit his ship, after bouncing over the wooden dockside first.

Upon recovering after about 30 seconds, there being no sign of the taxi driver who fled, he met Mullah.

"Mullah, start-up that crane, we'll lift this taxi on board, and then we'll hide it."

"Where do we hide it captain," came this somewhat lost response.

"For 100 rupees, tonight you pick it up, swing it clear over the top of the compressor house and then lower it into the dock, leaving only a very light line between the top of the taxi, which has a stronger one attached, that no-one can see. And then tomorrow, when it gets dark, we can pick it up, strip it to bits, and sell on anything that we can recover."

"But captain, how do I pick it up?"

"Do I have to do everything? Go to the fo'c'sle, get 60 feet of heavy Manila rope, and meet me back here. I'll get the sail twine and beeswax. Now Move! We are going to make a snotter."

A few minutes passed, as each sought out their requirements.

"Mullah, I said Manila rope, that is Polypropylene rope!"

"Yes I know captain, but this rope is easier to splice," Mullah replied.

A pause followed, with the inevitable sigh, "Mullah, we are trying to hide this car and what you are proposing to use, and to pick it up with also floats, so go and get 60 feet of Manila rope, which does not,.......... float!"

A rare smile came from Mullah, no teeth showing, mostly because he hadn't any, as he scurried off and eventually arrived back with the rope asked for, then busied himself with the task in front of him; this captain really knows what he is doing. He thought, or might have done, if he actually had the ability to think.

"Okay Mullah, the roof of the car is worth nothing, so feed the snotter through the front drivers and passenger windows, and heave away. You might need to go high, so forget about the cranes limits. We need to change the wires anyway."

To which he did. Anyone noticing might just be a bit puzzled, as it was during the night?

"Okay Mullah, drop it here," as he indicated for the cranes hook, outward from the top of the ships compressor room and the main deck, by now, this being on the port side of the ship. (To none nautical readers, port is left.)

"But where do I put it captain?"

"I've already told you Mullah, it is going to be hidden in the dock, alongside the ship, so lower it gently down onto the port side, take your time, and when it settles onto the dock bottom, then keep on lowering until the 2nd eye of the snotter comes within my reach, then I'll put a light line on."

A few minutes passed as Mullah did so, then went to shut down the cranes hydraulics, he not really understanding the logic of it all, and went back to finish his watch puzzled, how could a bit of fishing line, bring up the weight of a car, even an American car, from the bottom of a dock, back onto a ship? But then, he wasn't all that bright to start with.

"Oh, hello, who are you," as the captain arrived back in the ships offices, glad to be appreciating the coolness of the air-conditioning. Being met with a rather lost individual, who appeared to be somewhat, perturbed.

"I'm looking for my wife, and I know she has been coming to this ship, is she here?"

"Well, first of all, take a seat, in here in my office," as the captain unlocked the door, and invited him in.

"Care for a cold beer? Or a cold soda if you are driving?"

"A cold tinny would be nice, thank-you," as the beer he was given was opened with a gentle fizzing sigh. "Take a seat."

"I trust that your wife is called Christine Harris, who works for Been & Co?"

"Yes. I've just only gotten back from Houston, and she wasn't home, nor did she meet me at the airport. I'm John Harris."

"Okay, relax, Christine comes down to this ship every evening, to collect a letter that I write regarding our main engine repairs, to which it must be faxed off. For some reason, she did not come tonight, so it was faxed off from the hotel up the road. Christine was here earlier, but left just after lunch, after she came to up-date us on other matters. She has started using her lunch break to do this as my Chief Officer is also German, and I rather think that she enjoys a few minutes gossip in her native language."

"Is he on board, can I see him?"

"I'm afraid not, he and the Norwegian Gas Engineer, at this time of night are competing to see who is best at holding up one of the local bar tops, the competition ending usually at about 11pm, when they declare a draw. I rather think that you may know what I mean, as from your accent, I'd say that you are one of my antipodean cousins."

"It's a long time since I heard that, yes I am Australian."

"Could my wife still be on board?" asked John Harris.

"Highly unlikely, as visitors only ever come to the ships office, unless they are invited to dine with us, as the rest of this ship is so complex, that anything they may see would most likely be lost on them," said Doug, the captain.

"But we'll ask around anyway, come on, if you want to find out anything that is going on, on-board a ship, we start by asking the galley radio."

Who fortunately, were still mostly ashore, but a few crew were still in the Dayroom, watching TV, although how anyone with an IQ of over 10 could watch American TV was lost on this captain. "Hey guys, turn the sound down will you, at least for a minute or so, or preferably until the end of the decade."

The gesticulation from the captains' hands not being visible to John Harris behind but caught by all when asked. "Anyone seen Christine? Is, she still on board?"

A general consensus of opinion was mainly in the negative, although one Filipino hand was very quickly in motion to cover Mullah's mouth.

"Sorry John, but come, we'll have a quick look round anyway and we'll start on the bridge which did rather fascinate her."

No joy, she wasn't there, nor in his or The Chief Engineers cabin, not even the Chief Officers cabin, although even a scabby dog would probably avoid this. A few words in the morning reserved in his memory for the next day.

"Sorry John, can't help I'm afraid," as they both stood at the bottom of the accommodation ladder. Now back on the dockside. "Could she perhaps have gone to visit a friend?" asked Doug.

"Possibly, well thanks Doug."

"John, can I ask you a personal question? And don't answer if you think I should be minding my own business, but is your marriage with Christine in some sort of difficulty?"

The rather hopeless rocking of the shoulders, the hollow eyes with little apparent focus and the tired arms requiring no answer, but one to which was given anyway.

"Yes Doug, but please keep this to yourself. We are from different religions, and both of us thought that we could make it work when we married."

"Take care John, if I find anything out, I'll let you know."

He then, got into his car, started the engine and gently pulling away although oddly going in the opposite direction to the one that, Christine usually took. Well, well, well, a Jehovah's Witness married to an Anabaptist, that should make for some interesting discussion over Sunday lunch. Even more so given that one was Australian, the other German, and in The United States of America, where religions take on other meanings, if also involved in politics.

The captain sitting on the bottom step of the accommodation ladder thinking reflectively, and not noticing as Mike and Einar arrived. Or would have been seen arriving, had the driver actually switched on the cars headlights, or any sort of light, their arrival being announced, by hitting something, possibly metallic, most likely car shaped. Which next day, could, present another un-foreseen problem? Such as, what had they hit? But that would have to wait, for now.

"Who was that Doug?" asked Mike, getting out of the hired car, a curious Einar slightly behind and commenting, "and where did these dents and scratch marks on the hull come from and all of these oil stains?"

"Eh," as he looked up, evidently sublime to what had just happened.

"Oh my taxi had little in the way of brakes, but don't worry I've gotten the taxi hidden, and that guy driving away was Christine's husband. Care for a cold beer while I see if I can find Christine. Let me have the car keys please."

After running up the accommodation ladder to his office, where Doug sought out a powerful torch, questions abounded in abundance, the only reply being, "I'll tell you in the morning, and Mullah can tell you where the taxi is, if you can get any sense out of that Sub-continent brain. See you later."

Puzzled looks passed between two confused faces, as they watched him leave. Upon which, both sought out the coolness of the ship's offices.

"He's left his office door un-locked, that's not like him. Do you think he'll be long?" said one.

"Don't know," said the other, "but we might as well drink his beer until he comes back, and in the meantime, we'll quiz Mullah."

To which they both did. 30 minutes and several beers later were now no closer to finding out just where this mysterious taxi was hidden, than when they had first set out.

Meanwhile, the captain had found Christine's car, and with his bright torch in hand, found that the car was empty, although strangely, the keys were still in the ignition.

The night was absolutely dead still, not a breath of wind, the surface of the port waters eerily reflecting the light from above, only a gentle lapping coming from the rocks below. Strange he thought, why lapping, when there was nothing to lap with. His torch beam found the answer why.

"Eh, Christine, just why are you swimming in the harbour at this time of night?"

The response being a little jaded, and lacking in any sort of humour.

"Well I first of all fell asleep in my car, then I got hot and stripped off to cool down and get clean at the same time and I've been swimming ever since as I can't find where I left my clothes. Could you help me please Doug?"

"Just exactly, what are you wearing Christine?" he offered, although most probably already knowing the answer.

"Nothing at all," came, the rather lame and wet answer.

"I'll have a look around, you just keep paddling."

A few minutes later, "okay, out you come, don't tell me not to look as it is pitch dark anyway."

Even later, with many German swear words, the most common being the one that describes that emanated from one's solid expulsion system on one's rear, Christine declared herself ready to go home. Looking like a rag doll not even coming close to her original appearance.

"Christine, you are not going home, and you are not going back to my ship either, now where, is your nearest friend's apartment?"

"Why?" she asked.

"Your husband has been on board looking for you, including looking on the bridge and my cabin, plus various other places."

Her face fell, "oh no!" she said.

Now listen carefully, he told me about your marriage, and this is what I told him.

It took about 5 minutes to explain.

"So for tonight, you are staying with a friend, the one you told me about that you join in learning Spanish together, and I am going to drive you there, then when you are getting presentable again, I will bring your friend back down here, who will collect your car and leave it looking as though you parked it there yourself, at her place. Then get a good night's sleep. Call your husband in the morning and ask him to meet you for lunch, but whatever you do, don't come aboard until you pick up tomorrow night's fax, and if you can, bring him with you. Okay."

The logic of this took a little time to sink in as Christine appreciated that her previous behaviour and desire to be with someone else might just have been uncovered as an affair, to which her new love had sorted out even before she was aware of it.

The plan worked, albeit taking yet another hour.

"Find her?" from Mike as Doug arrived back in his office, "Yep," as he opened his fridge door for a cold beer, to find nothing there.

"It is not going to take Einstein to work out just why my previously full bottles of beer are now empty ones in my bin, how many have you had?"

The answer was not forthcoming, as he continued.

"Fortunately, I have a few more in my cabin, care to join me?" Silly question really, as he was already on his own.

"So where is the taxi?" both asked in unison as he entered his own cabin, met by two very curious engineers, already enjoying more of his beer.

"Well, if its' brakes had worked, would probably still be on the starboard side, had it not gone through the entire ship, is now on the port side, and submerged."

"Care to explain?"

"This ship is metric, the taxi is Imperial, and we now have all of the little bits of bolts and nuts that we need to dismantle the boxes of bits that The Americans are giving us, to adapt our own tools, which are a whole lot quicker than Coastal Iron, don't you think, seeing as the US is still Imperial."

"Eh! Yes, but what do we do with the rest of it?"

"We let someone else tow it out of port. Like the Department of Agriculture, who came down this afternoon, when you were both busy and you will not believe just what **they,** came up with!"

"Which was?"

"All of our garbage has to be sterilised, in a container, and by steam, with lime added, by boiling it for 30 minutes, before it can be disposed of for landfill. Unless, we can show the documentation relating to every single piece of stores loaded on board and this includes, fuel, and for the last 2 years."

"So how the hell do you sterilise fuel?" asked both incredulously, before being informed, that they also had to sterilise the half sealed empty drums of lube oil, supplied by the same company as well.

"It gets worse. You know all of the empty cans of Gatorade that we are getting through at the rate of 5 cases or so a day, they have to be sterilised as well. And they all came from here."

"But why the Department of Agriculture, for a gas tanker, or even a ship?" asked even more incredulously. "When was a ship, part of a field?"

"Eh, we'll not go into that just now if you don't mind," replied the captain before hurriedly continuing, the other two not picking up on this fortunately. "Believe it or not, and it took me a long time to understand this one, any uneaten cooked meat discarded has to be sterilised, and this includes these little bits of meat on top of a pizza."

"Are you winding us up?"

"No! They even have their own boat, although they prefer to call it a "Cutter," pretty much like The US Coast Guard "Cutters," only this one is a bit smaller, which by my figuring, is now parked on the port side of our ships main cargo deck. I don't think that this wee boat ever leaves the harbour, which as you know is pretty big, the harbour that is. Not overly wisely parked, but they are so damn arrogant, that they didn't think to ask for permission first. They ordered it, plus I am informed there is this silly wee chap stationed at the bottom of the accommodation ladder, making sure that we don't sneak anything off, before it can be sterilised. He's even got a gun, although they seem to call it, a sidearm. Seems stupidly dumb to me, as where else do you normally have your arms? Ever heard of a front arm or a back arm? And what use is 0.45 calibre bullet, or whatever size they use against a 6500 tonne ship. It's not as such that the ship can actually fire back. The Department of Agriculture's master then, after boarding, asked to use a restroom, to which I had to check first, he then went for a disposal of the bowels, and I, sort of being, an honest and decent Christian chap, directed him to the nearest one of the old cadet's cabins. Did you not see him as you came aboard?"

"Who?" asked both?

"The guy with the sidearm?"

"No." Coming from both in unison.

"Ah, that might be that he by now is in a car. You know how Americans are car dependent, just to get the air conditioning on, and the radio."

"Did we, or at least anyone sneak any garbage off?" the question being of no relevancy whatsoever, but asked anyway.

"Do pigs fly? Off course we have. While they weren't looking at us, they left the stern of their own 'cutter' unattended, so all off our garbage is now on the back of their boat, and their master, is currently trying to get out of the spare cadet's cabin toilet, or rest room, call it what you will."

"Why?" asked others.

"Because there is no handle on the inside of that door, and he could be in there all night!"

Mesmerised faces prompting something further, such as a clue?

"We cannibalised it last week remember, and an awful lot of the bits we removed are currently holding other bits of this ship together, seeing as the last owners did not leave us with many spare parts. The Propylene Oxide safety system pipework, which we don't need just now, is now on the fuel rack of a generator. We cannibalised that as well, plus one or two other places, which we hope to get fixed before the next seaworthy survey."

"And you expect to get away with this?" asked Einar, Mike also nodding his head hopefully, as it was he, who in the first place, had asked the captain, as to where he could get this bit of pipe for his generator.

"Einar, in my last company, we made our own spares, we had to."

"Now if you will excuse me, I'm just on my way to sink their boat or cutter or whatever they want to call it. That will get rid of our garbage at the same time, easy really."

The pause being somewhat silent, although protracted, as.......?

"Back in 5 minutes, just away to start a couple of pumps! Help yourselves to another beer, or six," as he quietly departed.

"I don't know about you mate," said Mike, as he left, "but I have this awful funny feeling that he has done this sort of thing before," as the captain headed downwards.

This thought being perceived simultaneously, although not as yet registering in two engineering minds.

"So do I Einar, but just exactly what pumps is he going to start?"

An incongruous look passed between them.

Oh no! Not them!

As both raced out of his cabin but to no avail, they being too late, a few thousand or so tonnes of water per hour from the cargo heater outlet now pouring in through the starboard wheelhouse door of their silly little wee boat, they being silly enough leaving the door open, and who could blame them really, as arrogance often takes over from common sense. The Department of Agriculture's Cutter, which when the back-up pump also came on, boosting this up by another 500 tonnes, left The Department of Agriculture's Cutter with a severe stability problem, some afterwards not being able to ascertain whether it capsized first, or just plain, sank. Irrelevant really, as it was now on the bottom of the dock, and all his own ship's garbage, happily drifting away. Fortunately, no lives were lost, although a few rather did get a bit of a fright, and, rather wet. Plus one in particular, rather forgetful, leading onto, expensive, VERY!

"Well boys, it has been a long day, I think I'll head off to bed. Good night," after arriving back in his cabin.

"Eh, just hold on a minute from his 2 engineering friends, how are you going to explain this?"

"Explain what? They parked their boat alongside without permission from the ships master, he being me, a pump started, to which if they had asked first would have been told that that was not a wise place to park their boat and as a result bent my ships rails with their ropes, to which in the morning, I will issue a Letter of Protest for the damage that they have caused to my ship. Good night."

The door closing quietly, which followed with, "I don't know about you Mike, but I think tomorrow is going to be one hell of an interesting day, especially as John Standish and his boys are coming in the afternoon with their fire engines, plus God knows what else."

"And our new crankshaft arrives tomorrow, which is really our priority, which should keep both of us away from what might just happen."

"I know," as both left on their way to their respective sleeping places. The masters cabin door already closed, but from another door in close proximity, came a lot of very loud curses, also noted by Einar and Mike, as both sought out to inquire why, life on board this ship running in between the curious to just, what the hell can go wrong next?

From the toilet/restroom in the cadet's cabin, there came sounds of a very angry Texan individual, with his trousers and underpants around his ankles, and an indescribable smell.

"Got a problem?" ventured one, stifling a grin.

"I can't get up from this seat," which did not come in pleasant tones, the swear words being plentiful, and there were many. Indifferently really as it was met with no sympathy, other than, "Good night then, see you in the morning."

Mike, with a little tap on the captain's door met almost immediately with a smug grin, as it opened, and told quietly, "he's been a complete pain in the arse since he came on-board, and before you ask, the toilet seat was covered in cyanoacrylate, where he is going to feel his pain not near his arse, but pretty close to it. Have you ever tried to sleep on a toilet seat? Either of you?" Einar being seen in the background, trying and failing miserably to hide, but only realising from a distant memory, that cyanoacrylate was known to most as, superglue! In the UK at least.

The reply being in the negative, to the captains question although that might not be quite true, as both remembered when they had fallen asleep on the toilet, but were not prepared to admit to it, especially to this captain, who would most certainly use such knowledge in the future and most probably at an embarrassing time.

"Are you going to leave him there? Like all night," from one asked curiously.

"Goodness no, I left a spanner over the flush valve, when he gets the bolts out, then he can easily wander off. It might be a wee bit awkward, but totally his fault, as he forgot to wipe the toilet seat first, there being a reminder on the bulkhead behind him, which currently he can't actually see, or didn't notice in the first place. Driving his car when he eventually gets there, should be a relatively simple matter, or a challenge, as long as he puts the car's front seat back. Mind you, explaining all of this to his wife might also just be a wee bit tricky, although anyone with a camera should get some fascinating pictures of a man trying to get down the accommodation ladder of a ship with a toilet seat glued to his backside, trousers and underpants could be anywhere. And if any of the crew can get a photo, let me know and I'll not only pay him for the photo, but charge The Department of Agriculture, a huge amount of money for one of their officials stealing a toilet seat, as a souvenir. Then I'll send the photo to The Corpus Christi Caller Times."

"Remind me," said one to the other quietly, "never to get on the wrong side of this captain," as Einar slunk out of his supposedly secret hiding place.

Both only later realising, and some hours later, that the unfortunate Texan still had to get the restroom door open from the inside, although from the clattering and banging suggesting, that the incumbent had actually found another use for the spanner, and it wasn't working. Nor had he come by car.

His sidearm being tried next, but after one shot, then a second shortly afterwards convinced even he, that this was not a wise way of getting out, as the bullets, just ricocheted off the bit where the door handle just used to be, disappearing somewhere else before the grey matter realising that he was firing at a steel door. Probably having gotten the idea from old Western Movies with the crooks trying to shoot the lock off a strongbox, which never actually worked! Well it did on screen anyway, but not in reality, as no mention was ever shown on screen, just as to where the bullet actually went after it hit the padlock.

Try the hinges then. If he could find them, which he couldn't as the door was hung from the other side.

The Filipino crew however, now having heard of this had conspired, not only to free him but were waiting with their cameras, and flash guns, just to see how he actually got off the ship. They now knowing of their captain's sense of humour, and that he always kept a promise.

But not quite! The distraction being welcomed on the starboard side, as not much later, the captain went for a little swim, on the port side and retrieved from The Department of Agriculture's Cutter, a modest sized briefcase, which upon returning, and not being seen, now had safely tucked away underneath the drawers of his bunk.

Next day, "hey guys, what is today's date?" as the captain, always an early riser, walked into his office, albeit a bit late this particular day.

No answer forthcoming, from the captain's question to all and sundry, no-one apparently having the first clue, as each day ran into the next. The Log Book from yesterday, an Important Norwegian Document, filled in daily by the captain to which, the Norwegian Consul would want to inspect, just seemed to have gone missing.

"It was on the bridge last night and it isn't there now."

"Right get on with the day, I'll find it." With the beginnings of exasperation as this was not the only important document that had gone missing.

"Now Blackie, they are ready to lift the block this morning, all 23 tonnes of it, and as soon as the crankshaft is out, it will be lowered back down, which is our key to re-trim the ship. Yes I know, we have already discussed this, but we also have to take into consideration that dumb stupid Department of Agriculture's boat which is about to get somewhat squashed."

"I can't wait," he said, "the skipper on that boat, cheats at Poker."

"How do you know that?" although instantly said, also realised just where his Chief Officer had been going each evening. "Okay, you take the front bit, I'll take the back bit, where we keep the cranes and not another question!"

A few hours passed, although there was a distant memory of someone attached to a toilet seat whose cries for help couldn't be heard anywhere, mostly because no-one was within earshot. Well, those who were having a big grin on their faces, thinking otherwise, and many winks exchanging between them both. He'd been in there all night.

"Okay Blackie, start putting the bow down, when she is even keel, and after getting the nod from the engine room, I'll start to lift the stern, then push the bow down even more. You look after the longitudinal trim as we agreed. I'll do the transverse trim, providing no-one else gets in the way." This being on their portable radios.

The hole being already cut in the hull, did not present an easy transfer of the old and bent crankshaft from the ship to the dockside, or for the new one going in.

Trimming a ship being relatively easy to do, either lengthwise or transversely, but in this case, it was necessary to 'twist' the ship as well, effectively pushing her starboard bum up onto the level with the dockside, while her port bow went the other way, at the other end. But it wasn't totally working.

"Okay Blackie, Plan B it is, "Start flooding the chain lockers, port side first please."

After about an hour or so, this worked splendidly, getting one old bent crankshaft out of the ship, to be replaced by her new one, with just about everyone pulling in all sorts of different directions with chain blocks, until the big crane could no longer be used.

"Blackie, The new crankshaft is now in, I'll trim her back to even keel, and I've already taken the twist out. Oh and you can drop whatever went into the chain lockers, back into the port."

"Yes captain," as a rueful smile crossed his face.

Unfortunately for the Department of Agriculture's cutter, it got the opposite, and became somewhat, squashed, to their alarmed consternation as they came rushing on-board, from shore side shouting "STOP STOP, you're crushing our cutter!" The master not being one of those expressing sympathy, as would be un-covered later.

To be met with a rather indifferent reply of, "Well, you put it there in the first place, and now is for us, not a good place to stop, as I now have just un-twisted this ship, so bugger off and see if you can find something useful to do, like driving a combine harvester, if you can find any floating wheat fields in this port."

But there was something close to it and not that far away.

"Captain, I demand that you stop what you are doing!" the level of facial expression suggesting to the captain that a visit to the poop deck was called for, with his subordinate in tow.

"See that bit over there," with a broad scan of his arm," as they all arrived onto the poop deck, "I hope you can swim, just don't come back," as this pain in the neck was lifted by his collar, and the seat of his pants, and thrown overboard, his entry into the water not being in any way painless, "you have the choice," as he looked at the other whose horrified face now scant with fear, "either jump, or get thrown." He jumped, a great pity that where he chose to enter the water was alongside his ship mate who copped for his elbow onto the middle top of his head. Strangely enough for the second one on his funny bone, rendering both with pain that only a few seconds earlier had not existed, but to which now, both found swimming awkward, and a few seconds after this, worse, both getting bonked on the head by the lifebuoy thrown in after them. It was only later, that both had to explain why they were there in the first place and not convincingly in the least with their explanation, as to why just how both were entangled in the lifebuoy's rope, which included a few knots, which some might explain away as the rope being tangled. Great spectator sport for those above, watching two trying to release themselves from this muddled rope in the water, their language certainly not being suitable in any way to anyone with a parent with a child in close proximity. Most of which contained a word which didn't always come out properly, it being necessary to spit out harbour water at the same time, apart from a few other things floating by, which they most certainly didn't want in their mouth in the first place.

"Come on, Blackie time to set up a false fire, after watching 10 minutes of this struggle," neither of those in the water realising that they now had both ends of the lifebuoys rope!

"Are you going to leave them there captain?" asked Blackie? With a problematic face?

"Well, they are bound to find themselves washed up somewhere, they do have a lifebuoy after all to keep them afloat, and look how far they have drifted away in the last 10 minutes. A couple of hours should see them on the other side of the harbour, and out of our hair for good."

The explanation not totally convincing.

"Right Blackie, do you remember that big box of time expired pyrotechnics that I found in a wardrobe, when we first came on-board. Where are they now?"

"Still got them, in the same place as you found them, what do you need? And where do you want them?"

"Put the 2 old smoke floats, one upwards, the other downwards and secure them to the rails just ahead of Number 2 void space. Shut the starboard entrance to number 2 void space, but leave the port side open. We'll use them to simulate smoke. I know that they make a mess, but these fire brigade boys will wash all it off anyway. Then take say, 6 of the parachute distress flares and wire them up in situ to the rails but take off the protective covers first, the one's covering the triggers, just so that they could go off at random, which should simulate that just blasting a whole lot of water at a fire on board a ship is not always the best way of putting a fire out, which, as we both know, a little is better than a lot. Just for the hell of it add about a hundred feet of rope to each one, so you can trigger them off remotely. You'll get the rope from the expired line throwing rockets. That should get their heads down, don't you think?"

"Can I use some of the old hand flares as well?" suggested he, hopefully with eyes inviting the word, yes.

This came in the affirmative. "A hand flare taped backwards to a rocket, and set off at the same time should make a good contribution to chaos I think, when the rocket runs out of propellant, and ignites its parachute flare, should be enough to set off the hand flare. I'll leave you to get on with it."

Down aft they were oblivious to this, but the new crankshaft was now lying nicely alongside the ships main engine, with the balance weights in the process of being fitted, not a big job as such, but one which took longer due to the confines of the space. Plus the unbearable heat, it now daily being over 110 degrees Fahrenheit.

In the ships office, another problem had arisen, to which the captain was already onto, if in doubt, delegate...... "Been and Co, Christine speaking, how may I help you?" inquired the other end of the landline 'phone just called.

"Christine, Doug, the captain and your forever busy friend, does your company know of any scrapyards? We've got this wee bit of scrap steel that we need to get rid of, but under marine insurance clauses, I need a receipt for."

Christine, now knowing that her Scottish friend was the understatement champion still risked the question, of "how wee, is wee?"

"Oh pretty wee, know any company that could come down and buy it?"

"You haven't answered the question, how wee, is wee?"

"Christine," in reply, from the captain, "it might take 2 of us to pick it up. Providing that you can find some bodybuilders, and I was not one of the 2."

"Six and a half tonnes give or take a few grams or so, and sort of, crankshaft shaped. They might just need a bit more of a truck to take it away, but I think we could supply the crane. As a guide price, we are looking at about in US Dollars terms, say $200."

"What! For something that costs $250 000 dollars?"

"That is the new cost, but this one is bent, so if you can find an engine that has 9 cylinders, but only needs 8, then we can give it to them for free, they just won't need the bent bit."

"I'll get onto it Doug, and call you back," the heavily strained reply conveying its own weight. "Oh, and before you hang up, John Standish and his boys are coming down at 2 this afternoon, are you all set up for a fire? Oh sorry, a simulated fire?"

"That we are, but with an odd surprise thrown in, see you later my darling Christine."

"That isn't fair Doug, trying for her to find a 9 cylinder engine that only needs 8 cylinders, she is after all, your new girlfriend," said Mike overhearing this in a little aside in the doorway of their ships offices.

"Well, we limped this ship in with only 8, but her boss doesn't and he needs taking down a peg or two. She's already delegated the task onto him," speaking softly. "And Christine will be spending a few more hours with us, while that arrogant Texan, tries to find a 9 cylinder engine that fits an 8 cylinder crankshaft."

"Do you think that he is that dumb?"

"Do pigs fly?"

Little did he know at the time of actually finding one, the ninth, the bent bit, of which could be straightened out.

Meanwhile, and back on the 'phone to their agents.

"You might just have a wee bit of trouble getting on board Christine, unless you are here in the next 10 to 15 minutes, as we are just about to lift the accommodation ladder. No point making it easy for the fire fighters, they've got their own ladders anyway, oh, and we've added a little bit of grease as well……………………………… hello, hello, are you there Christine?……………………hello?"

"I don't know what you said to her captain," said Richard, after picking up the 'phone, but I've never seen Christine move as fast as she just did."

To which the Corpus Christi Police had also noticed a few minutes later, as she flew past their radar trap, registering an incredible 110 miles per hour! And not showing any intention of slowing down, until at the very last second, with all four wheels locked and smoke pouring from all four tyre's, she got out of the car, and jumped onto the bottom step of the accommodation ladder, as it was starting to lift from the dock, ready for a fire drill, unsurpassed in the training of safety of ships at sea, only this one was in port, to which it lifted no more.

"Erling, here's $300 bucks, get her car keys off her, and get 4 new tires on her car, then park it at Einar's hotel. Don't argue, just do it." To which in the confusion he managed to do, just before the Police arrived, getting away that was.

"Your car Christine, is going to get 4 new tyres fitted," as she breathlessly landed into his arms, "only thing I could come up with to explain away 4 flat spotted tyres, and these massive long skid marks, that The Police are bound to wonder about. What speed were you doing, when you hit the brakes?"

"No idea my darling Doug, but it was pretty fast."

The Police, way behind in the catch up stakes, now found themselves mixed up with four fire engines going hell for leather to Cargo Dock 12, and at a speed that was easier to keep up with, than to argue against, this coming over their radios.

"It's an exercise boys, we've only just found out, and look for yellow smoke." Coming over the Police radios.

"Okay Blackie," on the captain's radio, "set off the smoke floats," to which he duly did. A rather satisfying sight as the Fire Engines arrived with all of the TV crew's wagons and some very confused Police officers.

"It rather reminds me of The Keystone Cops Christine," as they both stood back, he leaning back against the coaming, with his arms folded around Christine's shoulders and below her breasts, she settling in against him and watching the mayhem unfold from their vantage point on the starboard bridge wing, "I think Blackie and the boys may have just been a bit too liberal with the grease."

"What grease Doug?"

"Oh, to make it all look a bit more realistic, as they are now pumping masses of water onto **'the fire'** we greased the deck as well, oh, and also the handrails, which now that they have got their ladders up, is probably why they are having just a little bit of trouble getting over, or keeping their feet!"

"Okay Blackie, phase 2. You know what to do," over his hand held radio on his ships frequency. The other tuned into the same frequency as the Fire Department and The Police.

"What is phase 2 Doug?" alarmingly from Christine, her head turning to look at his face, and where did you get that other radio from?"

"It was in my back pocket darling. And as to phase 2, just wait and watch." Said with a little, wry and smug smile.

"Christine, to put out a fire on a ship, you do not just blast masses of water at it. Once you have located the source, you cool down everything around it, known as 'boundary cooling' and then carefully work your way in with a minimum of water. Only this is a simulated fire, and as we cannot simulate what fire-fighters might find on their way to the source, it could be anything..................oh! There goes the 1st one! That should keep their heads down."

Which it did! "What the hell was that?" from John Standish on his radio to his other fire fighters. "Don't know boss," came one reply, "but it came from in front of me, can you cut down on the water, as I'm having one hell of a time keeping my feet."

Somewhat heard un-surprisingly, from the viewers above, knowing that grease was not an overly good thing to walk on, far less trying to oppose the thrust of a fire hose. The jet going everywhere other than where it was meant to go, but taking out those other fire fighters, also having trouble keeping their feet, from other directions.

"No problem, we'll only spray water to each side of the fire."

This coming over the 2ⁿᵈ radio, with a gracious and smiling grin coming over the captain's face he already knowing just what was coming next.

"Christine, they are starting to think as fire fighters, and that ships are different from buildings. Okay Blackie, let 2 more go." Christine lying back in his arms and watching in amazement, as TV crews trying to get the best view, got in the way of fire fighters and the local police, all of whom were getting thoroughly soaked in the process.

But there was something puzzling the captain, as he held her close to himself, something to do with which he would need to uncover later, something to do with her bra.

"Now this next one Christine is bound to scare the hell out of them. I've used this before on another gas tanker. It is something that no one on a gas tanker should actually do, until they understand all of how a gas tanker operates. On these ships, a little bit of knowledge is a very dangerous thing. Now watch them all jump. I'm going to simulate just what happens when a fusible plug melts, and with this being a 'fire,' will shut the entire deck down, only I'm putting an entire 50 litre bottle of nitrogen into the deck piggy system at the same time. That's the bit that vaporises liquid gas into vapour if a line safety valve should lift before it goes up the riser and water is the very last thing that we need near the bottom of the riser. On the piggy yes, but not, on the bottom of the riser!"

"Eh, what is a fusible plug? Doug."

"Tell you later, come on, we need to get inside, this way," he coming off from leaning against the coaming, then entering the ship's bridge. A delightful Christine, finding that her feet were not still actually in contact with the deck and had to go as well, but appreciating that one of his arms was now supporting each of her breasts and the rest of her top, his other arm having moved downwards to a position of which was most welcoming, well to Christine at least.

Now inside, "Blackie, throw the Emergency Shutdown Switch and let another one go, no, make that 2," from the captain he then closing the bridge wing door, in order of not getting any wetter than both he and Christine now were, she rather dumped unceremoniously as he tripped on his way carrying her in, getting the door closed taking priority to getting his girlfriend upright. But a glance in her direction rather satisfying, as this dishevelled young beauty, trying to work out how her bra had become so entangled with her other clothing, that both breasts were now fully evident, and there did not seem to be a way out of. A sort of, new type of nautical knot. Going to be good unravelling though, later, providing no-one got there first.

But there were other matters to consider, although this distraction would have to wait, somewhat reluctantly.

"Onto it, and I can't wait to see where these go!"

There was an almighty whoosh as the deck pneumatics air reservoir dumped its charge, held at 6.5 bars. Valves open, now closing on their spring returns, alarms going off everywhere, leaving everyone within earshot wondering just what the hell, was that! But letting 250 bar of nitrogen loose from a 50 litre bottle into the piggy, saw the firemen on the deck, beating a hasty retreat, grease helping them fall onto TV crews who had gotten too close.

"I don't know what the hell that was boss," by radio to John Standish, "but fighting a fire on a gas tanker is far from easy. We've either got too much water, or not enough! And this only a practise exercise. Oh no! There's now new smoke, only it isn't yellow, it's white."

"Which is what happens when a bottle of compressed nitrogen suddenly meets water at atmospheric pressure, it freezes it, then a second or so later, de-frosts it," explained the captain to a rather lost looking lady, now partly disentangled and upright once more.

Unfortunately when the Emergency Shutdown Button was pressed, 3 more pumps came on, as the deck spray system started, with the entire deck, bridge front and the compressor house now enveloped in a fine mist of spray, well initially, but after a few seconds, just massive torrents of very fast moving water going everywhere, and on top of the grease, which was when the old 6.5 tonne crankshaft disappeared.

Not noted by those on the ships bridge, they not being able to see anything, but were at least dry. Off a sort, with Christine still trying to sort her bra out, there being no shortage of volunteers to help, mostly of a Filipino nationality, and male, she seeking sanctuary in the bridge toilet, locking the door, and desperately hoping, that no-one on the other side would be other than the captain after she had sorted herself out.

Not so from The Corpus Christi Fire Department, who were seriously getting increasingly wet, plus a few others.

"That is the least of our problems, abandon this exercise, we've now got a real fire to put out," said somewhat exasperatedly from John Standish.

One of the TV crews vans appeared to be on fire, it being on the wrong end of a parachute distress rocket taped to a flare, the crew, no-where in sight. And a police car, with no windscreen, also on fire! But strangely also had a satellite transmitter aerial from the TV van, or what was left of it sparking away, this being the most probable start of the fire in the police car. With the officer and his partner also nowhere to be seen, at least from 80 feet up, although they might be underneath something, that being the preferred place, as many others had already sought. The overhead police helicopter having to veer off, as yet another distress rocket fired, its' stabilisation not working until about 500 feet, when the flare fell off and was now discharging red smoke towards the garden of a soon to be non-too happy Texan.

"Blackie, did you set off the one that I made?"

"No captain, that one, you can set off yourself."

"Oh go on, just fire it."

The "NO!" being very convincingly sounding, as to "YES," being not the reply expected.

"Okay, we'll keep it for later. Coward"

The competitors TV crews loving this, and recording it all, from a distance despite previously getting very wet, when of all people, the Corpus Christi Mayor arrived in his limousine.

That should be helpful. No need for The Police to explain to The Mayor's Office, just why one of their Police cars had now exploded. Fortunate too, that he, now sheltering in a ditch watched his limousine roll towards the dock, its handbrake not appearing to have been applied and with the engine still running, helping it on its way towards its' floatation point. The driver's side door not completely closed either. An awkward introduction by 2 police officers, now protecting the Mayor where in their enthusiasm, found later that his face had been pressed, accidentally into the mud, despite his struggles. The ensuing language not becoming of someone in high office, and most certainly not available for putting into print, apart from the other hacks of who were tripping over themselves trying to get this into copy. One of whose cars just happened to collide with a fire engine after getting its front wheels nicely mangled up with a fire hose, which some fireman had carelessly left lying around, the water of which also going nowhere near where it was intended to go, mostly as because, on the other end, the nozzle had already become partly detached, as it flailed around with 2 firemen, trying in vain, to catch it. Others earlier having the same problem, and with the same lack of success, as in no success at all! The grease certainly assisting.

"You know Christine, you couldn't invent more mayhem. But I'll tell you one thing, when I take you for lunch tomorrow at the 5 star Windham Hotel, we won't have to look too hard for a parking space."

She, now having her bra and top sorted out, well after a fashion as the buttons didn't look like they were in the corresponding button holes curiously asked, why?

"Because we can use the Mayors private parking space, seeing as his car appears to be sinking, and in a not very fortunate position, for us all not to be, in the least, even slightly concerned."

"Why?" asked Christine. But she only got a rueful smile for an answer. "Oh no," she said, beginning to realise, that The Mayors Limo, was no longer on the dockside, but heading underwater, the bubbles as it sank being evidence as to its final resting place, well, temporarily at least. The driver's door, not being pushed closed even by the increasing water pressure doubling into letting the air out, as the water came in.

Educated minds, thought otherwise, as many sought out to see how to make a quick buck! "Come with me Christine, time we weren't here."

A few hours passed, most of which were pleasantly spent with Christine nestling in the captains arms, in his day room, as they chatted about, what she hoped would be their future. He already having started on the awkward problem of getting her buttons sorted out. "In Scotland Doug, what do you do when you are not sailing around the world? You are not married after all. How do you spend your time?"

"What I like to do most, after I have gotten my house and garden sorted out, is to fill up my rucksack with enough for a week in the mountains, that I do not always climb, I prefer the glens, oh, you might know them as valleys, take a good book and a good quality single malt Scotch Whisky, usually 'The Glenlivet' and go off to one of these little places that I know where there is a little waterfall with perfectly clear clean water, and as it falls into a little pool, pitch my tent alongside the pool, then totally relax. The waterfall is my shower, the pool is where I dabble my feet, and if it rains, which is inevitable, my tent is my home, and my camp fire enough to slowly cook my favourite meal. A carpet-bagger steak."

"But do you not get lonely?" asked Christine?

"Christine, in the Scottish glens, you are never alone, and I can tell you this, if you and I were to pitch camp together, it would not be long before someone came along and joined us."

"I'd love to try this Doug," she answered, snuggling ever closer and still not aware as to just why her tops buttons of her blouse were un-done. The sight from above though solving the problem as to her bra, it was still twisted in the middle, one side being inside out. Goodness knows just how she managed it.

"Yes, but it is what you find underneath all of these wee waterfalls, that makes getting cold all the more worth it. And not from the most obvious of places, not from the pool they create but from behind it. Try this for example," as he reached down and opened his briefcase, before handing her a bit of rock.

She looked with surprised eyes. "Is this what I think it is?"

"No, this is not a yellow diamond, but Cairngorm, and very rare in this carat size."

81

"The only problem we have Christine, is that you are married, if you weren't I'd have been with you on a plane to Scotland with me today, but I've got another 4 months on this ship, according to my contract. You might like to consider being with me in four months' time, but there is still the problem of your husband?"

She marvelling at the beauty of what she had in her hands, and not listening to just what he had said. That something as gorgeous as this could be found in Scotland and all that one needed to know was where to look for it. To which prompted the question, "how much is this worth Doug?"

The current desire of knowing having to be put on hold, as there came a frantic knocking on his cabin door. "Quick Christine, into my bedroom and stay quiet, I rather know just who this is!"

"Oh hello John, you look about on the sweaty wet hot side, care for a beer?" after opening his cabin door. She, Christine without hesitation, did as asked but sort of deliberately, forgot to close the door completely, listening carefully as all females tend to do irrespective of nationality.

He John, somewhat perturbed refused this offered beer and came out with, "this was supposed to be an exercise, now look at all of the damage. How am I going to explain this?"

"Well, as far as I see it, there is no damage to my ship, but to help you, you could start by explaining it all to The Mayor, or The Chief of Police." Who at the time, was slinking into a very dark corner, hoping not to be seen.

"What the hell has this got to do with The Mayor?"

"Because John, he is currently underneath one of your fire engines, and can't wait until you and your boys get him out. And as you do so, then you can ask him."

The look of askance wrote its own story, as he fled, not even hearing the request for a chemical suit and breathing apparatus.

A little while later, he forgetting that Christine was still in his bedroom, and still laughing within at the melee seen from his ships bridge, heard a rather distinct cough from behind. "Have you forgotten about me? I was seriously starting to perspire, and so are you, I've got the shower running, so join me."

Not that he had much choice, as this beautiful German young, well maybe mid-thirties, he not exactly finding out just how old his naked girl-friend actually was, yet, pulled him into the shower, he still dressed, but soon to be relieved of his clothes, stripped by this delightful lady, telling him how much she had fallen in love with him. He not overly resisting, much.

"I've been thinking all afternoon, just how I was going to get into your bed. Now, I don't need to think anymore. Make love to me."

The intended mangled making love position being both entwined in a hopeless position on the floor of the shower, but trying to get out, now that the shower was suddenly putting out very cold water rather than the previous hot steamy stuff, finding that their entangled limbs had now found their way into the captains bedroom. Not overly precisely, in a bit of a heap really, with each heads feet, at opposite ends of their respective heads.

To remedy the situation, as both got up, she in a different way trying to preserve her dignity sought something to cover herself with and found a face towel. About 30 cms square, which did cover one breast, but not much more, the bottom curly bit, between her legs, not covered at all.

However, this not being the immediate priority, though, as the captain's intercom 'phone went off, with "Captain, you're needed in the office and urgently." Followed by a banging on his cabin door. "Captain............"

"Mike," as the captain unlocked his door with a towel wrapped around his waist, to be met with, "Need you in the office Doug, and pronto, we've got two big problems, including something unbelievable."

"As soon as I get dressed, I'll be straight down." The captain replied.

"Sorry Christine, but the ship comes first."

Her face said it all, so near but so far, and then went on to do what all women do when frustrated, the logic of which no man in the world could even begin to understand, choose this particular moment, to wash her hair. With, in this case, a rather frustrated temperament ensuring even faster fingers than before, that the curls were now well and truly clean, and more curled than previously.

"Okay Mike," as the captain entered his office, "fire away. I've been master before, and nothing new even begins to surprise me."

"Someone or some others have stolen our old crankshaft, which as you know was lying on the dockside, opposite the hole we cut in the hull," said Mike.

The response was not immediate, but followed with "could the Corpus Christi Mayors car have hit it and knocked it into the dock?"

"What Mayors car?"

"Oh you don't know about that then, you being in the engine room." And went on to explain just how his Limo was now submerged, and somewhere on the dock bottom kind of close to the ships rudder.

"You seem to have developed the art of hiding cars underwater, that's 2 now. And although I am not superstitious, things happen in 3's you know."

"Mike, you said that we had two big problems, what's the other one?"

"When we got the new crankshaft in, did you organise a pair of welders, to weld up the hole in the hull?"

"Yes, you know I did, they should be finished by now."

"We need to open it up again."

A bright red face could not explain it better, so to avoid any embarrassment, Doug asked, "is it the wrong way round, and there is not enough room in the engine room, to turn it round, so it has to come out again, only this time, goes in the other way round?"

"Yes."

"Okay, forget about shore leave tonight and as to who is going to be blamed, we need to get it the right way round, before anyone finds out and if anyone is to blame, it's me. Make sure everyone understands this. Especially the Filipino crew!"

"We'd be quicker just fitting a door," not realising at the time that in a few months' time, that was what they were going to actually do.

Several hours later, it was the right way round, with many exhausted seafarers, deeply in need of a very cold beer. For which was already provided for. Bloody awful stuff, it being 'Bramha,' from Brazil, and left over from the previous owners of the ship.

It tasted well enough, it cooled the neck and stomach well enough, it took an awful lot of the perspiring's persons heat out, but after about 3 cans, did have the irritating habit of producing from the lower intestine on its way to the anus, an awful lot of gas, mostly methane, the other parts no-one bothering to analyse, the smell being an indicator that hydrogen sulphide was about to clear the room. And that was before the individual sought out the nearest toilet, about to experience a red hot arse occasionally with a bit of slight elevation, he also trying to get away from the dreadful smell.

Well, thought the captain, only about 10 more cases to get rid of, before he could get some better stuff.

Going into his shower, he having lost count as to how often he had been in that day, finally relaxed, and let the water just flow over him, before towelling himself dry and climbed into his bunk naked, seeking well deserved sleep.

Drifting into the land of nod, unaware that Christine had, very quietly, also been sleeping in his bunk, but both being so tired, had failed to notice the presence of the other. Sleep as his head hit the pillow, being instant, or pretty near it, the smell seeming a little familiar.

But not for long, well, after several hours anyway, when two heads came into close alignment and started sharing the same air, with neither actually snoring but unknowingly, enjoying their closeness, and without actually being aware of it, both drifting into a deeper sleep entwined in each other's arms.

The both being naked part, not a problem as they awoke together during the night, and early enough to enjoy more sleep, but both being slightly puzzled as to how each had gotten there, where just after a few and private intimate words, confirming that making love was what they both desired.

But differently, with no rush, just a gentle movement from each other and against each other, and totally en-wrapped in their un-declared love for each other. A stopwatch spring most probably having run out, as he left her beautiful intimate private part, before falling into a deep sleep, with Christine snuggling back into her former position, of breathing close to his shoulder, and trying with all of her might of trying to getting closer still.

Hoping that during the night, they could make love again, although her hand was straying, and from her contact, meant that she was going to wake him up. How to?

Kiss him awake, which after a few minutes, did succeed, as she to her surprise, found that ship-masters do not sleep very much.

But unfortunately, husbands, left alone, also didn't, as one rather angry one had just arrived. And Australian, who tended to be a bit unpredictable when full of beer. Well, they are up-side down after all.

"**Where the hell is my wife**? **And I know that she is here, somewhere,**" this not being expressed in any way of a calm manner. Or truth be told, he was somewhat angry, in a way that distressed Australians reserved for their selves and transportation not a good word to mention at the present time, reminding them of some of their ancestors.

"Hey, calm down," as he was intercepted by the Chief Engineer.

"Well where is my wife?" the anger level on overdrive and more than just a bit, loud.

"There was an awful tight schedule last night, and she and all of the rest of us tried everything that we could think of contacting you, but got nowhere."

The cold 'tinny' being refused, and noted as being odd for an Australian.

"Christine flew to Washington last night with the captain, to get our Sub-Chapter O Endorsement renewed, and your wife has gone with him as she knows her way around The US Coast Guard rules and regulations, of which you should be proud off, because very few others do. And it was the US Coast Guard here in Corpus Christi, who recommended that she go as well."

The anger not subsiding in the least prompted the inevitable question, "**is he sleeping with my wife?**" in rather angry and irate tones.

"Hey, slow down pal," in an effort to placate him.

"The captain was very specific before he left, as in Washington, where we have partner shipping agents, they would stay in different hotels for the night, then get our new certificate, and fly back as soon as they had gotten it. Getting anything fast done in Washington usually means an overnight stay, in this case on arrival there as they, The US Coast Guard are about as slow as the second coming."

"Why, separate hotels?"

"Because our captain hates 5 star hotels, he prefers quiet little hotels, usually up some back street, and away from flashing lights, and more importantly, noise."

"And where is my wife staying?" With a degree of exasperation.

"Knowing our captain, probably in the very best hotel in Washington, now I suggest that you go home, and wait for her to call you."

"So who is paying for all of this?" asked without thought.

This single frustrated remark confirming that the love of money, and beer, more important than the love of two diverse individuals, one from Germany, the other from Scotland, the other just being his wife, who he from Australia, gave no, or little regard to the fact that his ignored wife could actually fall in love with someone else.

"Take it from me, this captain knows many things that even I didn't know off, she'll probably be going home with about $1500 cash in expenses. He'll have taken care of it. Trust me, he will. Even allowing for the fact that he is 20 years younger than me, and a hell of a lot more knowledgeable than me, especially in marine insurance, and gas tankers."

The angry Australian reluctantly slightly more at peace than he had arrived with, but with still a little doubt in his mind, left the ship, his doubt expressed by occasionally looking over his left shoulder, as he descended dock wards.

And who could blame him, seeing as both the Captain and Christine, his German wife, were just a few decks above, and nowhere near Washington, DC or State. Snuggled up closely in a very loving embrace and perfectly fast asleep.

Only one other matter to clear up, on the distant and yet close master, distant being 1000 false miles closer, to being about 30 feet, to report to The Corpus Christi Police, that somehow, someone had stolen their bent crankshaft, previously on the dockside, and now no longer there.

All 6.5 tonnes of it. But it was worth $200. And could be un-bent. If you knew just where to hit it, after being heated to over red hot.

To which a Scots master reported to The Police as lost property. Well it didn't quite get reported as lost, initially, leaving The Police a little bit more than, confused. Well, that is how you get things done in Texas. The crime reference number could be useful though, especially as this could be expanded into covering almost everything in an insurance claim, including horses.

"Captain, you can't be serious," after this being explained to Blackie, the German Chief Mate, 2 days later.

"Why not? Americans blast rockets into 'space,' so why can't we blast our garbage into 'space?' Well, not into outer space as such. More of a diversion of getting them to look the other way, and have you seen how much others garbage there is, washed up on the coast of the bay. You could make a fortune selling some of it. We'll just add our own in," the sceptical look suggesting that this thought still had a little way to go yet, but heading in the right direction.

"We can't be violating any USCG rule, as they don't cover 'space,' well inner 'space' anyway, might just be a bit ambitious trying for outer 'space' just yet. They only cover what happens at the waterline of ships, and the bit above and below it, the above bit being ending at the top of the tallest mast. Or when someone dopey enough comes along and bumps into a bit of the harder bit of their coastline that is stronger than steel, **Such as rocks!** For the, below waterline bit.

"Involving what?"

"Blackie, we are already in port, so what happens next, they have no law to back them up with."

The sceptical look, with raised eyebrows arousing more doubt.

"The remainder of our out off of date rockets, plus if need be, a few of our over-supplied new ones, plus the one's that I accidentally came by last night, which this ship doesn't actually need."

"And just how exactly, did you come by these, 'out of date distress rockets', accidently?" asked an even more doubtful Chief Mate.

"Who said distress rockets had to go vertically up?"

"You haven't answered the question."

The thought process being a little slow, mostly as it had a few beers to addle the brain prompting the next question.

"Has this got anything to do with the one that I refused to fire yesterday?"

"Mmmm, well, I might need to re-design that one a bit."

"Re-design it a bit!" in horror, and voiced such that all could hear, **"Captain, that thing is fucking lethal!** And how did you accidentally come by more rockets?" asked even more curiously and for the second time.

"Sort of lost my bearings a bit, and sort of stumbled on board that laid up Greek tanker a little further up."

The reply not in the very least convincing, but with the effort none the less tried anyway.

"How can you stumble on board something of 80 000 tonnes, 600 and a bit more feet in length and with no gangway, with the deck 30 feet above the quay?" asked with just a little dis-belief.

"Well in response, it helps, sort of pro-rata, just how many beers you have had," hopefully, the pro rata term not being within his knowledge of the English language. It wasn't, as he carried on.

"And how many distress rockets did you acquire, or put more succinctly, steal?"

"Oh, just a few, and succinctly is a big word for a German."

"How many?" The disbelief now becoming evident! "And don't change the subject!"

"Oh, all right, if you are going to be pedantic, thirty six ish. But I got twelve line throwing sets as well."

"From one ship!" asked even more incredulously! And in a loud voice!

"Not exactly" He answering in such a way of trying to divert this line of questioning, "four ships actually. But on the others I was given all of their time expired rockets, which might just be a wee bit unreliable, or perhaps, unstable. A few were 10 years out of date, which makes them 15 years old. Come on, let's test my 3 stage one."

"NO," he replied vehemently, just as Christine arrived, "am I missing something?" she asked curiously.

The conversation in German, being somewhat heated, at least between one of the three, before resulting back into English, "okay, you explain it to her, and if she agrees, we'll try it, only, if **you** set it off, I'll be inside somewhere made of steel, very thick steel!" As his German Chief Mate stomped off, but not going far.

"He seems a bit upset," said this young delightful blonde.

"Christine, a parachute distress flare, when fired goes up to about 1800 feet, when the top pops off, the parachute ejected and the rest of the solid rocket fuel ignites the flare, which comes slowly down and very bright red underneath a little parachute, glowing to about 1.2 million candelas."

"Well, I've got three of them, one above the other, in a plastic tube, and the triggers of no 2 and no 3 set up such that when the flare ignites, it not only sets off the rocket above it, but melts the plastic tube at the same time, so that bit falls off. I've also taken out the parachutes. Just want to see what happens, when I elevate the tube at 25 degrees above horizontal, and what sort of load it could pull."

"Seems logical, can I fire it" asked Christine.

"Off course, it is still set up on the foredeck. Let's go."

"But captain, it still has no guidance," pleading the mate still trying not to get involved, but failing miserably. His stomping off not getting him very far.

"Blackie, you worry too much, each rocket only burns for 3 seconds. At the very least, you only have to duck, for at most 10 seconds. Right Christine, let's go."

"You know Doug, said Christine, "in the short time that I have known you, you have changed my dull boring job and life around into something now exciting, as I never know what is going to happen next. Now what do I do?"

She, not at the time beginning to realise, that she would be spending the rest of her life with him, and with many adventures on the way. The being married bit, hopefully, would sort itself out and somewhat harder to do, the private investigators paid to snoop on infidelity not being able to swim as fast as a ship. That's if they could find it in the first place.

"Just let me check the trigger, and if it is okay, just gently pull on that rope when I get back, and as rockets go off with a massive amount of smoke, stand well to the side, or in the compressor room."

Word must have gotten around as the entire crew were now cowering behind any part of the ship, waiting to see just what might happen, this never having being tested before, far less thought off.

"Okay Christine, we're all set, so when you are ready, just pull up all of the slack on the line, and when it starts to tighten, pause and then give it a sharp tug. I've aimed it for the Bay."

"Okay, here goes," as she tentatively took up the slack. "Do you want me to give a countdown?"

"Just pull the bloody rope!" in response, to which she did.

Not a lot was said for the next 10 seconds, as all marvelled at just how brilliantly it had all worked, well the dry rockets, anyway, the guidance system would still need a little bit more thought, as into rather a lot, as to where the last bit was seen to be heading likely to probably cause a little bit of embarrassment, or maybe more than just a bit, one's superintendent might just being a little none too sympathetic as it landed in the swimming pool of his hotel just alongside him, but well, the water at least putting the flare out, eventually, after fizzing around under the surface first, it not being inclined to sink. The guy on the diving board, preparing to dive backwards falling off, after being slightly tapped by the incoming missile. Landing flat on one's back in the water, not to be recommended, to those who not as yet having tried it. It sort of hurts a bit, as in, a lot.

But rockets no's 2 &3 were also going to be a need a little bit of explaining as well, later perhaps, hopefully. There was a small field of dry grass on fire, which might just lead to being a bigger field on fire, should the wind suddenly change and a dumper truck driver unaware that his load was also going to give him a few more problems than what he had set out with from about 10 miles or so ago.

"Anyone for a cold beer?" as the smoke cleared. The question being rhetoric, as everyone cleared the foredeck, running after their captain, and heading for the nearest place to hide.

A period of about one hour considered enough for those on board reasonable to wait before going ashore. From various directions, mostly dry, but a few wet.

"Doug, why are the crew trotting half crouched with their right hand vertically up in front of them?"

"Tell you later Christine," just for now, try to keep up with them. "And do the same."

Eventually, after negotiating several dimly lit backstreets, they all arrived via the backdoor of a familiar bar, which was from the front, at least closed. Fortunately, the back wasn't.

In a gregarious welcome, "Hi guys," from the barman, "what are you all doing this weekend?" in a slurred manner. "Ever been rattlesnake racing?" As they came in, their eyesight yet having to come to terms with the gloom, mostly of stale cigarette smoke.

An intoxicated barman could spell only one of two things, trouble, or even more trouble, especially as the Corpus Christi Police were trundling around outside in their cruisers. "About 10 beers will do for starters, please." As he sort of wobbled off, in the general direction of more beers, hopefully not hearing for what came next.

"Now listen carefully you lot, and don't interfere with anything, apart from this, "I seem to have been told about this before, so for tonight, let's just humour him, as we have more than enough to do tomorrow, providing we can get back to our ship tonight, which I rather doubt, as we might just need to walk back.

"Ever been rattlesnake racing?" as 10 or more beers were placed in front of them, although the wobbly bit accounting for the spillage."

It was a Briton who replied, "Considering that we don't have rattlesnakes in The UK, or to the best of my knowledge in the Philippine's, Germany or Norway led to a fairly conclusive, no. India however might just have a few, especially among the money changers."

Not that that made much difference to the barman as he went onto explaining the rules of rattlesnake racing, the only important one being that you were not allowed to hit the snake as it runs or any way it can up the 80 foot lane, not exactly running but sliding backwards, and the fangs, or the bite bit trying to keep out of range of the stick, trying to help it on its way. Whichever rattler has the shortest time, wins. But they do have heats which run over 2 days

"We bet seriously on this, if you want to come along?" A pretty stupid question to this bunch, but risked anyway.

"Give us a few minutes, we'll discuss this over another 16 beers, if they eventually arrive intact this time?"

To say that rattle snake racing might this just be a tad dangerous, until it was revealed that the competitors wear thick paddings over their legs, just in case the rattler got so angry that it might actually have a go at relieving him or her, of its' fatal venom. Plus the 2 wee holes on any exposed skin where the venom went into. A tiny pin prick being no more than a hypodermic syringe, although with less intention or accuracy, seeing as most doctors and nurses only use one at a time. And even if a cannula is already in place on the back of a hand. They could duplicate this technique, although veins don't tend to be overlaid and placed within dual range. But at 50-50, it being fairly certain that at least one bite would score, unless off course if the rattlesnake was cross eyed.

The concluded huddle agreeing that this might be rather fun, finished their beers, and agreed to a bet of $1000 that their ships rattlesnake was faster than any one of theirs one.

The inebriated barman confirming the bet, only that the $1000 that he put down, was actually $2000, spotted immediately by one of the ship's crew who slapped a $1 bill on top. The barman not realising that the $3001 he held in his hand, including the extra $1 was betting with him but also against himself, as he placed the wad of notes into the safe for overnight safety, and giving a receipt to the ships master. The smug grin, in a few days' time perhaps might just change into one of,....................mystery.

But he wasn't alone.

The only slightly small problem being that the ship did not actually have a rattlesnake. Rats perhaps, although on a gas tanker unlikely, but rattlesnakes, no.

A few hours later, and back on board ship, as a few awoke up to their problem, to be announced of their captain's remedy.

It was held in somewhat awe.

"Well, have any of you got a better idea?" said Doug.

Apparently not! As most just shook their heads, somewhat despondently.

"Let let's see if we understand this," from those collected, minus their captain who had set off for a few cold beers, their spokesman saying "first off all, we need to catch a rattlesnake, without getting bitten, and then we need to get it drunk."

Their captain replied upon his return.

"Well it is going to be the same way as you lot go with too much alcohol in you, constantly trying to go in a straight line, and not fooling anyone, and snakes have more legs than you, although inside their skin should be relatively easy to steer it in the right direction. And as they all slither from side to side, should if they are drunk, go in a straight line."

"If it wasn't that I'm in for part of this bet," said one, "I now am, because this ludicrous concept, might just actually work, but I am going to lay off a few other side bets first." Many concurred.

Only a few hours later, side bets being taken on just how a ship master could actually capture a rattlesnake single-handedly and very successfully, and then get it drunk.

Luckily the next day, was a day off day, as the ship was waiting for specialist tools flown in. And everything else that could be done was actually already done.

Next morning as Einar entered the ships offices, he said to Mike, "is Doug up and about, as I came aboard, I noticed that the blinds were still down in his office, and there is a "Do Not Enter" sign on his office door. He only usually has his blinds down when he has the safe open, or paying the crew."

"Oh, he's up all right, you don't want to see just what he has come up with this time," he having little clue into how to change the subject, not that that was going to make much difference.

"A funny thing happened to me last night, as I went for a swim, before you both joined me for a beer," said Einar.

"Does this have anything to do with parachute distress rockets?" asked Mike.

"Yes, how did you know?" In reply.

"You just don't want to know, believe me you just don't want to know!"

At that point the Chiefs 'phone rang, "right Mike, I'm all set to go, are the boys ready to lift the hatch on number 4 void space, so I can change the detector head for the gas analyser?" from the captain.

In the annuls of merchant shipping inventiveness, did not prepare anyone, far less his 2 highly experienced engineers, and rather a lot of the crew, well, all of them apart from the cook and one of his mess men, who had been assisting the captain, for what came into the masters office.

He, apart from his swimming trunks and with a 10 minute escape breathing apparatus pack on his back and trainers emerged a captain completely covered in Cling film. Fathoms of it!

A home-made chemical suit!

Two minutes later, the gas analyser detection head being changed in Number 4 void space, the captain emerged back on deck, and deciding that this possibly wasn't such a good idea, as it took several others some time to take the Cling film off, and a lot longer than it did, to put on.

But 3 beers helped, pity it being Bramah, three cans being de-canted carefully into a glass to which the ships master drank gratefully, he not sighting the cans.

"How long do you think it will take Chief?" asked Einar.

"We'll give it an hour, or so, bit unfair really, but then, he did it to us first."

To which one ship's captain emerged, with some odd red patches on his skin being apparent. "Next time we go into dry air around the cargo tanks, we'll blow the fucking dry air out, and then re-dry it!" Not projected at anyone in particular, as most within earshot found themselves rolling about the deck in laughter, metaphorically speaking. They all by now knowing that the ships' master could laugh at himself as much as to others.

The coffee break not throwing up anything useful, apart from, "Blackie, I know you've had your doubts, so, let's see if we can make this into a four stage rocket, we're up to 3 miles down range, only need another few hundred yards, before we start seeing how much garbage we can land in the bay, and I've got another idea of grouping the rockets, but this might need a wee bit more testing. I think we'll change the launch trajectory angle to 45 degrees."

"NO! NO! NO!" Came the response, "I want nothing to do with this, so far you have scared the shit out of just about everyone, set fire to a field, left a very confused lorry driver with a burning load, and a swimming pool needing to be cleaned out. A four stage rocket is never going to work."

"Okay, calm down, let's get through the rest of today first, as the only important thing is to get this ship back operating and as soon as possible and you know how just much extra stuff there is to do at the same time."

Later, during dinner the captain and his other 3 senior officers sat around a table in the ships restaurant with his superintendent, enjoying butterfly prawns, none of which had come across before and trying to avoid the white wine, which the captain had offered as this wine came from China, and named 'Ming Palace.' But it was at least cheap, at $10 a case for 12 bottles. The ship-chandler in Houston somewhat relieved that he had off-loaded 2 more cases onto yet another un-suspecting ship master. The after dinner conversation drifting back to an earlier one, the wine having eventually being sampled, before being declared, hey, this isn't that bad at all. Liars, each and every one of them, the captain being called away to answer the 'phone, who upon returning found his wine glass full, others empty as was the bottle the opposite.

"So you don't think a 4 stage one will work then?" said the captain, taking a sip of his wine.

"No, I didn't say that, but a 5 stage one might. When can we start building it?"

"I thought you were against this concept?" from the captain somewhat astonished.

"I was, until we and a few others realised, that when the second one fires, and then the 3rd then fires, that they are no longer static, but moving at an incredible accelerating speed."

"And just who, exactly, are **we**?" asked the master.

"Well there is The Norwegian gas engineer for a start, and most of the crew."

"Which might explain just why all of my plastic tubing has somehow disappeared, you didn't perchance, in any way, let the crew know where the line throwing rockets were as well?"

"Didn't need to, they helped you carry them on board remember, when you actually managed to get them to the bottom of the accommodation ladder."

A faint memory had to agree.

"So, where are they now?"

"The crew, oh they set off to find some 3 inch plastic pipe, and were last seen setting off towards the superintendent's hotel."

"Did any of them perchance, be seen to be carrying a hacksaw?"

"Oh none were carrying a hacksaw, in their hands anyway, but a few of the smaller one's had something poking out of their collars, and were walking in a rather strange way."

"Just after a long day, that is all I need. They've got them up their backs and under their shirts."

A diversion being called for, to get his none too intelligent crew out of inevitable trouble, the only bits of 3 inch plastic pipes being the down pipes from the hotels roof. And into just where line throwing rockets, did fit exactly. Someone, despite their heavy shipboard on-board workload, had puzzled out just how to get metal cased line throwing rockets to work in multi-stages, putting out about 4 times the thrust of distress rockets, the extra thrust needed to pull out a line behind them. Or in the next planned stage, something that might be attached to the line, such as empty aluminium cans, or what the lesser salubriously parts of Corpus Christi hadn't as yet, actually stolen. They had already 'acquired', or put another way, stolen, the best part of a tonne of garbage, in brown paper shopping bags. They having, also tried many times so far of trying to steal the hired cars wheels, to little avail, even to the extent of shattering a socket on the end of a 6 foot bar and those who had tried to hot wire the car's ignition found themselves thrown backwards out of the car, not expecting to find an independent 15 000 volt and fully charged capacitor hidden within the wiring. They also not noticing the warning or reading the advice of, 'Do Not Touch' written on the capacitor, just at the same place as the 2 wires required to hot-wire the intended theft already wired up in such a way to produce totally the opposite of what they expected. The cars horn went off, and all of its lights started flashing and even when the wires were separated, didn't stop any of it.

Kind of hard to read what was written on this capacitor in the darkness, though, as most car thieves don't really know how to read in the first place, nor expect to make a realistic claim for compensation within the ludicrous American Legal System by claiming that they were not forewarned of the risk, and suing for damages, for 2 burnt finger tips. Then having to wear a neck brace after coming into fast backwards contact, with a hard bit of the car that they were trying to steal. And they were not alone. Others were also busy, and no more fortunate. Mostly because they failed to notice the 'Do Not Touch' sign on the most awkward corner of their next target, beside the exhaust pipe, well in American logic, who said it, had to be logical.

Those would be thieves trying to release the somewhat awkward to find bonnet/hood/trunk catch finding to their extreme discomfort something that this particular captain had learnt from the British Army before actually going to sea. That to as much as touch the bodywork, after the release attempt on the catch gave out one hell of an electric shock, early indications suggesting, that a second attempt at touching anything up to 600 volts, not wise, as two did try it, the 3rd attempt never being tried. Common sense suggesting that it was time to be somewhere else, and PDQ, ie, Pretty Damn Quick!

The recalcitrant remaining few deciding that this might be a suitable time to slowly melt away into the gloom, or put another way, hide.

And it was not the captain, who organised the diversion.

Although trying to find the captain was proving to be a little bit difficult, but the usual way of searching from starting at the top of the ship and working downwards, did eventually produce a result. Even although the engine room was in total darkness, apart from the emergency lighting giving just a mere hint of light.

"Where have you been?" asked a curious Chief Engineer to the

Ships master, after he arrived back in to the engine room through the hole still cut in the hull by climbing up a Jacob's ladder.

"Isn't it obvious?" He struggling to get the compressed air bottle up at the same time.

"I would have just switched off the lighting down here, had I been able to find the switches', so I shut down the generator instead."

"Eh Doug, just how did you shut down the generator?"

"Oh, the easy way, I shut off the fuel. But not to worry, when I'm finished, you can start it up again."

The strained and mystified look on Mike's face conveyed nothing other than total dis-belief. "You do know which grade of fuel we are burning just now in the generators, or not perhaps?"

"A minor consideration for just now Mike, it is some of that black stuff that keeps leaking from just about everywhere.

"I would have borrowed some diving gear from Christine, but this is the only way out and in without being spotted by that clown at the bottom of the accommodation ladder.

"I've been having a closer look at the mayor's Limo, well under the bonnet, or hood anyway, and from below."

"Ah, thanks Abner, can you re-charge this bottle for me?" asked of the third mate.

"No problem captain, are you going back down again?"

"Yep, as soon as it is re-charged, thank-you and I'll only need my mask again. I'm not going deep this time."

"And," curiosity no longer coming surprisingly from The Chief Engineer, he knowing that his Captain and fast becoming friend had rather a lot of different ways of doing things, slightly differently, or put another way, unbelievably, which might be changed into, just plain stupid or even borderline legal.

"I had a closer look, at the starter motor. On there is one of the gears that we need for our own lifeboats."

"How do you know that? And more importantly, how did you get it off?"

"Well there were only 3 bolts holding it on, and with a little persuasion and with a bit of wire, ripped it off. The 3rd mate gave me a hand."

"And to just what was on the other end of this 'bit of wire' connected to?" asked, he probably already knowing that the answer would be odd, or just plain stupid.

"The Ships rudder Mike. Before I blacked the ship out, Abner switched on the steering motors, and swung the rudder hard over, first towards the car, and then after the wire was attached, swung the rudder over the other way, and it came out just a treat. Mind you, it did tend to bring out a few other bits as well."

"Such as," in a questioningly, curious sort of way?

"The Mayors Limo is going to need a new engine. When they actually get it back up. But they won't be looking too closely at us, as I found something from the inside of the Mayors Limo, which I'm going to install inside The Department of Agriculture's still sunken 'cutter.' Well, a bit of it anyway."

"Which is going to take one hell of a lot of explaining away no doubt," words not being heard, as the captains' attention being elsewhere.

"Ah thanks Abner, 100 bar should be enough, I'll be back in about 10 minutes," as the captain jumped back into the dark waters of Corpus Christi Harbour without any conventional Scuba gear. Just a mask, and his air bottle.

After a little pause, "Okay Abner, just what is he up to?" The overwhelming presence of Mike, the British Chief Engineer, to this very young Filipino 3rd Officer procuring nothing other than, "but Chief, I do not know. I only do as I am told."

About 10 minutes passed before the captain returned, this time for good, or at least for that evening, most fortunately timed as rather a lot of un-marked cars, cranes and some very dubious people rolled up.

"Care to tell me just what you are up to Doug, asked Mike," after the master surfaced and climbed back in through the hole in the hull, although a little awkwardly.

"Let's just say, that something has gone missing from the Mayors Limo, and is now partly in The Department of Agriculture's cutter, and what was in The Department of Agriculture's cutter is now in the Mayors Limo, with a slight difference. Only what is now in each of both is not what each actually started off with."

"But you had no Scuba gear!"

"Yes I know, but there is a way of getting around underwater without it. I learnt that when I went on a diving course, not something that you want to advertise overly much, just in case some nincompoop comes along and tries it for themselves. I just needed a good old blast of air, to set up a wee place to hide something, which is underwater, but not being in contact with air above the waterline. Mind you, there isn't a lot of room between the ships bottom and the dock bottom. And not as much as a bloody lobster or crab in sight."

"So what have you put in there, in this mysterious place?"

"Between you and me, around about, a brief case contents full of which might be cocaine, I don't know much about street values but it might just be rather a lot. I reckon about 5 kilo's or whatever system Americans use, and it was all in sealed little bags."

A few moments passed, this taking a little time to sink in, before the inevitable question being asked, "So what are you going to do with it? The drugs perceived that is?" asked Mike.

"You'll soon find out, because nothing is attributable back to us," as two bemused heads looked at each other, not knowing what was coming next.

"I just swapped the briefcases contents of both around, when I was underwater, the first time around, and on the second later dragged back, hid what I found after just popping up for a few seconds. These guys tend to get really nervous before any sort of exchange and don't pay too much attention, to anything which might be constituted as a lack of trust between themselves, such as on board a boat, where the swap is very easy to do."

"The movies are make-believe, you know," he said, and ignored.

"Oh, and I changed the combinations of their brief cases as well," he not really listening, or at worst, thinking.

"How did you manage that?" asked Mike with a scant beginning of new respect, but no closer to solving his problem.

"Because my friend, when something is sinking, no-one expects someone to come up from below. Good eh? Done it twice now, get me a cold beer."

"Mike, while I get dried and dressed, re-start the generator, or at least one of the other two, and then I'll explain later."

Later and over a few beers it was explained.

"Now I got this from a friend, who I will restrict this to his Christian name of Martin. This guy, if he can stay out of prison for long enough does what we do all of the time, we do it with figures, cargo, fuel and so forth, he does it with material things, otherwise known as a pick-pocket. And he should be joining this ship in a day or so, as I talked The Sheriff in a Scottish Court into not sending to prison, but instead doing something useful as punishment. And this is what he told me. Martin, not the Sheriff."

"Easy really, when the latch of a briefcase case is sprung, instead of setting the right combination, you just push the latch the other way, and set it up for anything you want. Then when drug dealers meet up to make an exchange, then the one's with the drugs can't get their briefcases open, and the ones with the cash in the other can't either. Pretty handy knowing that both sides had the same type of briefcase, give or take a few identifying scuff marks and scratch marks but then, you know crooked drug dealers; they consider everyone else to be stupid because the previous combinations are now set on the one with the drugs and the other on the money. And not a single one of them thought of changing the combinations first."

Puzzled looks being exchanged, as to what might come next.

"And their meeting has been put back for all of the activity around this ship," no doubt? Before continuing, "Just one question Doug, just what does exist in their respective briefcases?"

"Well, the drugs, at very short notice, are now plain flour, a bit of icing sugar, and a bit of salt, except the package in the middle, which is one of the original pure white powder. They always sample the one in the middle just to test the quality, and with tense individuals, with guns not very far away. They are in, what was the money briefcase." Conveyed to two puzzled faces.

"In the one that had the drugs is a Chop Chop note, good eh?" This latest remark, only causing more confusion, but prompting a question that could only be called, unique.

"Hang on a second, to see if I understand this. So you have now got 2 opposing sides, or drug dealing gangs trying to carry out a drug trade exchange, with one side now only having a load of nothing other than a small amount of drugs and rubbish, although they started out with all of the money, while the ones who started out with the drugs, now have not got the money but a Chop Chop note."

"Good eh?" The smug smile, not really helping matters.

"Yes...................but where does the Chop Chop note come in?" Being an engineer, not having had the same convoluted training as required for a ship-master.

"Just wait and see, because both sides will now be looking for a Chinese connection, and very soon. They will blame each other. Or in the annuls of time, the first ever money/drug exchange where both sides started out with what they actually hoped to have ended up with, in exchange, should with a bit of luck, need a bit of head scratching, in the way of an explanation."

Curiosity had most definitely been arisen, mystique even. But that would come later.

"How much money was there in the briefcase, don't tell me as I've already lost track of just what is where?" asked Mike.

"Haven't had the chance to count it, which is a bloody difficult to do anyway underwater, although it was all in plastic bags, but it is in the same place as the drugs."

"Which are now in the only place where you can hide air underwater I suppose? Even compressed air, and not in a bottle."

"That's about the size of it Mike. Care for another cold beer, got some British stuff on my way back from the agents this afternoon and it should be cold enough by now?"

Mike just shaking his head, and there being nothing helpful from Einar, who seemed equally lost.

"Anyway mate, I've got a report to write and that is where the British beer is. Just need to pop up to the bridge first, I'll be about 5 minutes. The gyro compass should be balanced by now."

It didn't take long, and the first ones up the accommodation ladder were the Corpus Christi Police, fortunately led by the same police officer who had had a run-in with them before.

"Oh hello Mike, is the captain on board?"

"I'll just get him for you," hitting the Intercom button, a bit pointless really as he just chose the same moment for the captain to walk in the door.

"Oh hello Bart, bit late at night for you to be coming on board for a beer or a look around."

"Sorry captain," he not declining the offered can of Gatorade or any of his fellow officers now crowding into his office either, all sweating a bit profusely.

"We need to raise the Mayors Limo. And tonight, goodness knows why it can't wait until tomorrow."

"So how can we help Bart?" asked the captain?

"Can you rig up some floodlights over the back of your boat, sorry, ship for the divers?"

"Off course, no problem, might take about 20 minutes or so to shift them. Okay with you Mike?" A nod and departing Chief Engineer already on to it, plus now more than just a few Filipino's all eager to help. There was bound to be a laugh somewhere, and better than watching American TV. Might even get a free cold beer!

"Doug, after tonight, I and my fellow officers are going for our 4 days' rest. Could................"

"Say no more gentlemen," the captain's hand being shown palm up, "we dine at 5, so you can all come for a second sitting at 6, bring your wives and children. We are not cargo gassed up just now, so it is safe, just No Smoking on deck. We never really know as to where

103

there might be a bit of gas that got missed. All are welcome. It takes about an hour to show you all round, and then you can all join us in the Ships' restaurant. On British ships it is called the saloon, but on this wee boat which is Norwegian, for saloon, it is called a restaurant."

"Do we need to bring anything, wine for example?"

"The only thing that you need to bring is yourselves, and the one nominated child who wants to sit in the captain's chair."

A wave in the background from The Chief Engineer catching his attention, "oh ho, looks like we are all set to go." The 'that was quick,' being explained by what foresaw them.

Three big floodlights attached to the transom with varying types of clamps and wiring that could only be explained away as being somewhat dodgy, if not downright dangerous now though illuminating the surface of the harbour, the Mayor's Limo nicely also illuminating the 2 divers trying to attach some sort of slings to the back wheels.

"You know Bart, there is something puzzling me, this afternoon there did seem to be an awful lot of bubbles coming up, not only from the Mayors Limo, but also from The Department of Agriculture's cutter up amidships."

"Is that on the dock bottom as well? How did it get there?"

"Oh, one of them was dopey enough to leave a door open when one of our pumps started at random. We were checking out the control phases at the time."

"Let's captain just concentrate tonight on the Mayor's Limo. Tomorrow, that is someone else's problem."

Couldn't agree more thought the captain smiling inwardly, the seed of doubt now being sown into The Corpus Christi Police who if a complaint was to be raised into The Mayors or one of his assistants missing drugs, and probably unlikely at that, that one of The Department of Agriculture's crew would also have to explain away, just why they had lost an awful lot of money. To which both would have to admit that their perfectly infallible scheme wasn't, and that those to which they were responsible, not in the least way, at all pleased. A satisfactory nights work all round. All that was left for later was, "I haven't got a clue as to what you are talking about."

The crane taking the strain as the Mayors Limo was rather quickly lifted from the harbour, when something very unexpectedly happened. The sheer amount of water inside this Limo, or as all non-American readers would only know as a stretched car suddenly became too much for the bulkhead between the interior and where the car's engine bay was. The windshield being bullet proof as was the rest of the car, stayed intact, but not so the radiator and grille as both now joined the motor/engine on the bottom of the dock. Which was useful, no-one now having to explain just where the starter motor was, or a few other particular bits?

The rescued Limo from the crane, after a period, landed onto a flat trailer, with rather a lot of people guarding it, and for some peculiar reason, all wearing sunglasses. Oh you see it in the movies all the time, but why wear sunglasses when it is pitch dark. They also seemed to be having a rather big bulge on their suits where most people keep their left shoulder, the under part anyway.

"Well goodnight captain, see you tomorrow night," as Bart and his pals shook hands with the captain," before departing homewards. The ship's captain heading for bed. But for some reason, there was still a guard at the bottom of the ships accommodation ladder. Better not chance it tonight thought the master, in a couple of days' time would be soon enough to see how much cash lay beneath the ship, and as for the drugs themselves, as soon as he eventually fired up the main engine would see them disappear, saving more than just a few from even more misery, if not preventing many deaths.

Next morning:

"Remember me?" pushing himself into the masters office, and not wisely timed as the captain, senior officers, plus engine builders engineers were totally ensconced in a very serious discussion, as to how to get specialist tools out from Helsinki, Finland to Corpus Christi, USA, and as fast as possible. Christine, stopping off on her way to work, rather trapped in the background, but thrilled with the thought that this could go anywhere, it having being explained to her during the night, that "this captain does not suffer fools gladly."

"Yes I remember you, so go back out again, and knock this time, and do not come in, until you are invited," said Doug, the captain.

The already bright and fuming face, nearly at bursting point now lost for words, but did sort of try to comply.

Knock, Knock, Knock, being answered with, "come back this afternoon, we're all a bit busy just now."

This proved to be too much from the Department of Agriculture's Cutters master, as he exploded, various bits of spit going in all directions.

"It's your fault that my cutter is on the bottom of the dock, and my boss wants it back afloat again to-day, and you are going to do it." In a tone that could be construed as threatening.

"Okay," said Doug, "just sign here, here and here," offering 3 different documents, before resuming his previous discussion.

"What is this?" the tone getting slightly more agitated by the second.

"Well the 1st one is Lloyds Open Form, like No-Cure No-Pay, so if I do get your boat back afloat, I'll be claiming salvage rights, based on the hulls insured value of your cutter, and this one? as he looked at the next, with a degree of doubt starting to permeate the grey brain cells.

"That is a bill for the damage that your ropes did to the railings to my ship, and you're getting off cheaply at $50."

"And this one?" as he looked at and read the 3rd, "$1000 for stealing a toilet seat, and for the damage that you caused to the toilet/restroom by firing your sidearm, we can forget about the dents to the bottom 6 steps to the accommodation ladder when you slipped. How is your back by the way?"

"I won't sign any of these, ever," the facial sweat glands now on overdrive.

"Well, that's okay, you don't have to," said Doug.

"Why?" came a dry throated response.

"Because I faxed all of these off to your boss this morning, and he has already signed them. Christine, if she can get through this melee is on her way to collect them."

Time for a little sympathy to be shown, "have you had any breakfast?" asked the captain. Any answer having no relevancy whatsoever as he was steered towards the restaurant anyway.

The cushion brought from his shoulder bag, suggesting that getting the toilet seat off his posterior may have left a few parts of his outer skin covering not as yet wholly repaired, and in a somewhat embarrassing area. Hopefully, as getting that fork off his hand, might just present a comparable dilemma after he had his breakfast. It also covered in Superglue. Might just going to be difficult explaining, just how Texan's cut up their food with a fork and knife, try to change hands, and pick up a new fork, to which they are not going to need another fork for.

Not half as difficult though of driving home. Mostly as a few had already stolen the fuel from their respective cars. Martin's presence and knowledge already being passed on.

"Christine, confirm to The Ship Chandler that I need the 2 cases of X-100, previously flown in from The UK and then hire me a portable generator, same as we had before, and 2 submersible pumps with 60 feet long discharge hoses, plus enough cabling for 2 X 200 feet, okay?"

"Sure," as she gave him a little kiss on the way out, nothing of any significance to both but noticed by everyone else. "Are you flying the tools in?"

"Yes, we are just on our way to order them. Let you know later what the airway bill number is."

"Now let's get busy, we might actually today manage to get watertight again, with as we agreed last night, 2 more inter-costals welded in as well. This from a captain who didn't seem to need much sleep.

"Doug," asked Einar and Mike, what is X-100?"

"Well if you don't know what that is, then you haven't been around gas tankers long enough. Now, I have to go ashore, see you both later," leaving the office in the direction of the galley.

"Christopher," as the captain entered the galley, "I'm sorry it is short notice, but we need a second sitting for dinner tonight, our usual at 5, then a second at 6 or thereabouts, we have The Corpus Christi Police and their families coming for a ship visit and then joining us for a meal. Set it up as a buffet."

"No problem captain, I've taken extra out from the freezer, we can cope."

"How did you know how to take extra out of the freezer Christopher?" asked the captain, curiously.

You can always tell with Filipino's, their eyes being rather shifty, and not focusing on anything, the body language being a dead giveaway as to covering up something.

"Come on you lot, out with it, you know that you can tell me."

"We all got arrested last night captain, and it was only when we told the Police the name of our ship, that they brought us back, and told us to behave ourselves in the future. Pretty good of them really, they even let us keep the downpipe, but we lost the hacksaws."

Relieving them of their embarrassment, so that they didn't lose face, a smiling captain, just smiled, shook his head and left.

Half an hour or so later Mike asked. "Where has Doug gone?"

Puzzled heads around the ship's offices not knowing where their captain, had actually gone.

"That's not like him, he usually tells us where he is going. Try 'phoning the Agents, and try The US Coastguard, The Corpus Christi Police, even The Department of Agriculture, or anyone you can think off," said Mike.

"Any particular reason why?" asked Einar.

"No, just get 'phoning."

To which all of those free, started doing.

Several hours passed, with no news as Christine arrived on board for her lunch break, concern written across her face, and of many questions being asked, no-one seeming to have known where the captain had actually gone.

Suddenly, with many wailing sirens, and blue flashing lights, a dozen or so DEA cars arrived at Cargo Dock 12.

"Stay where you are," came over this loudhailer, "this area is now a crime scene." To which about half of the dock was cordoned off, with that tape that said, "DEA, do not cross." The tape of which they seemed to have mile's off.

"Off all the days when we need the captain, it has to be the day when we don't know where he is. He would know how to handle this," said Mike.

"I agree," said Einar, but it looks like it is going to be just me and you, as if we don't already have more than enough to do in the engine room, we were meant to be getting the overhauled cylinder heads back today, now that we have most of the cylinder water jackets in place and already have some of the cylinder liners in as well. I hope this is not going to mean another lengthy delay. We've even got the pistons ready to go in as well."

"I'm looking for the captain," as this tall Texan strode into the ships office, gun drawn."

"Well you can put that thing away right now," said Mike, with a rapidly drying mouth. "The captain isn't on board just now," swallowing deeply.

"Well until he does get back on board, no-one is to leave or attempt to board this ship, or attempt to break the cordon."

"I rather think that you may want to re-phrase that a bit," said Mike, as this tall arrogant Texan swaggered on out, heading goodness knows where with his gun.

"What the hell is going on?" asked Einar.

The Chief engineers landline 'phone rang. It immediately being snatched up by Mike with, "who's calling?"

"It's me you dimwit Mike, Doug, the captain."

"Where are you?" consternation and surprise alerting others in the office. The open speaker now being engaged as the door was closed.

"No time to talk, now listen carefully, both of you, after this call, put the 'phone down and disconnect both 'phone lines. I know all about the cordon. Lower the coiled up 'phone lines into the dock on a long length of fishing line. Then after about 30 minutes lift the accommodation ladder completely up, all damage accepted as it comes into line with the hoisting blocks. Don't say anything to that Department of Agriculture clown on the dock, or do a thing that he says. Get the engine room stores crane ready to lift 9 main engine cylinder heads up 3 at a time, and don't put them down through the engine room stores hatch, just land them on the deck, doesn't matter where, no niceties, just get the next 3 up. I'll be there in about an hour, take in the port side aft fire wire and replace it with a pilot ladder, but do this as quietly as possible, and alert all of the crew, and again, as quietly as possible, get them ready to warp the ship astern on her stern lines and forward springs. Have someone on the forward and after breast lines, just keeping them in check, as we still need to keep the hull close into the jetty. Coastal Iron with these 3 lifts will not be able to break the DEA cordon, but their flatbed truck can stop just outside it.

As soon as it stops, get the crew to warp the ship back on the winches, until it is outside of the cordon, then get the hook down to lift these cylinder heads. Just go as fast as you can and we'll check how fast the ship is going backwards, sorry astern when the crew check her by holding onto the headlines and back springs. Don't be surprised if the guy doing the 1st hook up suddenly disappears by sliding into the dock, I've got 2 others ready for the next 2 lifts, and the 2nd one will escape the same way. Each lift has a few extra bits, just put them to one side for now. Got all of that Mike and Einar?"

"Yes, but where have you been Doug?"

"Tell you later, and don't use the ships rudder."

A bemused look passed between both as the line went dead.

A small time passed while the intended instructions were discussed by everyone stuck on board, including the hastily mustered crew, one of whom asking just what the DEA actually was, and being told, "Mullah, you are Indian, it means Drug Enforcement Agency," the information registering in such a way that if he had been told, 'Dogs Enjoy Apples,' probably making as much sense.

"Christine, grab a radio and let us know as soon as you see him coming, and remember, it could be from anywhere, said Mike."

"Onto it Mike." Her heart beating quicker with respect for her new found different, oh so, different man as she sought out a radio, last seen on her last visit to the ships bridge.

A surge of excitement ran through all on board, as they took up their respective positions, no-one yet realising as their captain had earlier worked out that the tape 'DRUG ENFORCEMENT AGENCY, DO NOT CROSS' and repeated every 6 feet or so did not actually go around the ship as well, but stopped on the nearest point closest to the ship. And moorings ropes within the cordon didn't know how to read.

A slight tremor on the pilot ladder indicating that the captain had arrived as Christine gently and quietly asked, "is that you Doug?"

"It is, let me just catch my breath darling."

"Mike," said Christine quietly on the radio, "Doug's here."

"Good. Let him know that we are all in position, we're just waiting for the cylinder heads, which I think are just about to arrive. Need any help getting him out?"

"No, he already is out, but looks absolutely knackered."

"Time to change numbers," as previously agreed, just in case others were listening in. This being code for changing frequencies.

"Okay boys, is the accommodation ladder up yet?" asked the captain on his radio.

"We had a slight problem, but we are ready to go now Captain."

"Right boys, we'll move her back now and lift the accommodation ladder at the same time. Go."

This rather light, and buoyant gas tanker moving astern perfectly out of the DEA cordoned off area abreast of it coming within range of the overhauled cylinder heads and the cranes hook lowering nicely into position for the first of 3 lifts, completed beautifully by now lifting all of the first of three. The hook-up man sliding gracefully into the waters of the bay as a second moved discreetly into position, ready for the next lift. This being achieved as the ships accommodation ladder having become stuck under The Department of Agriculture's car, to which from both now came scraping noises, and the car losing, as the lazy incumbent abandoned it. A welcome distraction as the cranes hook was now back down for the next 3 cylinder heads, which went up as swiftly as before, and the hook-up man also sliding gracefully into the dock as his predecessor before him.

Only one lift to go, as the hook was lowered once again, only this time, by instruction, she stayed with the lift and came up with it. Nobody being stupid enough to shoot their guns at her with so many witnesses around, especially as no-one expected a woman to be involved.

"Okay boys, tie her up here for tonight, and join me for a cold beer in my cabin. Well done all of you," came the voice of the ship's master, as yet un-seen by anyone else, other than Christine, who now, seemed to have lost him.

The earlier arrogant DEA (Drug Enforcement Agency) clown back on his megaphone, bawled out in a very angry, if not frustrated tone, "captain, lower a gangway, I'm coming on board to arrest you."

To be replied with, and on a megaphone, "If you are coming on board to arrest him," the Chief Engineer replied, "then you can get your own fucking gangway!"

Which didn't seem to go down at all, well, or even slightly?

"Not bad at all Mike, you might make captain one day."

"Not on your life Doug, my job is hard, yours bordering on nigh on impossible, and where did you come from?"

"Mike, Christine and I are going swimming, join us tonight in this location with Einar, in about 4 hours' time, don't let on to anyone just where you are going. Okay?"

"Sure, but how do we get past that DEA cordon?"

"Have you not as yet worked out, that the closed off area is 30 metres ahead of the ship amidships, throw a pilot ladder over the starboard side at the end of the main deck, and climb down that, but take some grease with you, and whoever is first down, a generous coating on the right hand side ropes to be followed with another generous coating on the next ropes down a step, but on the other side, with he who comes down next, using the ungreased ropes, and then greasing the bits that you both came safely down on. Which leaves a completely greased pilot ladder, which will be nigh on impossible to climb up on?

"And how exactly do we do that, without being seen, as that DEA guy looks worse than furious, he does have a gun after all!"

"We do have a spare parachute distress flare, take out the flare and the parachute and fire it towards his feet. That should divert his attention, and when you are outside of the cordon, all that you have to do, is walk away, simple really."

"In about an hour or so, he won't be there. See you later, oh and tell Christopher not to set up for a 2nd dinner tonight. TTFN."

"Mike, where does he get all of this from? And what's TTFN?" asked Einar.

"I have this feeling, that as yet, we have been kept in the dark a bit," said a pensive Mike.

Meanwhile, arriving at the bottom end of the other pilot ladder, on the port side Christine asked, "do you expect me to swim all the way over there, that must be about half a mile?"

"Goodness no, just slide in and follow me."

Very quietly, and with a slow breast stroke and in the darkness provided by the overhang of the ships stern, Christine deciding that this would be a good time to kiss her new love. What could be more romantic, telling her children and grandchildren just where they kissed in the near total darkness, while he unexpectedly formerly treading water, now in a sunken mode did respond, for a few seconds, the moisture of their kiss, fleeting before he at first climbing from the water and into a small rowing boat, hidden under the dock, she assisted in as well, a few seconds later with, "keep your voice down, and try not to move too much." Passing her a large towel, as both started drying themselves off gently. She, still having a glint in her eye, for more intimacy, but that would have to wait. Probably for quite some time yet.

A slight splash alerted the captain, that 2 were now about to become 3. "Shhhh Daniel," as this slightly camouflaged man emerged from the gloom, the only white parts being his teeth as he smiled and the stunning whites of his eyes. Night camouflage perfect as long as he kept his eyes shut and didn't smile. Black skin had many benefits, especially at night with some jealous of this and no-one being in any way, racist.

"I didn't think we could get away with it Doug," as Daniel was helped into the boat," he gratefully accepting the rather large towel and drying himself off.

"All we need now is Ben," said Doug very quietly, this bringing a puzzled look coming across Christine's face with, "who's Ben?"

"Shhhh, keep your voice down," as about 10 seconds later, one other surfaced alongside, but not trying to board the boat, and accepting the cold beer offered, as three other beer bottle tops were released from captivity.

"Christine, meet Ben, you already know Daniel, well slightly."

"Cheers" he said very quietly, offering up his beer bottle before taking a swig, "nice to meet you." Clinging onto the side of the boat, "You'll meet Susan later," and said in a much whispered tone.

Yet another mystical look came over Christine's face.

"Susan has all of the equipment that came up on the cylinder head lifts that we needed to raise The Department of Agriculture's Cutter, and Susan will set it all up tonight, less the X-100, which none of us has a clue just what it is, or actually for," said Daniel.

113

"Got the car keys Ben?"

"Christine, if you haven't worked it out yet, Ben is the tug, and all that we have to do is get across to that point over there, about 100 feet away, and quietly, then slip ashore and into his car. The wee boat will slip quietly back under the dock as we are pulling a light line out with us, which is pre-weighted, every 6 feet or so."

To which in almost total silence was achieved. The mystery, though, still deepening.

"And why" Christine asked quietly and said, "do you need the wee boat back underneath the dock, when we are going the other way?"

"This my darling, is called insurance."

Meanwhile and earlier, in another place.

"Okay truth time," to all assembled from an individual high up in the DEA. "We have known for some time that cocaine has been brought in through the Port of Corpus Christi, Texas, but could not understand how it was done, until someone came to see me this morning, as if he didn't have enough problems with his own ship, which he is in command of a foreign flag ship. His identity remains for now, private."

An attentive many, their hearing now considerably sharpened.

"So that is where he went to this morning, when we couldn't find him, chorused Mike and Einar," in subdued aside whispering.

"Now I do not know how he has achieved this," from this high up DEA official, "but we are going to carry out a simultaneous 3 timed raid, first of all on The Department of Agriculture's Cutter, then on the gas tanker which he is in command off, which will take about 200+ of us, in and then the garage where the Mayors cars are stored and maintained plus one currently lying on a flatbed truck, within a DEA cordon. "He's not doing this terribly well," said Mike to Einar, a few seconds ago, it was a foreign flag ship, now it is a foreign flag gas tanker, and there is only one in port at the moment.

"The only thing that I can tell you is that we will only find a very small amount of cocaine, but enough evidence to support the case of how they are getting cocaine in through this port, and onto our streets. Oh, and simultaneously being timed to coincide with the time that damn Department of Agriculture's cutter is safe to board, which is, as we speak, remains sunk, or also perhaps, a little squashed.

We have already this afternoon put the equipment on board this Norwegian gas tanker to raise it, the Dept. of Agriculture's cutter not including the cutter's crew that is."

"There he goes again," said Mike, "he might as well give a news broadcast from the foredeck."

"Any questions?" to which there were a few, and answered quietly to those who had asked, taken aside and given the low down in whispered dialogue.

"What do you make of that Mike?" asked Einar, whispering.

"I rather think that Doug has uncovered that there is someone who within The DEA is involved in this highly skilled smuggling racket."

"But what I don't understand is to what this stuff X-100 actually is, nor seemingly do the Americans."

"Well we could ask him, if we could find him. He was here a minute ago, where has he gone? Or more to the point, Christine as well!"

Smuggled out the back way, and both with Ben and Daniel in tow, all four eager to meet up with Susan, the only problem, getting past, the DEA Cordon, when who could not have come at a better time than Mullah.

"Fancy making about 300 Rupees Mullah" asked the captain, "for about 10 minutes work."

Eyes agog, "what do I have to do, and when do I get paid?"

A greenback US Dollar bill to any of his native countrymen, taking more importance than just exactly what he had to do, the mind-set now so focused on doing anything, legal or otherwise, just to get the US$ bill of whatever denomination.

"Right now, here's $100 US and a bit more than 300 Rupees do you know how to drive a car Mullah?" asked the captain, "and did you bring your spectacles?"

Whether he did or didn't wouldn't have made much difference as the eyelids were now so far apart that on both the upper and lower lids, the in-differing colours of corneas gave way to whites.

The pupils focused on a very narrow beam. A blind man would have most probably had more of a clue as to direction.

"No captain, I don't know how to drive a car, and I haven't brought my spectacles, do I have to give you back your $100?" Not as anyone from the Sub-Continent was liable to actually do.

"Ocht, no," in that momentarily lapse back into Scots, "you'll be perfect then, a crash course into how to drive an automatic gearbox hired car in The United States of America, with less emphasis on the crash, and more emphasis on the correct course. We'll just overlook the minor details that you don't have a licence, or insurance, or have never actually driven a car before, or can actually see where you are going. Have you seen how kids of 16 years old in this country drive, at 50+ish, you are years ahead of them."

Age from tired, and wrinkled faces, always being difficult to judge. "You don't need to pay all that much attention as what you have to do is keep looking forwards, and ignore the various mirrors. And anyway, the top speed is only 55 mph, Okay?"

"Perfectly Captain, I've always wanted to learn how to drive," said with a degree of excitement, before being told, "now keep this key in your right hand, and whatever you do, keep your mouth shut, and I mean, very tightly shut!" Not that he was expected to comply, but worth a go anyway.

Little did he know at the time was that he was going to get away with just about every motoring offence imaginable in the State of Texas. And an additional few that no-one had as yet in fact dreamed up. While scaring the hell out of everyone else, when who just came into view! Or could possibly have gotten away with it all, if he had heeded the advice just given. His perfect excuse, being the hidden one, on the ships port side, such as how he was somewhere else at the time! It not the time to explain the difference between a misdemeanour and a felony, mostly as the captain hadn't a clue about the difference anyway.

"There it is over there Mullah, the dark red one, you slither up onto the left hand side, and I'll follow. When we get near the car, press that little button on the key fob, and you'll see the indicator lights flash, the yellow ones, that means that the cars doors are open. Get quietly into the driver's seat, put the key into the ignition, it's on the right hand side on the control column, but don't start the engine just yet. Put your seatbelt on first." To which he duly did. "Now slide the chair into a position you feel comfortable with, with that wee lever underneath the front seat. Good, well done. Now handbrake off, that's the bit in the middle of your right, near your hand, put your right foot on the big pedal, that's the brake, and hold it there until the engine starts, as you turn on the ignition and then select **Drive.** Yes the light that just came on with that other lever in the middle, push it forwards until the light goes out. Okay, I'll switch on the lights for you, see, and off you go. Just remember this, as this is your first driving lesson, and that Americans drive on the wrong side of the road, it is they who are wrong and not you, now in a minute or so, when you are ready, move your right foot from the big pedal on the left onto the other pedal, the smaller one, which makes it all go."

"Okay captain, I think I've got all of that."

Not the most convincing statement in the circumstances.

"Now the final part of your first lesson is the steering wheel, to go left, you turn it left, to go right, you turn it right, to go straight on, you keep it in the middle, okay?"

"Okay captain, but which is left and which is right?" said an excited Mullah.

"Think of it as port or starboard, port being left."

Not going to be overly useful as a ships' lookout, this being filed away for the future, should this particular captain ever succeed in getting his ship operating, hopefully sometime soon. Best to get today over with first.

"Try converting just where your feet and fingers have just been into hands that now need to rotate, on this circle thing in front of you. Just don't press the bit in the middle," to which he duly did, having now located the horn. A new found toy to which those, being from a particular race seemed to think that continuously using it, could keep them out of trouble. It never permeating their brain cells, that no-one could tell one horn from another, with a dreadful cacophony going on all around, at least periodically covering up the sound of steel to re-shaping steel. Mostly because those coming the other way, didn't understand just what was left, or right, and were tempted to use both sides of the road anyway. Fortunately, this being the USA would relieve him of the additional problem from his own home country, it being highly unlikely that there would be a cow or two in the middle of the road. Or anyone in a rickshaw, or even more dangerous, on a bike with no lights.

"Just swerve away from on-coming lights, you'll soon get the hang of it. Good Luck." Hopefully.

"This is the easiest $100 dollars that I have ever made Captain, thank-you."

"One last thing, if it gets a bit bumpy, don't use the brakes, and if you hit anything, don't stop as it is their fault, they are after all, driving on the wrong side of the road. Just aim to miss that one up there on the flatbed," hoping that he would in fact, hit it, or at least enough to dis-lodge it. "Good luck, and when you get the car to the Agents Office, there will be another $1000 waiting for you."

A pretty safe bet, not to lose as Mullah had no idea where the Agents Offices actually were but for an Indian AB, $1000 was an awfully big carrot, "3 miles that away, left over the bridge, and left again onto Leopard, stop outside 3076, at the back, were his final directions." Which unfortunately would have worked had he heeded the advice of The Royal Air Force in that eating carrots doesn't actually help you see in the dark. At least, he wasn't wearing sunglasses. Or come to that matter, spectacles. Tunnel vision occasionally having its odd advantage, in a limited sort of way.

A bit of satisfaction then to those who had been eating carrots, giving them adequate time to avoid this hopelessly out of control car, accelerating out of the dock area, having completely missed the car on the flatbed, but making up for it in other ways, as the first power line came crashing down, with sparks going everywhere, as it shorted out, and an awful lot of other lights also going out. The only one's still glowing on Mullah's car, heading towards more mayhem. He not quite, but working on it though, getting the hang of the cars steering system, and making a thoroughly useless job of it in his learning, although to be fair, each car scraped as he fought the steering wheel the other way diminishing correction, but only just. Just as well each panel guarding an American car containing more air, than their European counterpart's. The dents, just being bigger dents.

Christine, Ben and Daniel looking a bit perplexed, before one dared to ask, "how far do you think he will get Doug?"

"I'll be surprised if he gets it out of the harbour area or in the next 5 minutes, who cares, but judging by the way Indians drive in Bombay, and they have driven there before, I'd give him at least a minute in a straight line, or 5 seconds if he has to turn a corner. Remember, all we needed it for was for a distraction."

Eventually, Mullah makes it, the long way round, involving just a few warehouses on the way, some now devoid not only of their front doors, but large parts of their roofs as well, explaining this away, to come later. Apart from the house, missing its Christmas tree, now in the next door neighbour's yard, and the wrong way up. Christmas was a few months away yet. Not too bad really, only 8 miles to find out just what the brake pedal was actually used for.

Meanwhile!

"Anyone see where that arrogant DEA man went?"

In the confusion, no-one knew. But he was close-by, and suitably attired.

"Right, X-100 time, Grab an air bottle, a mask and follow me. This we only do once tonight as I'm getting rather tired. Shake up and down a can vigorously, screw in the plastic tube into the nozzle, then squeeze till the hi-exp foam comes out, open your air bottle and breathe in through your mouth the bubbles that come out, and as you go down squeeze the hi-exp foam into anything with a slot in it. The foam cures faster when it gets wet, so use plenty of it. Follow me," as the ships master slipped beneath the surface.

It took a little time before all got used to it, surfacing occasionally to follow his lead as it took several cans to seal the Cutters engine room air vents, although only one venturing inside to seal them from the inside, and Christine having the most beautiful face giving hard concentration to what she was doing.

Giving the 2 fingers signal for underwater communications, and follow me, drop your tanks out with the cutter, the four swam away and surfaced in the darkness, ahead of the Cutter.

"Now we know who the bad penny in the DEA is," said Doug, and confirmed by both Ben and Daniel. Christine not following their lead, because Susan was nowhere in sight."

"Come on, let's quietly get out of here," a gentle slow breaststroke in the shadow of the cutters and ship's hull bringing them to the pilot ladder at the aft end of the main deck, on the port side.

One at a time, quietly, and softly up the outside way, and into the masters cabin.

The captain being the last to arrive, greeted by Susan, and asked, "did you get all of the photo's Susan?" The smile said it all. She had.

Picking up his 'phone, and dialling, to be met with the answer, "we're already sir."

"Go for it Blackie, and remember, I only want the ship warped forward, enough, as we agreed. Then get the 'phones re-connected."

The head of The DEA, also present, asked, "Doug, we've got most of the evidence, what are you doing now?

"Making sure that the bad pennies don't get away, I'm moving my ship forward into the inside of the DEA cordon, well a bit of it at least."

"Do you know who they all are?" asked, by the DEA, Head Man.

"Yep, and it is not only one on board The Department of Agriculture's Cutter who is involved, they are all involved in bringing drugs into Texas."

"Only, they don't know that when we re-float their cutter, it isn't going anywhere."

The preferred route of not asking how, watching as submersible pumps were lowered over the fo'c'sle and into the sunken boat, then after about an hour or so, discharging the water from within, as their cutter slowly came back afloat.

A delighted corrupt smuggler from within a Government Agency, totally unsuspecting, as to why he was going nowhere, as the others involved frantically trying to clean out their diesel engines, previously being submerged in dock water.

Puzzled looks emanating from all, most now expecting something odd as, "Okay Blackie, lower it away," as a 5 tonne port anchor steadily took up its position on the after part of the cutter, ensuring at least its stern was now relatively back towards where it had been just a few hours before, and not likely to move under its own power, as another 2 tonnes of anchor cable arrived on top. Afloat, but only just.

"Captain, I need you to sign Lloyds Open Form, if you do not, then a signatory from your agents will do," the arrogance of this man about to be brought up short.

None appearing to be forthcoming resulted in the following, on dock-side. And not what this arrogant individual expected, in the very least.

"Right captain, (of the Department of Agriculture's cutter), is this your briefcase?" From the Head of the DEA.

"Well it looks like mine, but I can't be certain, it is where we all keep our official documents when we go on board ships that come into this port."

"So the simple fact that it has your cutters name on it, you suggest that other members of your crew also use it as well."

"Yes off course, we take turns."

"Good. What are the combinations to get the catches released?"

He gave them, and un-surprisingly, didn't work. To which the Head of The DEA, and assisted by the local police, said, "Okay, arrest them all, and get this down to the lab, and if the lab can manage to find the combinations to get it open, don't reveal anything until we get all of them to witness its contents. Seal it completely with red tape, and cable ties. Then get them to witness the seals, and take photographs of everything. Take them away boys."

Their protestations not getting them anywhere, and swearing in front of Police Officers, not to be generally recommended. In any country, particularly that of the ships' master who were strict on this. Well Scotland in the main, are a polite nation.

Bit hard to argue in handcuffs behind their backs, but all were a bit vocal as led away into what American Police call 'cruisers.'

Again, from the head of The DEA, addressing The Mayors Limo driver, and asked, "Just how exactly can you explain why you have a briefcase in your possession, with the same name as of The Department of Agriculture's cutter written on it?"

"I don't know sir. I just get told to collect it and drive it up to the Mayor's office."

"Do you know the combinations to open it?"

"Oh no sir, but I'm sure the Mayors Head of Transport does."

"Okay, arrest him, and get this up to the lab as well, and same conditions as the other one. Only we'll use blue tape this time. Plus cable ties. And get the photographs."

Again voicing his innocence profusely, sitting in the rear of a 'cruiser' and driven away.

Out of visual range, so that no-one could identify him.

"Okay Doug, we've got most of it, all that we need now are the drugs and the money, and if you can find the time tomorrow to be interviewed by The FBI."

"Why the FBI?" asked curiously.

"Because our department has been seriously corrupted, my young Scottish friend, who we owe you an enormous debt of gratitude for exposing it."

"Okay, no problem, might be a bit dirty, but you'll find me dockside in about 10 minutes or so. I'll deal with The FBI tomorrow."

"Ben and Daniel will go with you, and Susan has the underwater camera."

"Are you not coming as well?"

"Sorry no, I can't swim." Conversation being limited to quotes. "Well to be truthful, I kept sinking."

Christine chipped in with, "can I go too?" the captain not having the strength to argue, meekly relented.

Only one compressed air bottle being required, as 5 disappeared underwater, with a few keep sake bags for the hard evidence, although some of it might be slightly damp.

Susan taking photos, with an occasional break for more air, as the captains hand reaching up into the air space where the rudders stock came down from the steering gear flat, and through the hull, and passed down to those below, he getting his air from the bubbles sent up by Christine, with both Ben and Daniel sharing in the same alternating sequence.

The head of The DEA more than just a bit surprised at the sheer quantity as it was eventually brought back to the surface, and spirited away very quickly, as The Press were beginning to arrive.

"The less we say tonight the better," said Doug, "I'm going for a beer, and anyone care to join me?"

Silly question really, as all did making their collective way to his office.

No sooner were the tops off and the first swig having been taken, when the 'phone rang.

"Is that the captain of the MV Norgas Challenger?"

"No" as the chief engineer replied, but I'll just pass this 'phone onto him, who is calling?

"Corpus Christi Police outside 3076 Leopard sir" he said before passing the handset across.

"Yes, Captain here, can I help?"

"Captain, it is the Corpus Christi Police, know anything to do with 3076 Leopard?"

And continued with a question to which he suspected he already knew the answer to, however implausible it might be, "Sir, do you have any knowledge of an Indian individual, who goes by the name of 'Mullah?' He has just arrived at this location leaning against a car, which might have been involved in more than just a few accidents, and all that we can get out of him, is "I've come to collect my $1000."

"Can you describe him?"

"About 140 pounds, 5 feet 6 or so, dark in colour, and for some reason, isn't wearing any shoes."

"What about the car?"

"Very badly damaged sir and we are getting reports that it may have hit a bridge, and a few other things."

"That sounds like the one that was stolen from beside my ship earlier. Sorry I've been so busy with The DEA, The FBI and so forth that I've not had time to report it."

The mention of both of these departments changed the attitude from being threatening to submissive. But in a nice way.

"So what do I do with him sir?" asked the young officer, "he seems to know you, and claims to be one of your crew."

"Look, for tonight, just leave the car where it is, it is a hire car after all, providing it is the same one and after having a day like today, I'll sort it all out in the morning. And in any case, Mullah can't drive a car, what else did you get out of him?"

"He keeps repeating that he has come for his $1000."

"Ah, I just remembered, ask him if he was one of the crew who joined the ship, just at the same time as I did."

A few minutes passed, before the police officer came back with, "Sir, all that I can get out of him, is that he has come for his $1000. What do I do?"

"Point him in the right direction of my ship, and if he did come from here, then he should be able to find his way back, shoes or not, because it is only 3 miles, which might just defer the problem until I have had some sleep."

The Corpus Christi Police, not without heart did give Mullah a lift across the freeway, before pointing him roughly in the right direction, which unfortunately was almost immediately met with a collision with trash cans. Asian eyes, emanating from a tired face taking a little longer in acquiring his night sight. The police not hanging around too long, to investigate, the incoming smell being suggestive that they should be somewhere else. Plus, they had already had enough of Mullah!

Meanwhile, back on board.

"What was all that about Doug?"

"Mullah managed to get to Leopard 3076 in the hire car."

"WHAT? AND HOW?" from just about everyone.

"Now, it has been a long day and I am going to bed, goodnight all."

The intention, being usurped by Christine though who had other plans, and explained to her husband, just what a day she had had over the 'phone, and was not going home that evening, but had been invited to use the spare pilots cabin, the Chief Engineer insisting that she being so tired was not a wise move to drive when thus so.

"Nothing to worry about darling, the captain isn't here, no-one knows where he is. See you in the morning."

As she retired to bed, taking a cold drink from the captain's fridge, leaving his cabin door open, with the curtain drawn across, then retired to bed in the pilot's cabin. One deck up.

It only took 30 minutes or so before a furious husband arrived, hell bent on finding if his wife was in a sexual relationship or any other relationship, with the ship's captain, finding nothing in the ships' offices, shut down for the night, and in partial gloom.

He then, searching every part of the ships accommodation block, much to the consternation of the crew, awoken from their slumbers, as he frantically sought out his wife, and finally arriving at the masters door, with now more than just a few trailing him.

"Hey, you can't go in there" from behind, but he did so anyway.

"WHERE IS MY WIFE?" and in a tone not to be argued with.

"She is in the pilots cabin, one deck up," said Mike, the chief engineer, "but she is exhausted, so to put your mind at rest, just look in quietly, and then let her sleep."

He did so. But was not content with what he saw, his suspicious nature not being appeased by much, prompting his next question.

"So where is the captain, he's not in his cabin?"

"If you knew just how hard that man works, then you will realise that where he goes to sleep in the little time that he has for sleep, you'll find him in The Rope Store. Come, I'll show you."

Raised eyebrows accepting that he could be wrong as he looked at this ships master fast asleep curled up on a mooring rope, flaked out ready for use next port, when it eventually got there. "This John, is one of the few places on board a ship, where there is no vibration, so move back, and let him sleep."

Just afterwards "You mean he sleeps every night here, why?"

"Because, with the time differences from our various charterers around the world, this is the only place where he can sleep, without the bloody 'phone ringing, at some un-godly hour when it is usually some really dumb secretary who hasn't got the first clue, as to where the ship actually is. Now either go and join your wife in the pilot's cabin, or go home. Breakfast, if you are still here is from 7 in the morning to when anyone not already working has found about 10 minutes to spare, and that might include you."

He choose to stay with his wife, and after-undressing, snuggled up to her, to be met with, in a sleepy way, "John, make love to me."

"How did you know it was me, petal?"

"I know that smell anywhere, come, it has been a long time since we made love."

She had been forewarned, as the captain gave up his rope bed, and sought out his real one.

Unfortunately, caught out on the way by Mullah! As he veered into his own office.

"Okay Mullah' before we get down to the money bit, just where is the hired car, the one that you were driving last night?"

"$1000 dollars sir!" A light sallow skin palm, empty, but expecting to be filled at short notice, "One thousand dollars," coming from a face that one could very happily punch the smugness lights out of it all day, with no regrets or remorse, and coming very close to doing so.

"Where is the car Mullah?" in a tone suggesting violence.

A total waste of time, to which this tired ship-master, gave into, but not in the most obvious or coherent of ways.

"Out and close the door while I open the safe," the recalcitrant one having to comply. "Okay Mullah, here is your $1000," handing over a $1000 bill. Its' source hopefully would trip this one up later, but ship-masters do need to be devious and lie, with a completely straight face. The unfortunately now smug Indian, in possession of a counterfeit note, courteously provided by one of the two other drug dealing sides, with still an awful lot of explaining to do, seeing as he had already lost his spectacles, the torn ear of the bill being a dead give-away.

"Now bugger off, I'm going up to my cabin to sleep."

Mullah though having other ideas, jumped in front of the captain as he tried to leave his office, which was not a wise thing to do, as he protested "but captain, the money changers in Bombay will not accept a US$1000 note, especially as this one is damaged, see it has a little tear on the corner."

"Well take it to a bank then Mullah, and change it there and for now, just bugger off. Or alternatively, put on a little bit of sellotape."

"But I won't get the same rate of exchange as they charge 10% commission. Now if I had it in $10 or even $20 dollar bills, one's not damaged, then I would get much more from the money changers," the octaves in his voice ramping up a scale or two. The point noted as the stress levels coming to the ears of the captain, would be recalled later sharing this with others.

The captain, more than just being a bit pissed off, tried again, "where is the hired car? Tell me and you'll get your $20 bills."

"It's at the bottom on the accommodation ladder sir."

"And where are the keys?"

"They are here captain," offering them to him. This leading to a little bit of confusion, which prompted another question, "according to The Corpus Christi Police, the car is supposed to be at the rear of 3076 Leopard, and you were supposed to be walking back to the ship."

"But I don't have any shoes captain, now $1000 in $20 dollar bills!"

"You might have more hope of getting it, if you said please, stopped jumping in front of me, and waited till after I have had some sleep. **And stop jumping out in front of me"** As he did it again. "Anyway, all of your countrymen have soles like leather! And you don't need shoes."

The captain finally accepting that he was not getting him anywhere, with this dumb brain that could only focus on money, and the only way of getting rid of this nuisance, was to deviate from the normal.

"Right Mullah, you are coming with me, only this time, I'll drive, and we are both walking back to the ship, after I have hidden the car, for the final time, and DON'T ARGUE!"

Rather satisfying as they both took off, in that Mullah still had no shoes on his feet. A point not unduly missed. Looking for something that was hard to walk on, might just being an alternative distraction.

Mind you, after looking at the state of the hire car, most of it looking as if it had had an argument with a herd of stampeding elephants, prompted the remark, "Mullah, you are getting no more driving lessons! It's not as much as what you hit, but more of a case of just what you didn't! And I cannot for the life of me, think of anyone dumb enough to sit in a car with you as an instructor. Apart from me that is. So hang on! And seat belts do help you know." Mullah being so thick, trying to puzzle out just where his seat belt actually was, forgetting that he was now on the other side of the car, and struggling as he might trying to reach it from his left would have had more success, if he had sought it from his right. "At least here Mullah, there are no cows walking down the middle of the road." Not that that made much sense, the general rule in Bombay, being, you either drive on the right, or the left, or even the middle, as long as you don't hit the cow or cows. The unfortunate part being that to avoid the cows, the on-coming traffic, followed the same logic, but due to the congestion, slowed the collision speed down to an almost complete stop.

Only, there was a wee gap.

The pressure on his back however from the accelerating car, convincing enough that he should be somewhere else, like anywhere other than here and pushed back in his seat. His singled minded and arrogant attitude, now about to have the shit scared out of him, "I used to race cars Mullah. You okay there?" Knowing that he wasn't!

"Let me out please?" coming as a whimper, the expression of the eyes conveying to those who might just have had a fleeting glance of abject terror.

"No can do, anyway, getting the door open at 90 miles per hour, you might have to struggle with, and did you recognise the word being 'please', you might like to try that again when you refer to money."

Followed by.

"Found your seat belt yet Mullah? Better be quick, as there is a bridge coming up. We might be flying."

They were, although they now being perhaps, a little lost.

Approximately 5 miles later, the captain swerved off the road into a field of corn, the corn-on-the cob type and which grew to an approximate height of about 7 feet, and following a pre-thought out plan, eventually brought the car to a halt, or put another way, the car having had nearly enough.

"Right Mullah, out you get, there is enough moonlight to see by, just follow the tracks we have made through this cornfield, and when you get out of this field, the ship is only about a mile away. Now off you go."

It took only a few minutes for the passenger, who had spent the last few miles upside down in the foot well, to ask, "just how fast were you going when you hit that bridge?"

"Does it matter? You survived didn't you? And which bridge? There were 3 of them. Your bruises might fade into the same colour of your skin is perhaps, just as we see them in the morning. You might need to point them out to us."

"Now off you go, that way." Pointing anywhere, being anywhere other than the correct way.

"And when I get back, you will give me my $1000 money in $20 bills?"

No comment was required, but tendered anyway.

"Yes, that is what I promised, now get going, although this will be paper currency, of the only country in the world that accepts this as legal tender," his temper struggling to maintain composure. "Oh, and take the car keys with you." The voice deliberately lowered from the referred "now get going" part, until the "take the car keys with you."

He set off, with a slight skip in his step, apart from the limp, thinking that he had gotten the better of this captain, but corn fields are not smooth to walk on, especially re-arranged ones and his progress was somewhat slow, and only had to get through about 2 miles of cleared corn? Getting hopelessly disorientated in the process, and with feet and knees that were getting somewhat sorer, from continuously tripping. The odd bits of blood now suggesting that setting off without shoes, probably, not considered being overly wise. Seeing as some who within the crew, just couldn't stand this particular individual either. Racism, within a multi-national crew on board a ship inevitable, and those of the non-Asian race, had massive sympathy with their respected master, dealing with this individual, hell bent on milking his position to the full, and at their cost, although there might just be a way of turning this around.

The captain's progress was considerably faster, as he forced his way through about 5 metres of corn, to the edge of the field and completing his journey back to his ship in a little under 20 minutes.

Cooling down in his office, feet up, for the best part of an hour or so and with the vague idea of the intention of going to his bunk, and for what was left of the night, only to be met by The Corpus Christi Police

"Sorry to disturb you Captain," from this very junior, but pleasantly polite police officer, "I'm sorry to have to tell you that your hired car, behind 3076 Leopard has been stolen."

"Can we leave this till the morning, I know you mean well, but I would rather wake up on the next day after I went to bed, and not as everyone seems to think that I am someone who doesn't need to sleep at all."

"Off course sir, I understand, but my sergeant wants to know if you have any information about an individual, who might be one of your crew, and who is now wrecking a corn field."

A moment's hesitation, lost in suddenly awaking this particular master, with a glint of a smile onto his tired face replied.

"Just how exactly is he or she wrecking this cornfield?" asked the ships master.

"A person seems to be driving a car around in it sir, could this, perhaps be the same person, who earlier one of your officers told me about, who may have stolen the car from behind 3076 Leopard?"

No answer was required, at least until later, as there was a horrendous bang on the dockside!

Those still awake on board rushing down to investigate, to be met with Mullah, and a few others staggering around, amid an area of carnage, well of the twisted and dented variety one of which just happened to be on the back of a flat-bed truck, and all, mostly made of steel, originally, but no longer complying with their part reference number, it now being bar coded.

"Hello captain, I'm back, $1000 in $20 dollar bills, and no torn corners." As he wobbled in front of him, again with that smug face, which did not get punched out just yet, but coming very close to being so.

"Officer, I do believe that this might just be the car thief that you may be looking for, and I suggest that you ask him first of all for his driving licence, then his Insurance, and then his passport, with no doubt, also his work permit."

"But captain, it is me, Mullah!" Wailed from the same shocked place, the brusque arrogance, now being replaced with fear. And jumping in front of the captain, not realising that this was still not a wise thing to do.

To which the young police officer asked, "Can you identify him sir?"

"Well the light isn't good, But I think that I can safely say that I have never met this man before in my life, although that might not be totally exact, as he reminds me of a waiter who I may have come across, as The Norwegian Consul who served us as we both had an Indian Lunch a few days ago. A lot of these from foreign shores just look a lot the same and will stowaway on ships, no matter where the ship is going, as long as it is out-with International Waters."

Listening carefully, and ignoring the wails from behind.

"I suggest to you officer, that you ask him where his passport is, and if he cannot come up with it, then I suggest you apprehend him. I don't want stowaways on my ship."

It not being explained just how it was possible to stowaway on a ship, with the individual, not on a ship but on the dockside. After all, whoever stowed away on a dockside? But then, there is always a first time for everything.

Apoplexy could not have described this face better protesting individual, now being led away by The Police, still demanding US $1000, voiced vociferously, and in a way suggesting that $20 bills being more important than visiting the inside of a prison cell. Well, he at least would be fed. Of a sort! He might even be given a shower, which should soften his feet up a bit, and at least washing the blood away.

Going to be one hell of a job though explaining just how he actually managed to get into The United States in the first place. Although his name was not included on The Crew List, as the ship had already gained Inward Clearance. He at the time of going ashore, had, and been warned of this, to take his passport with him. Which he did, sort off, only the entrance permit, stapled to his current passport, and had now seemingly found its way onto his previous out of date passports. And he not noticing.

This may take even more of explaining away, just why he is now in a police cell in Texas, and his passport in another country, as in the interim, the captain had found out what his actual country of origin was, and it was not India, although it was, sort of. He wasn't married after all. Doubtful, as most of his age had many wives, and goodness knows how many offspring he had, it could be anywhere. Where obscure? As the captain already had 3 of his other passports, as each one going out of date, was stapled to the already out of date ones.

Plus the original one in another drawer. For some obscure reasoning, just why anyone needed to present not only his original one, but the other entire out of date one's at the same time. And they from this nation, not only vociferously objecting to seeing the out of date passports, detached from the current one and handed back to them, as they came to sign on a ship. Which they had to do, as the ship had now changed owners, even although they were already on board, well give or take a few.

Mind you, just what exactly the ships master was supposed to do with their chest x-rays, as they were filed in the box, marked. "For float testing," they being thrust into his face by the incumbent new crew, who didn't even bother to knock on his door first, the rush of which being explained later. Well, sort of. As one more was added to the box. Not actually tested as such, but 5 or 6, the dark patches anyway, and compressed together, made very good arc welding eye masks.

"So what are you doing now, as we've now gotten around spares for welding masks?" Asked The Chief Engineer?"

"Watch and learn." Came the only response.

Shouldn't be that difficult, with a chart correcting pen, and a bit of glue covering up the staple holes, a few minor details adjusted so to send him on his way.

To which the captain, with a magnifying glass and a very steady hand, did achieve, and didn't have to part with $1000. Even if it was counterfeit.

"A bit ambitious Doug, although I have to admit," Einar watched on, "India does look alike as Indiana."

"It just needs a hypodermic needle to get underneath the plastic, and a few more wee squirts around the edges to make it as look as though this particular passport may have gotten a little damp. Then flatten it with an iron."

"What about the barcode?" asked a curious Chief Engineer?"

"Oh, I changed that as well."

"To what?"

"It comes up with a resident of Sri Lanka. Amazing just what you can do with a scalpel. You don't actually take a bit out or add a bit in, you just move it a little bit of the numbers sideways. Plays hell with the bar-code."

"And does this work?"

"Every time so far," but I like to keep it quiet.

"Well, if he ever gets there, he should be able to walk home."

The wee bit of water in between the island attached to India and rather a big island though might present a further problem. Trying to lose oneself in a country of 1.2 billion people, could be a tad tricky with a forged Sri Lankan passport, and 3 out of date Indian ones, which had gotten a little damp. Somehow.

But only time would tell.

The others from his crew, witnessing this, and from the ships offices, preferring not to get involved, but watched with a degree of amusement, and in total agreement with their ships' master, as they had another request, now that The DEA, and the local Police had left, Captain, would you like a cold beer?" one of the group volunteered, although with a bit of trepidation. Raised eyebrows and a face not conveying patience, suggesting that tip-toing around would be better addressed if they just came out with what was on their minds.

The question being somewhat pre-empted as a cold beer was thrust into his hand, followed with, "Because we've got a 5 stage rocket ready to go, and a 3 stage line throwing one also ready to go. And it looks like a nice quiet night to test them."

There was a pregnant pause.

"I thought you guys were kidding when you stole that bit of pipe?"

The apparent blank faces conveying nothing. They having already noticed, that their captain could deduce who was lying, by where their eyes were looking, and all were nearly closed.

"One night, I am going to drink myself senseless, down a bottle of Scotch in about 30 minutes, and during this time, wonder just how I ended up with a crew like you lot. Off course you can test them. Where are they?" A level of ingenuity at last.

"Roughly where the new Radome stand is due to go. We thought that if the paint got a bit burnt, then we could cover up any burn marks with a coat of primer."

"You may not have noticed, but the primer we have is grey, and the deck is red, which one is onto due to go first?" asked by someone looking for anything to brighten up the remainder of his day, "and where are they aimed?"

"Well, they both are sir, all that we have to do is move them into position," enquired cautiously, "or perhaps you may know of a better place?"

"I meant, not where they are going, but where they are going to be coming down."

The askance looks suggesting that this had not been considered.

"When something like this gets set off, and it's a 50-50 chance that it may not work, you might just need rather a lot of water, so I suggest the dockside, quite close to the ships stern, but on the watery side, and that you can all hide in, with a modicum of cover. Actually, the deeper you go, might be for the better."

Lying back against the nearest bridge wing, with legs crossed, head back and several decks higher, and after a very long day, watched as a newly invented 5 stage parachute distress rocket, without the parachutes just actually went. This should be fun.

It was.

Mind you, judging by the amount of smoke, no-one involved in the firing of it hadn't much of a clue as to where it went either.

But others did! And not overly pleased either.

But not to be un-abased, "Well that went well? Now let's try the 3 stage Line Throwing One."

"Now hold on a minute," as the ships' master briefly thought, fighting his way down and trying to breathe through the cloud of dispersing smoke, each one of these requires a detonator, and that is on the base of the rocket trigger required to ignite it, so how are you going to ignite the second, and even third stage, without a detonator?"

"Watch and see boss," was the reply, "we modified it."

"And just how did you modify it? And, who, are we?"

"Well we calculated, that if the initial burn time was about 1 and a bit of a next second, then that would be enough to crush the detonator, to set off the next one, and 1, maybe 2 seconds later would set off the 3rd one."

"And just exactly, how did you calculate this?"

"Oh sir, we used all sorts of things......................."he not getting much further as someone, dopey enough actually fired it. Rocket science apparently not being one of his or hers, extra-curricular studies, smoke ingestion not also ever having being considered.

About 5 seconds later, or perhaps longer, given the degree of surprise from all, as this very successful prototype, scared the hell out a civilian airliner pilot on final approach on landing at Corpus Christi airport. And 3 rockets capable of pulling out a thin rope for at least 1800 feet per 2 seconds each, minus the rope now suddenly plopped down into the same sort of area that it had now been earlier, fortunately missing the ship, but only just, and most fortuitously, in a place where no-one was likely to look.

"I think boys, after tonight, we need to give a little bit more thought on guidance. Or alternatively, we just take our garbage down to The Bay and throw it in."

"Now here's 30 bucks, go and see if you can find where the 5 stage one came down, as if it is not in the bay, would most probably be somewhere now, on fire. And remember, we've still got a ship to put back together, and time is pressing. Now I'm going to bed, good night!"

"We could always change guidance into stability," thought one aloud. "It doesn't need to pull all of its line out, just enough for it to get stable, and then we after 200 feet or so, attach the rest of what we want it to pull and deposit it in the bay, Even if it might, just, not, get, there." The trepidation in his words to which some might doubt, but not all.

"You know boys," said the captain, he listening, from behind his not quite closed door, "that might actually work. But after a day like today, I'll let you try it out, but just first, go and find where the bits of the 5 stage one actually ended up. Then you can play with the other 9. Call me if you need me."

Gleefully as many fun filled Filipinos, set off at speed, with more than just a few extra dollars, the first thing being fun, usually fuelled with beer, and a few suitably ensconced females, also appreciating that their new friends company was different, even if this meant going back to a ship to collect what looked like very strange objects, and spirited away to the local, in put no other way, as a house of ill-repute. But for one very strange reason, the fireworks on the beach, taking favour over from the usual carnal intentions.

It would have been a relaxing night of sleep, well for most of it, if Christine's husband hadn't needed to rise early to go to work, leaving his wife a little cold with no-one to snuggle up against, and sought out the only place she knew where there was warmth, and invited herself in, quietly, and mostly naked.

She, in her slumbered way, quietly forgetting that who she really wanted to be with, was one deck beneath, and got into bed with The Chief Officer. On the same deck, but he was at least German.

Well directions can get a bit muddled, when you are half asleep, but the screams of both awoke the whole ship, but not fortunately, the captain he being so tired that he blissfully slept through the commotion. And strangely enough did not appear in his office, until 10 am next morning, yawning a bit as he laid his coffee cup on to his desk.

"Right chief, main engine, what stage are we at?"

"Oh you've come back to the land of the living have you?" with quite a lot of sarcasm. "Had a nice sleep have you?"

The strained eyes, and much yawning, not being appreciated, so early, or was that late, in the morning.

"We should have probably, most all of it back together in the next 3 days, then we have to test it, which is not going to be easy, as some clown in the harbour masters office has given permission for The Department of Agriculture's cutter, now that it is no longer aside us, to park it astern of us, just right in the way of where our prop wash is going to be. And to make matters worse, they haven't dipped the eyes of their mooring ropes under ours. Effectively, we are stuck in port." The consternation being understandable, but placated with, "finish re-building the main engine, and leave the rest to me."

"How?" The joint multi-national reply sounding a little exasperated!

"Know how to make thermite? From things that most gas tankers carry? Apart from one, the puzzled expressions conveying that they did not." The smile conveyed it all, as Doug, with a little skip in his step left after making a 'phone call, and left a few even more puzzled heads behind.

The 'phone call, asking Christine, for "I need 1 kilo, sorry, 2 to 3 pounds of silver magnesium, and held under distilled water."

More confused heads, now just being one more.

Meanwhile from the head of FBI.

"Captain, we've never tried this before, but as you will be sailing out in the next few days, we need as much evidence as we can gather to break this drug smuggling ring, to which we are now in receipt of a little bag of cocaine, goodness knows how much of other substances, one of which we just cannot identify, and rather a lot of pure cocaine, plus, and it took us all rather a lot of time counting it, of just under USD $500 000."

"No problem, and by the way, the other substance was all that I could find at the time, which is custard powder," said to rather surprised faces. They knowing of him decided not to ask until later, although smiling within themselves that the lab chemists would never work out just what it was.

"What we are going to do, is wheel in individually those who had briefcases seized, and ask them to identify the contents, they not knowing at the time, just what the combinations were, although we now know them."

"And you want me to tell you if they are lying, as no doubt you will already have subjected them to a polygraph test, which in my opinion, doesn't actually tell you if they were telling the truth or not. We tend not to use them in The UK."

"Doug, would you like a full time job with us, how are you always one step ahead of us?"

"Minor skills that most gas tanker captains pick up on their way, although I may have rather refined the techniques, look closely at their throats, especially the 'Adam's Apple,' whenever the subject is asked a question out of the blue, they will swallow, and hard, they not expecting the question, and their face will get slightly redder."

"That, is not something, I'd thought of before," as others in the room nodded in agreement.

"Now here is your first line of questions."

"Eh, now, slow down a minute, I was just going to ask you what they could be." The others in the room, as surprised as their boss, but ready to listen, as this might be their chance to wrap this all up, and watertight, especially as their prime witness would be leaving the country shortly."

It took a little time to explain, but which all of them, after a short discussion involving the legal implications, decided to have a go at. The smiles all around, were conveying that they could not wait in getting started. Leading questions, usually reserved for The Courts, now masked under what the unlikely never expected.

Sitting behind one way glass, and viewed as the 1st was led in, dressed in the usual orange boiler suit and manacled in chains that if ever one was to escape from, being no use whatsoever as some spoil sport had gone and locked all of the doors and built very high walls, with razor wire on top. This in European eyes, seen as somewhat demeaning and counterproductive. Seeing as yet, the accused hadn't actually been charged with odd words such as a felony, a misdemeanour, or what other words cropped up in the

American version of plain English, that made no sense to those of the country, from where their language actually originated. Mind you, dialects from various parts of The UK, probably not helping that much from immigrants in previous years.

"Recognise this?" as the first was brought into the room, and released from his manacles. As he and his lawyer were invited to sit.

To be met immediately with protestations from his lawyer, who did not sit, and being told in such a way, that his only protest could be as to the comfort or cleanliness of his intended seat, and told also, that it had not as yet having been established just what the accused man's name, actually was.

To those watching, and there were many, already impressed, and who couldn't wait to see what came next. They now being a bit suspicious wondering just how another countries legal system could now be so easily showing up the irregularities of their own.

Now looking at a briefcase sealed with red tape, and cable ties, and still inside a large plastic bag? One did swallow, and picked up by their investigators, the newly learnt technique already working.

Various photographs of the time of his arrest being placed in front of them, and to which very strangely brought no protests from his defence council lawyer.

"Right gentlemen, before we remove this brief case from the bag and break the red seal and cable ties, would you like to tell us what we are going to find, before we set the combinations on the latches?"

The accused suddenly having a dry mouth, his heart beat on overtime, and then unable to speak, was met with. "You can't deny it is yours with your fingerprints and a few others fingerprints are all over it."

No answer forthcoming, as the face reddened up.

"We'll take that as a no then. Proceed."

"Okay, left hand combination being 8-6-4-2 and right hand combination being 7-5-3-1," to which both were set."

The setter keeping a well-disciplined straight face.

"Last chance, what are we going to find?" The strain eventually taking over from The Department of Agriculture's Cutters master, much against his lawyers instructions to the contrary "Oh all right, in United States Dollars $500 000, in sealed bags of $10 000 each," spluttered forth.

But not lost on the many watching from The FBI and The DEA. "Well, let's take a look then," as the catches were sprung."

"Doesn't look like half a million dollars to me eh, looks more like a load of drugs?" from the investigating officer.

You could have heard a pin drop. Even if falling into open mouths and bouncing off the teeth not producing any more audible noise.

"Right, get this off to the lab and get it analysed," said the boss, and hold them all for importing controlled substances."

As one very confused individual was led away, no objections from his lawyer even, as the rest of his crew, waiting to be interviewed, were about to be singly put under the same line of questioning. The manacles being re-fitted before one arrogant individual, now in a very confused state was led back to his cell, the only gratification being that when all of the others had been questioned, they could discuss this among themselves, even if it meant shouting from cell to cell.

The Engineer fared no better, he being of the breed of those in the opinion that ships masters and deck officers, appeared to stand on ships bridges and do apparently nothing. After all, he could run the engine room, and do the same as they did, it not entering their grey matter that looking at a radar screen didn't actually tell anyone just where the ship was going, but displaying something that had already happened. Plus the myriad of other things that on a ships bridge which have to be continuously monitored, and no amount of electronics could replace the human brain. Such as where the ship was actually going! Or the most important and most difficult thing of all, just how to get the ship stopped and just where the captain wanted it. Plus those on the other side, who also wanted it in the same place as the ship's captain.

"Right Chief? Can you tell me what is in this briefcase; after all it has your finger prints on it?"

He a little thrown off by The FBI, and stumbled a bit, before he had been given the chance to say anything.

"You do concede, that you do know just what is in this briefcase," came in from the boss of The DEA. Care to tell us first?"

"Oh all right, it is drugs!"

It is always better getting things off your chest, don't you agree?"

The forlorn but angry face indicating otherwise.

"Now before we set the combinations on the latches, do you agree that they are the opposite of the briefcase we opened earlier?

"I wouldn't know, I wasn't there," without a hint of suspicion.

The still confused lawyers not having a clue where this was all going, left and strangely for an American lawyer, did not object.

"So on the left hand side, the combination will be 7-5-3-1, and the right hand side will be 8-6-4-2."

The case being sprung................and revealed a 'Chop Chop Note.'

And not any drugs in sight.

Which did instigate more than a little alarm, Panic more like, where the hell have the drugs gone?

"Well that went well Doug, and as you suggested we don't need to send it to the lab, as it has already been there, only they don't know that. Care to join us all for some lunch?"

"Sorry, but no, I need to get back to my ship, but tell you what, come and join us for lunch, then I can do two things at the same time."

Does this man never stop, wondered more than just a few, as they all left together, and set off for lunch on board.

"Okay, here it is, 2.75 pounds of magnesium underwater," as Christine arrived, in the ships restaurant, "do you know how many 'phone calls I've had to make, to get this stuff," to be met with, "Ssshh, keep your voice down," fortunately not heard by The Head of The DEA, The Head of the US Coast guard, The Chief of Police and quite a few other dignitaries all ensconced in sampling a delightful buffet, which was, even by Texas standards, a way of getting thoroughly full stomachs with not a single burger in sight, or any other filler, not full of fat. Even the tablecloth not objecting, as the American habit of only using a fork in the right hand, with which to shovel food into one's mouth, appreciating the short distance from the plate to the mouth, sympathising that overloaded forks, with those not in contact with their eyes bit, tended to slightly drop off.

But the captain had disappeared, without as much as a by-your leave, although 2 in the background, who had been keeping a special eye on him, did notice the wink that he shared with Christine, as something was most definitely afoot, and neither just knew what the components of thermite actually were.

Celia Barnes didn't either, but she knew something else, and why she was here, been given the note of thanks from the missing master and from his bosun, an arising trusted crew member, who now accompanied her to an odd place, where in the annuls of shipping, no master had ever tried to hire 3 horses and pay for it on his ships insurance, the word 'cuddy' referring in one way as a place on board a ship, as a cabin, not exactly first class, more steerage level, while in Scots parlance, also did actually refer to a horse. Getting the cost into the insurance claim might need a little imagination. Or written off, as a translation between two different languages from the same country, not having the instinct as to which actually coming to court might reveal and how both being in English. Just also a bit tricky in Scotland, who on maritime manners were dependent on English Law.

"We only need one more Celia, know anyone else who can ride a horse?"

"Doug, even I just don't to know how to ride a horse!" in abject horror, "these things bite you know, and there is no way of knowing just where the feet go. Usually at high speed in the direction of human flesh."

"Well it can't be that difficult, you just sit on the top bit in the middle, behind its neck and before its bum or tail, then get it to go, and hope for the best. After all, we only need one more of them long enough to find a rattlesnake."

This news not being overly welcomed as both arrived back in the ships restaurant.

"Why do you need a rattlesnake?" and asked, with a high degree of curiosity from all assembled, the food rotation order from plate to mouth, temporarily halted.

"Because I've been invited to go rattlesnake racing, and tonight. Well I should have all of my day's work done by then. Plus there is a $1000 bet running on this, and, as I suspect, there might just be a few more side bets."

The curiosity from others within earshot on overdrive!

"But they supply the rattlesnakes, the protective leggings, even the sticks, which you are not allowed to hit the snakes with. Have you ever tried this before?" asked a concerned Celia, her voice increasing in pitch.

The 'no' not being overly convincing, but countered with a degree of enthusiasm, by way of explanation, and as something not worth worrying about. Much.

"Yes I know, but in my country if you go horse racing, you do take your own horses, even if they come from abroad, they bring their own horses, the race course only supplying the course, stables, straw and hay, a few grandstands, quite a lot of places selling rather expensive booze, goodness knows how many Turf Accountants, and a car park. Well, maybe more than 1 car park, which on the busy days might include a few helicopters. Same thing if you go greyhound racing, only difference being they supply the fake furry rabbit, a bit tricky getting people small enough to act as jockeys, and on a track consisting mostly of sand, so I'm taking my own rattlesnake tonight, just got to catch one first, before, shall I say, adjust it."

There were many shaking heads, as the captain wandered off, with Celia in tow. "Doug, I might be The Norwegian Consul, but this is way out of my league, officially you know."

"It didn't seem to concern you Celia over lunch on Norwegian Consul Business, and then when we sailed around The Bay on your little yacht." The sympathy not being overly truthful.

"We didn't, as you full well know, get all the way around the bay, it was far too hot. We only got as far as that little island, and as soon as we got into the shade, I fell asleep and losing about 4 hours of my memory. Is this blackmail? Doug, or did I say or do anything that I might regret," the question inviting a devious answer, one of which might be forthcoming, or perhaps not, the non-response exactly set to add to her intrigue.

"Well, that Indian lunch we had together, the Indian food being rather hot, you did quaff rather a lot of wine trying to cool your mouth down, and your steering out of the little marina where you keep your boat, requiring a little assistance. But when I got you under the palm trees and into the shade so you wouldn't get sunburnt, the over-indulgence of wine as an internal cooler did reveal a side of you that I didn't expect."

She was trembling, as to what might come next, her memory missing about 4 hours, and struggling hard to recall.

"For your size, you are remarkably light to carry, and after covering you in palm leaves, and myself lying in the shade found out something that only very beautiful women have and even fewer men recognise."

"Which is" the question being somewhat dreamily asked? "That beauty does not conform to what glossy magazines say a woman should be like, but in your case, a very gutsy and highly intelligent woman who can lie in the shade with a relevant stranger who has been up for the last 20 hours. Palm leaves make for excellent covering do they not?"

"Well now that you mention it, they do. Anything else?"

"You asked me to marry you, see, on your ring finger of your left hand, is your engagement ring, the 1 carat diamond on white gold that you told me about selected earlier. I hope that you still like it."

She hadn't a clue, but beginning to accept her predicament, not realising that she was now the victim of a very complex practical joke. Going to be hell explaining this to her current boyfriend, and long term partner.

Meanwhile.

"Just a minute," said Mike, "I know about this 'adjust it' bit. I got this from a friend of mine who knew our captain in his last company, and this I can tell you, takes a bit of believing, but he did it, not only once, but twice."

Tell us more being in anticipation; this had to be worth listening to.

"He was Chief Officer on a smaller gas tanker, but a highly sophisticated one, and the cargo they carried loaded at the terminal at Flotta, which is in The Orkney Islands in Scotland. And everything was on the limits, and Doug was only one of a few in the company who knew how to gas the ship up, say after dry-dock. They often had to wait for a few days, so anchored in Scapa Flow, and go ashore for a few hours in the evening. There not being a lot to do after having already seen the tourist bits invariably ended up in a pub. And so it was this particular evening, as The Kirkwall Ladies Hockey Team wandered in.

Now this being a friendly little place, and with a bit of banter ended up, after a few beers, with his ships' crew challenging them to a game of hockey, which most had forgotten about until next day, as they all sobered up, or became less pissed.

Only problem being that no one on the ship had actually played hockey before, but they were all held to a game, if it was to be for charity.

It was our now captain's idea as to how they would need an edge if they were going to win. They would all run around chasing the ball all over the place in the first half, only one of the engineer's was not overly fit. Whenever the ball came his way, he first off all, put his cigarette back into his mouth, screwed the top back onto his half bottle of Scotch, before replacing it back into the back pocket of his 'shorts', by which time, the ball was long past him, but he chased after it anyway, and when it did come his way, he elected to stop the ball with his leg as opposed to his hockey stick. A repeat of this not being attempted, as the language changed from being downright bad, but elevating to, something that even a normal person would wish not to hear. Even hardened seamen, who were now glad to hear the half-time whistle, rather than more relieved, than not wishing to be associated with where this engineer desired to lodge the ball, and not in a pleasant place, it being suggested that surgery might be required to remove it.

It was at half time, when they, the ship's crew gained the advantage, and eventually went onto win.

"How?" came from many interested faces, listening attentively.

"On the ships bridge, when there was not much to do as they swung at anchor, and it previously having been agreed, that the ship would supply the oranges at half time, plus a few drinks in the local pub afterwards, that they started adjusting the oranges."

This drew even more inquisitive faces.

"They took a pack of hypodermic syringes from the ships medical locker, with various lengths of needle and very carefully from the little pip bit, where the orange hung from the tree, the longest needles first, drew out the natural orange juice, and replaced it with neat vodka, only this was the really powerful stuff that only shipmasters can only buy out of bond. And carefully working their way up until the shortest needle replaced the last bit. They only did one, so cut in half next day, to see if it still had its' natural colour."

"And did it?" even more attentive heads now asking.

"Perfectly. Fifteen more were duly doctored, plus another 15 not doctored added to the box, but coded, if the little pip bit was still intact, that was one to avoid, and if the pip bit was missing, that was the one to take."

"I don't quite understand this," ventured one, "how did they present them at half time?"

"Their trainer, who just happened to be an ageing 2nd mate, and also a bit of a queer, brought a chopping board with him, and duly cut them for all to see, in front of everyone." Both teams joining in during the rest period. It was after all a, 'friendly game'."

"So what happened next?"

"Well after the bully off, for the second half that's seemingly how you start a game of hockey, the ship's crew drew level, but the game had to be abandoned after the ship's crew took the lead. After the next, 'bully off'.

"But why?" asked many even more curious Americans, and a few others of various nationalities.

"Because it takes 2 players for the 'bully off', and the opposing 10, plus one of the two referees who had already left the field of play, wandering in all sorts of directions, the remaining one, a 16 year old schoolgirl, her hair in pigtails, not used to neat alcohol, but still upright, also not fully in control of lateral direction, and not making any sense to the whistle blown by the last remaining umpire, eventually falling asleep on a compost heap, and nowhere near the pitch. Mind you, not all of the compost was compost, sheep liking the warmth to sleep on, as compost rotted away, generating heat and leaving behind their own contribution, expelled from their respective arses. Great for the garden eventually, but not to be welcomed by one in pigtails, or in any hair style either.

Just a bit unfortunately that she was the local Sheriffs' daughter, and his family being of a religion, who frowned upon alcohol, and just about everything else which could fall under the parameters of actually having fun.

She wasn't found until next morning, still taking a few more hours to sober up, and even the family dog steering well clear of the smell."

"And Doug did this twice?" asked by a few incredulous Americans.

"Seemingly 2 years later, but with a different crew, and a much changed Ladies Hockey Team. He even had some of the loading masters of the Oil Terminal joining in. Seemingly, they were even madder, than the ship's crew."

"Did the ships' crew win?"

"You have to ask?"

There was what is called a pregnant pause after this story, before one ventured. "So how is he going to get a rattlesnake, drunk? And why does he need 3 horses?"

"Well," said Mike, "if you have been laying off bets, then I can assure you, he will know how to catch a rattlesnake, and get all of its legs going straight towards the finish line, and in most probably, a record time."

"But snakes don't have legs!" as many pointed out.

"Well, not exactly! His theory is that if he can get it drunk, then its head, with the ears bit, will do all it can to get away from its tail. And the bits that do the slithering now becoming legs as such, from within its skin. After all, you walk in a straight line when you are sober, and when you get drunk, you are all over the place. He's just doing it backwards, assuming that the getting drunk bit will set it off in a straight line."

Seems eminently sensible. Various shaking heads thinking otherwise.

The American gambling fraternity, from those on board, deciding that inside knowledge could be used to their advantage. No doubt expanding this information, laying odds on how a merchant ship-master from the UK, was actually going to get near a rattlesnake, then catch it, and then race it, in just a few hours from now.

Later and following him off the ship, as he sought out a place to start, which for some very strange reason, just happened to be in a bar, which was also in Einar's hotel, which also had a 'kite museum.'

"Sir," to the barman, "set up 20 beers, and then 20 more, and then let me know when these US $200 bills run out."

Not a lot was said for a few minutes as dry throats from running became more normally rehydrated, but the question from Christine remained. "How do you become invisible?"

"Darling Christine, when I found out just why they do this, I was sailing with a Korean crew at the time, and they believe that passing in front of two or more others, it makes them invisible, as long as they crouch and hold their palm of their hand palm open and upright, in the middle of their, faces."

"Does it work?" asked a curious Christine.

"Goodness no, but it draws others attention away from them. I'll let you know later, as I've just had the nod. I'll finish my beer and leave quietly, time to make a rattlesnake catcher, kites made from rip-stop nylon perfect, as there with a smooth and almost indestructible fabric impossible for the old rattler having nothing to actually bite at, as long as it comes down fast enough in the shape of a cone, with the end chopped off."

It not being noticed by anyone, that The Kite Museum was now short of a kite, thanks to an inventive Filipino crew member, currently sneaking out the back way.

"And this works? What do you do after you've caught it?"

"Lower into a box, which my bosun has already made, through the hole on the top of the cone, which takes care of the swishing rest of it, then slide the door down at the same time as removing the kite/coney bit, and then feed it in time for the race."

"Have you tried this before?" asked one, the others deep curiosity suppressing their mouths.

"Only with lobsters, when my pals and I go Scuba Diving, and remember they have 2 damn sharp claws, a rattler has only one mouth. And we use clear plastic then. How we get them going is a secret."

The disbelief apparent to those others listening in.

"But what do you need horses for?" asked a doubtful Christine.

"Because horses can sense just where a rattlesnake is before we can, and I'll wager that in that wrecked cornfield, there might just be a few rather angry ones. Coming? All you have to do is sit in the middle of a cuddy, and when it rears up, no doubt a bit of whinnying as it does so, you just fall off the back, then run like hell, no doubt following the cuddy while I jump off my cuddy and catch the rattler. Only small problem is that you go about a couple of metres, or in American parlance, yards ahead of me."

"Does it actually work?" asked his new girlfriend.

"Well, I've never actually tried it with a rattlesnake, but it does work in Scotland when we go haggis trapping in the mountains."

Anyone dumb enough to believe this, obviously not fooled from the lobster angle.

"Indulge me," the level of scepticism, moving from the possibility of ridiculous, to a sport that Christine had never heard of before. Although in Great Britain, they did have some very eccentric games, such as cheese downhill racing and worm charming, and even, Lawn Mower Racing, and on race tracks, Car and Caravan racing. It having to be explained to their fellow English speaking friends, of Motor Home racing, not that many understood this. Or were ever likely to!

"Christine, a haggis has two legs, only one is longer than the other, but reversed for the female where the legs are opposite, To catch one, male or female, and they are elusive, and it takes a few others when you spot one, you chase it around the mountain, until it meets the others chasing it from around the other way, whereupon it gets a fright, and as it high-tails it the around the other way, falls over, its legs being the wrong way round to escape, as it then tumbles down the mountain."

"But does it work for rattlesnakes?" asked a sceptical Christine.

"We'll soon find out, coming? Now let's get back to the ship, I'm expecting Celia back any minute now."

They did not leave alone, or when they arrived back at the ship.

"Sorry Doug," as Celia alighted from the tow car, with a horse-box behind, "best I could do at short notice, but I could only get you 3 mules."

"All right the rest of you, bugger off, and help yourself to a beer or anything else we have on board. If you follow us, on your heads be it, if you get bitten, but what would help most of all, if you stayed here until the 4 of us get back. It'll have to do Celia, thanks."

That fell on deaf ears, the shear curiosity being arisen, as none of the mules had any form of saddle, a pair of reins yes, but no saddle.

"Mike, got any grease handy?"

"Yes off course, why?"

"A liberal spreading on the back of Christine's mule should help her slide off faster."

"Are you serious?" Christine wishing to be somewhere else.

"No, off course not!" came from another similar voice, not too far away.

But the remark defused the tension.

"Ah thanks bosun, just what I need. Well done. You got the box?"

"That I have captain, but where is my horse, sorry mule?"

"Well, for the outward leg, you walk, or double up with me, until we get into the cornfield, then you slide off, and after we've gotten the snake into the box, you have your choice of any mules hanging around, to get you back to the ship."

"You really haven't thought this out completely captain, have you?" Coming from a very curious Filipino.

"This my friend is a little fun, when I joined this 5 year old gas tanker, I did not expect it to be falling to bits, and so far on Insurance, have spent nearly $1.5 million of the company's money, and I am going to have to spend an awful lot more yet. Now let's go get us a snake."

Getting on board a mule was initially a problem, solved only when it was distracted by giving it an apple, although Doug was the first to try it. The bonnet, no sorry hood, of the nearest car helping. Pity about the dent from his weight, but that should push out later, hopefully. His well-used trainers not leaving a sole mark that if it came to it, forensic chappies couldn't match with anything. Thank goodness the reins were short, but as for sitting on its back soon became hanging on for dear life and in more of a horizontal as opposed to the more normal vertical position. No chance of getting saddle sores on this mount, at least on the backside, but the upper inner thighs compensating most admirably. The testicles and lower ribs also taking a similar and more painful beating.

It wasn't a particularly fit mule thankfully as it ran out of puff at the entrance to the somewhat trashed cornfield. Its initial acceleration more than compensated by its braking facility, leaving its rider now in front of it, but fortunately still holding onto the reins. Although getting out of this bush, with prickly bits and back upright, not overly endearing Doug towards a love of animals with four legs, as he sought one with no legs, well, outward legs anyway.

"Sorry Doug," as Celia arrived, the bosun with the box, also on the back of her mount. "If you'd had given me the chance to explain before you jumped on, as you insisted on 3 horses, I could only manage to find 2 mules that were broken in, but the guy I got them from said that this other one was pretty gentle and should be okay, as long as it didn't get startled. Oops, sorry darling. Can you forgive me?"

"Well I don't think that I have much choice, seeing as we are going to get married."

This quietly said but overheard from German ears not going unnoticed. Well, that's the best things about practical jokes, people making conclusions with only part of the real picture. And women can get, oh, so, jealous.

"Well, now that you are all here, in sorts of different ways, we can continue." From an intrigued and growing assembling bunch, with what might come next. "Just stay back so that you won't get bitten, or kicked, or trampled." Many of whom had never come across Doug before, or what he was capable off.

"Now, here's the plan."

This should be fun, following a general consensus of opinion whispered among the assembling throng. An actual, plan?

"Right Christine, you go in first with your mule, I'll be right behind you on my mule with the kite bit. Bosun, follow me about a metre back, with the top of the box open. Celia, you keep that mad mule across the entrance, and stop any of these following lunatics from coming after us. If any try to get past, just brush this branch over the top of its private breeding part, I learnt this years ago, it drives them mad and they kick out their hind legs, which is enough to keep most out of range. And tell them to keep the noise down." Why keeping the noise down of dubious intention, and no hope of succeeding. Which unfortunately, just co-incided with one not overly following events, just happened to come within range off two hoofs, moving at a rather high speed from two different directions, about a second apart, the realisation of his error, only apparent before he lost consciousness. The sad part of which only coming out later. Something to do with The Mayor's Office?

Trepidation from all but Doug being very evident, as they set off, not diminishing as they ventured further into the field, whereupon a slight rattle could be detected, to which Christine stopped, well, not only her, but the mule as well. Trembling with the inbuilt fear that to all animals is akin to a sixth sense. The combination of rider and mule slowly starting to back off, as Doug slid slowly off his own mount, having spotted one very nicely curled up rattlesnake, and about a perfect size to fit in the box, with just a little room to spare.

"You see it bosun?" as he pointed towards this nasty looking object.

"Yes captain, it's a right big bugger, do you think it will fit in the box?"

"Well we might need to squeeze it in a bit, just remember, after we have adjusted it, we need it as mad as hell for when we let it go at the races tonight."

"Christine, slowly take the mules away," this already having been done with not a sight of either," but whispered anyway.

"Now bosun, we need to steer clear of its fangs, and as I read in a book this afternoon, the tail as well. These little buggers fight from both ends, usually at the same time."

Now he tells me, from a bosun, not fully acquainted with all of the facts, but concentrating all the same.

"Well captain, if you don't get it on your first go, I'm out of here," carefully whispered, with the pulsating heartbeat almost audible.

"Coward, just make sure the lid on the box is open, then slam it shut when it is in." As the captain moved in. "Ready?" No reply being heard, but suggesting fear increasing as it got closer.

"Right got it," and with a fairly dramatic scooping action, plopped it into the box, albeit upside-down, "now close the lid bosun." Hands frantically getting the latches shut and the padlocks secured.

"Captain, next time you come up with anything as dangerous as this," as the lid was finally secured, "get Mullah to do it. Just as well we've got 3 padlocks holding it in, as it is doing its best of trying to get back out."

"How do we get it back to the ship?" As the box was jumping all over the place.

"Oh we've been given a replacement hire car, Mike and Einar should be waiting at the entrance where we left Celia. It can go in the boot, sorry trunk."

"But what if it gets out, it's as mad as hell in that box."

"Air conditioning my friend, and if that doesn't work, or if it gets out, then someone at Thrifty Car Rental is going to have one hell of a problem, in about 4 days' time."

A cheer went up as a jubilant few arrived back, 3 mules backing away from this writhing box, as it was placed in the boot of this new car, and the lid, sorry trunk, closed.

"Ah, hello Erling, (The Norwegian Gas Engineer and the laziest human on board), "care to do me a favour?" asked Doug.

"How much does it pay?"

"$ 100, but on a Lloyds, 'No cure no Pay' agreement." The semi unbroken mule, now about to be even more unbroken. Hopefully taking a rather pissed Scandinavian head and torso with it.

"Okay, what do I have to do?"

"Take this mule back to the horse box beside the ship. Come on, I'll give you a leg up."

"No problem, I can ride a horse you know, we have a few on the farm that I live on in Norway, and we often go bareback."

A horse maybe, but this was an angry scared mule and not inclined to be ridden bareback, or even ridden at all. "Good luck, here are the reins."

If that were true, then he would have noticed that the reins given to him by Doug included a knot, to which no matter how he tried, only tightened up. And connected to the mules head! The new rider most not noticing being explained away, by having had too much to drink, of the serious alcohol variety.

"First of all, my friend," quietly under his breath, "you need to get this little bugger going in the right direction, and with it being American, doesn't understand, the Norwegian/English equivalents of, Whoa, or giddy-up."

A hard slap on its rump, and a branch across its private part certainly made it a contender for drag racing, as this wild mule and one equally wild Norwegian shot off in totally the wrong direction of the ship, more in the direction of Corpus Christi, or the bit which included an oil refinery, and staying on this piece of horseflesh most admirable, as in not as much as it galloped away, but flew, as did its passenger, horizontal along the length of its back, and bouncing, not overly comfortably. Rather similar to its previous passenger, whose testicles were slightly more to the front, although its current passenger's testicles were now in contact with the mule's spine.

"Well that's one problem out of the way, you know guys, he has been annoying me for ages, everyone else on board working their socks off, and all that he has to do, is train up the next gas engineer into how to use the gas plant, and at $1500 per week over and above his normal rate of $1000 per week? AND IN CASH! With a bit of luck, we might just lose him all together, and Mullah, with a bit of luck. What is the breaking strength of reins anyone? I can calculate for all sorts of ropes and wires, even chains, but leather did not come up as I sat my orals for master."

Vacant faces, of several nationalities, as clueless.

"Ho hum, onwards then."

"Right Mike, wind up the cars air conditioning, we need to calm this little bugger down."

"Here are the car keys," said Mike, "**YOU CALM! THE LITTLE BUGGER DOWN, WE'LL WALK BACK!**"

It did come across as this was your idea, so you sort it out.

Einar and almost all of the others in full agreement, with the exception of Christine and Celia, as the car's engine was fired up, and after a while as the air conditioning kicked in, did start to subdue this rather wild snake. Rather wild? More like f****** livid!

"Doug, it is only 3 hours till the start of the racing, how are you going to get it drunk? Snakes don't drink all that much."

"Who said anything about alcohol?" He replied.

"Well with what then?" asked in chorus, from a confused two, "and you are not getting away from here until you tell us."

"Well I've never tried this, but I read it in a book, that I read some time ago. Do you know how snakes keep tasting the air with these little forked tongues that fly out and in every few seconds?"

"Yes," as both acknowledged.

"Well, we just hold a little something in front of them to taste, before their tongues take it back into the snakes mouth, which then gets absorbed into the snakes bloodstream. Seemingly, it drives them nuts."

The conversation between 2 of the 3 as they arrived back at the ship, venturing only one question, "Doug are you going to take the rattlesnake on board this ship?"

A rotating head, eyes looking upwards, was indicating no. A practical joker he may be, but plain dumb stupid, not.

"You just keep the trunk closed. I've just shut down the cars air conditioning. I'll be back in a few minutes," as he disappeared.

Christine looked at Celia, and very jealously, "are you and Doug going to get married? You've only known him a few days."

"Christine, all that I remember is that we went to a jewellery store and the next thing I remembered was waking up with this ring on my finger on an island in the Bay covered in big leaves. Look, it is a 1 carat diamond.

A very capable and highly intelligent German blonde, who had already fallen in love with the captain recognizing that, that ring, was totally worthless but starting to appreciate again, should that be necessary, that Doug was up to more than one thing at the same time, as he came clattering back down and jumped into the car.

Just before departing, a shout came from above, "Captain, the Corpus Christi Police are on the 'phone, something to do with an........ out........of........control mule in the middle of to...................... ....wn."

Oh well, thought the voice, he'll deal with it later no doubt, pity about Erling being kicked in a private place, and now in hospital. Going to be interesting listening to a Norwegian male soprano. Even better if he was as usual, topped up with beer, and whatever highly alcoholic and volatile spirit, Norwegians drank. Maybe that the Norwegian Government should lift the extortionate tax on spirits to reasonable levels convincing their population that the higher the proof level did not exactly equate to consuming Scotch Whisky in equal quantities. But what the hell, when you are that pissed on either, logic has no boundaries. Until next morning perhaps?

"Right we need to be at San Patricio, which is just up the road a bit. I was just getting the money, it costs $7 each to get in, and $40 to enter, and there doesn't seem to be anything in the rules which says you can't bring your own snake. The winner is the one that goes the fastest up an 80 foot course, and seemingly they have heats, that last over 2 evenings, which is a bit unfortunate, as we have only got one evening to spare, so Celia, darling, if we qualify, would you mind entering our as yet unnamed rattler for the following day?"

The reply unprintable to print, but generally, "O.........ka......... ....y." Coming across though, as how the hell did I get involved in this?

"Right bosun, you figured out just where its head is just yet," as this very bad tempered and rather big old rattler started to thaw out from the induced cool down period, and back up to normal temperature.

"Well captain, when it was cool, we took off 2 of the padlocks, and tossed the box around a bit, well to be more precise, kicked it around a bit, and the bite bit is somewhere near this air hole. But it doesn't seem to have settled its' temper down much. Probably, made its' temper worse, with a bit of luck."

Unsurprisingly.

Indeed it was, "bosun, well done."

As a 2 pronged tongue flashed out of this hole in the box, and met with a dry powder, which was immediately withdrawn, not for long though as it was back for more, and several other times.

"Eh captain, it does seem to like this white stuff, just what exactly is it?"

"Only if you don't tell another living soul?" Pointless really as Celia and Christine were also listening in, and females usually don't know where or when to get involved in gossip. But they had very acute hearing.

"I had a bit of pure cocaine left, and at this rate, it is going to be well and truly stoned before we get to the races."

"And you expect to get away with this?" asked both, now with several others from his crew listening in. "Well yes, as these professional athletes get tested for drugs all the time, usually after being told to piss in a bottle, or give a blood sample. Providing we have now caught this rattlesnake, just where do you get a blood or urine sample from and expect the snake to co-operate? Holding it down while they do so will require quite a few pairs of hands and somehow, I don't think that those drug testers are going to be too keen on getting more than 1 idiot to help them."

A somewhat pregnant pause followed before one ventured forth, with, "Doug, who wrote this book about rattlesnakes and how they taste the air and so-forth?"

You have to ask, "I wrote it. Never, just, quite, got around to............ actually, publishing it, because I made most of it up."

Two females exchanging puzzled looks.

"Captain, it is going demented in that box. Who is going to drive the car up to the races?" From a very concerned bosun.

"Well if Mullah had been here, he would have done, so I suppose it will have to be me. Four spare seats, any takers?" From the assembled crowd with lots of money to lay bets with, suddenly finding that they had other means of transport, and hastily scurried off, not wanting to be anywhere near that demented snake, even more hell bent on getting out of its box. But a few Filipinos were. Plus one other.

"Captain, if we come with you, just what do we have to do?" They having already placed their bets in some of the most convoluted of places known to man. And against huge odds! Including odds of actually getting it to race again after the first heat. The American influence over The Philippines most evident, which most would describe as, cunning.

"We need to keep the snake in the box, so throw this tarpaulin over it and then pile your bodies on top, or alternatively, one of you lie on the parcel shelf and the others make sure that the back seat is held down. We'll worry about how we get it out of the trunk later."

"Captain, we'll go with the tarpaulin." Which somehow showed signs of actually working. Even although the tarpaulin was actually a waterproof jacket.

"You can trust me boys as we will be sailing together soon, as getting this damn gas tanker up and running is taxing even me! This mad snake is a minor hic-cup in comparison."

The drive up to where they held the races seeming to take forever, with the legal top speed limit of 55 mph, but they made it, arriving just in time.

"Right, boys, here is the entrance, get the box out, and wait for me here, while I park the car."

Easily more said than done, but tried anyway.

Upon returning was met with a new problem. "Captain they are searching every bag at Security, what do we do?"

"Let them search it, Texans aren't that bright, something to with the heat I think, who knows it might get our rather big snake even more angry, and with more angry, means more speed." The logic of this falling on not so deaf ears, as they appreciating that some one or two might.

The queue, or in American parlance, a line, showing a decided gap from others in front, and behind as this box kept jumping around until they arrived at Security.

"What is in the box sir?" Innocently asked concerning his position, although somewhat fearful. He not liking this at all.

Best to be honest.

"A snake, want to see it? You see we decided to bring an International Component to this sport, this is a Scottish rattlesnake that we want to race against your American ones."

Some, are that gullible, that a lie can be told, with a straight face. And this captain was an expert at it.

For once, an American was lost for told, "If it's not allowed, then you will need to confiscate it, but be careful, as this one is as fast as hell when it gets out of its box, and you want to be well clear when it does get out, unless you know the Scottish words to calm it down." The completely straight face as this was said convincing enough to be replied with and somewhat nervously asked, "what makes it Scottish?"

"Look at its markings, that's off the Mac-Queer tartan, which she is now displaying. See, from the throat and over its head. Good eh! It takes us ages to breed one like that. I trust that you can speak in Gaelic? Or even Scottish, and in the correct dialect?"

Followed with.

"You do realise I trust, that if you confiscate the snake, that we keep the box."

A very sceptical head and withdrawn arms replied.

"Okay sir, bring him in," he wishing to be somewhere else as it started spitting, and this, not overly friendly spitting.

"Oh, its' not a 'him, it's a her,' if it was a 'him' one, we'd need a stronger box." The satisfaction of getting one over an American, being kept for later. The Filipinos, not as used to such things amazed that anyone, far less their captain could tell such brazen lies with as such a straight face, but not ready for what came next, as they waited for their turn in the first heat. The two engineers preferring to be somewhere else, and both asking. "Where the hell did that bloody snake come from?"

The pre-race briefing going well. Sort off.

"Right bosun, I'll set it off, with a wee tap on its box, you go to the other end off the track and get ready to catch it, by which time, I'll have made it round the others with the box, to put it back into. The kite catcher after all, already works."

"Not quite captain, we'll set it off, you catch it. After all, we are not on board ship now. Good luck. For once RHIP, as you told us once, Rank Has Its Privileges, isn't somehow going to work here."

The smile from their boss said it all.

Shouldn't be that difficult, with an 80 foot strip of an advantage in front of him. Didn't reckon on just how fast a stoned rattlesnake could actually go, it not even slowing for enough time to even bite him on the passing. Fortunately, as he missed it completely. The snake from previous experience, not desiring that kite bit again. And who was it that said that they were not the most intelligent of vertebrates.

It came out later, that it managed 80 feet in 9 seconds, and maybe more or less, as the guy with the stopwatch, joined in with every other, assisted by gravity easing the pain in their throats, swallowing, both being on overdrive, utilising parts of their respective bodies, spectators fleeing simultaneously, that in American talk was, and translated into proper English as, "let's get the fuck out of here!"

Not helped by the other 5 rattlesnakes in their respective lanes, suddenly devoid of their tormentors, now also on the loose. And not overly pleased, seeking them, and in revenge. Which if one rattler was seen heading your way, was not a time to be just where they were at the present time. Amazing at times just how resourceful, people in a state of panic could actually be.

It only being a matter of time, before the cooling fan, hanging from the ceiling of the room she sought sanctuary in unexpectedly picking up a rather indiscreetly dressed female, did not fall, her dress, after a few revolutions, nicely tangled up, just as the motor burned out. The melee underneath, eventually confirming that, although, where she was, was better than more than just a few feet beneath, as punches did rather be seem to be a bit random, but those who connected, have now inherited that taught by a bucking donkey.

Later, slightly, back in the hotel, and somewhat cooler, thanks to the air-conditioning and the cold beer sliding downwards in throats not used in years, well apart from tea and coffee, not now having the strength to face alcohol, but making a pretty determined effort of replacing that lost by the sweat incurred as they, sort off, cleared a fence.

"The last time I jumped a fence that high, I was still at school," said one, and that was 30 years ago! "How did you get on?" from another panting for breath his mind still running.

"I didn't bother in jumping it, I just ran straight through it, anything to get away from that damn rattlesnake attached to a horse. Don't think the wife is going to be overly pleased about the state of my clothes though."

Most being in shreds, and trying to find a convenient tree, but failing as others had already found one, competition being fierce with no thought to those coming up behind. Anything to get away from that damn snake.

Later.

The ship's crew, slowly returning from elevated positions, tops of cars, and from other unlikely places, one Filipino having a little trouble getting down from a street lamp, unfortunately caught up on a traffic signal. For the first time, it was okay to turn right on a red, only this time going right went green, mostly because the lights were upside down caught in this guy's clothing. But not for long as the catenary did rather contribute to those being diverted above them, making to a rather good crash, and which would forever take a hellava lot of explaining away. Bloody handy that half-filled skip breaking his fall did eventually short out the wiring though, if you can call blacking out a couple of square miles of traffic lights, a mild inconvenience.

"Next time our captain gets talked into going Rattle Snake Racing, **HE, is going alone!**" Spoken by one, but the general consensus of all.

"Do you think that it might know how to slide up stairs?" asked a mild white faced Chief Engineer, still trying to catch his breath.

"Why?" asked another.

"Because only one was fast, there's another five still on the loose now!"

"By the way, where is our captain?"

"Well he isn't here, nor are Christine or Celia."

Who just happened to join them in the hotel bar.

"Got our captain with you girls?" ventured one, somewhat bravely, he luckily having access to another way out. Although that table might come in handy as a short measure.

Christine, not accustomed to swearing, unless it was in German, and even less accustomed to alcohol, having previously confessed to the fact that even wine made her feel sleepy, spared no niceties with the barman, "two 'boilermakers' and make it f******* quick."

Not a lot was said amongst the assembled throng, as 2 Scotches and 2 beer chasers disappeared in quick succession. Followed by others joining in, the barman having to call his assistant just to keep up.

"It was when it jumped the fence and got into the car park with the spectators sitting on their 4 X 4's.................."

"Who cares, it was going away from us," as more Scotch was consumed, this time without the beer chasers.

Meanwhile, back on board ship, the master arrived, sought out a cold beer from his office 'fridge, and offering one to a rather young policeman, who declined but accepted a Coke instead.

"Captain, this might sound like a stupid question, but do you have any mules on board your ship?"

"That's not a stupid question, on board my ship, no, but on the dockside, we did have 3. Why? Although in The Panama Canal, we use them, but they are steel tugs on rack and pinion rails, called mules. Why?"

"Because captain, in the middle of town there is one that we have cornered, but no-one is brave enough to go anywhere near it.

160

It was seen going at double speed before it stopped at the traffic lights, and the guy on its back flew into the back of a garbage truck. He seemingly is now in hospital but his voice and language are very strange, no-one can understand him."

"It's probably Norwegian, if there is alcohol involved. Have you still got one of my crew in custody? Indian, or Sri Lankan, devoid of any documentation? Goes by the name of Mullah."

"I can check sir," getting onto his radio, now even more confused than he was half an hour ago.

When someone else arrived.

"Are you the captain of the Norgas Challenger?"

"Nope." Considering that it was painted on both bows, the stern and he was now in the master's office. Yet another of limited intelligence far less visual powers, but un-daunted carried on anyway.

"Do you have a Pontiac 836?"

"Why?" the policeman equally lost, but fast learning that the only thing shared between Americans and The British was a common language, well, sort off. The logic at times being on a different plane.

"Because Mullah says that you have one."

There was a long pause, as this news set in, and followed with.

"Could I have it please?"

"Well you are one up on Mullah, you said, please. How do you know about it though?"

"Well you are going to have to sail with him, 30 odd hours in a police cell demented not only me but also the police, and they agreed that if I was to get the car, then that would get rid of 2 problems at the same time."

"I think that would get rid of THREE problems actually. How are you at catching horses, although this horse might be a mule, and a somewhat angry one at that?"

Not giving this much more thought, the response was understandable and naïve to boot, "anything... as long as I don't have to listen to Mullah any-more."

"Perfect then, go with this officer, collect Mullah, catch the mule and the car is yours, although it is slightly damp, and don't tell

Mullah anything about the car, he is under the impression that he owns it."

"Owns it captain? He can't even drive!"

"Between you and me, that is something that we have already found out about, as well as many others in this US Port."

The young US Police Officer, having now confirmed that an Asian individual was in custody only too eager to assist, his ear still ringing from the tirade of his sergeant, and left in any way in no doubt that the sooner he got back to home-base and collect this individual, the better.

Relaxing back into his office chair, feet up on his desk and alone did not last long, the vibrations of his ships accommodation ladder suggesting that a few of his crew, plus the squeals of several females were about to descend onto one who had lost a rattle snake, plus a few other things."

"Who were these guys captain?" as he and a few others burst into his office?"

"How did you get here?" being the most obvious question as all were very clearly more than slightly inebriated. Or put another way, just plain drunk.

"Oh, sorry, you haven't met Jim yet, he drove" as Jim was introduced.

"Eh, just why exactly does Jim have a white stick? And wearing sunglasses?" asked the captain.

"Because he is blind," the previously recognised level of intoxication not coinciding with any form of logic from any of the mixed nationalities.

"So how can he drive a car if he can't see where he is going?" asked the ships master.

"Oh he can't see, but he is the only one of us who is sober, so if he was stopped wouldn't be charged under US laws as, 'DUI' Driving Under the Influence. We just did the same as you do when sailing in fog, if it wasn't for RADAR, he does the driving, we are his RADAR and tell him when to turn left or right, or speed up or slow down. It worked perfectly, if you discount a wee bit of white fencing that got in the way, and a few other minor things."

The perplexed reply being, "So far, after the owners paying $23 million for the ship, and after us getting through 165 000 cubic metres of nitrogen, drying out the cargo tanks, and having only steamed 200 or so miles before bending the main engine crankshaft, we have not as yet, actually seen any fog. And in less than a month."

Bemused heads confirming that he might actually be right. The thought levels when so intoxicated taking rather longer than normal, or in another few nodding in agreement, had also found that the brain was no longer in contact with the muscles that controlled the mouth, but a few may have short-circuited and joined in with those required to making a stupid grin and the ones that produced a bobbing head in confirmation.

The captain, not overly sure if he also should ask, but did so with a degree of trepidation, "how WEE, is this WEE bit of white fencing?" As if that was the least of his current problems, as a certain individual from the Indian Sub-continent had arrived at the rear of this throng.

"Well, we didn't actually stop and measure it, we were too busy getting Jim back onto the road, he sort of misunderstood one of our directions, as someone told him to turn left, while someone asked if that was right, I think meaning if that was correct."

"How much white fencing?" from a rapidly becoming impatient master.

"Well Sir," accompanied a mob not risking speaking but nodding in agreement, "about 4 hundred feet or so, a few posts, a sign or so, a few mailboxes, the odd kids bikes, and possibly a few ducks."

Said surreptiously, a hint quietly and from the side of the mouth, the current increasingly red face indicating that he was not overly truthful, as they may have collided with something else, probably rather expensive.

Hopefully the ship would sail out of port before their master would find out about the tractor, last seen in the duck pond. It's bent bit rather similar to the bent bit on the car, although reversed. Well, only a bit of it could be seen, as American duck ponds tended to be somewhat deeper than British ones.

"Get to bed the lot of you, and just in case The Police happen to come on board, I suggest that where you go to lie down is not in your cabins, so that if I need to find you during the night, I won't be able to."

A general consensus of muttering, as the throng split up, coming to a conclusion, that the best place to sleep it off, and not be found was in the fo'c'sle, the mooring ropes making enough beds, not only for themselves but a suitable hiding place for the empties of the 4 cases of beer which went with them. As well as a few bottles whose labels suggesting that this was not something obtained from a liquor store. After all, the door was pirate proof and capable of being secured only from the inside. It not occurring to those with little foresight, that when the next anchor was dropped, using the anchor cable chain lockers, as a bin, including a bin for human excrement, that the usual 'what goes up, must come down' being reversed into 'what is down, is going to come up, before going down,' and hopefully onto to the one operating the windlass brake. Or anyone else in the vicinity not moving fast enough, despite already knowing just what flies off an anchor cable when the windlass brake is released. Scaled rust being the least of their problems. A practical joke seen years before, he trying to forget about, and after seeing the outcome off, would never use again. A pity that the windlass brake operator, the ships' bosun, started off with rather ageing grey hair, and overnight, went completely white, during his time in hospital.

Christine though not joining them, she knew where to hide as sleep starting to overcome her. Celia taking this opportunity of looking for an alternative place, and found out a few hours later, comfortable as it was, the Cook/Steward did need rather a lot of rice for the crew's breakfast. Her sleep pattern eventually broken, but not before a rather randy Filipino had introduced her to his bunk. The crew would have to just wait for their steamed rice. Seemingly, later, she was reluctant to leave, which probably explained why, it being a Sunday by now, the crew also had to wait for their lunch. The risk of her being seen by her 'fiancée' only adding to her concern seeing as he was the captain, and still not having the 1st clue to her missing 4 hours, as to how she became engaged to marry him.

The captain's respite did not last long.

"Mullah, why are you holding your ribs, and where did that black eye come from?" from a captain smiling inwardly, but trying to maintain a concern for one of his crew, and this one clearly requiring a few facial stitches.

The response predictable.

"Captain, $1000 in $20 dollar bills, and no torn corners or edges." The word 'please' not entering into the demand, as he wobbled in front of the master's desk.

"Mullah, do you not have any concern for others, you appear to be hurt, and does money not count for more than injured people? And what is wrong with your mouth, you sound half pissed?"

"In my country captain, we do not care about others, as long as we have enough for ourselves, now $1000 in $20 dollar bills, as we agreed."

"Well, I hate to disappoint you Mullah, but The Corpus Christi Police charged $100 dollars per night, by the time I had paid for all the damage, cost another $ 900 just to get you out of gaol, a new passport a further $ 200, so you are in debt to this ship to the tune of $ 300 dollars. How would you like to pay? I'll accept $ 20 dollar bills, as long as there are no torn corners or edges."

Lost for words, not expressed better than an arrogant mouth, lost in its ability to move, or capable of saying anything in any language, mostly having had partial and no doubt painful contact, with a mules hoof.

"Mullah, there is one final question, did you have to do anything to get back to this ship? After all, your record of returning to the ship isn't very good. I think that you may want to write this answer down."

Scrawled in a composite average of English and Hindi, taking some time to decipher, but eventually being agreed as follows.

"The Police said that we had to catch this horse, and as that we had sailed with you would know all of the commands to get it quiet. Then take it to a Miss Celia Barnes, who was waiting for it, beside the ship."

"And?"

"It wasn't a fucking horse, it was a fucking very bad tempered mule, who had encountered a snake hitching a free ride and desperate to get off, me included. Which is why, I fell out of a tree that I thought would get me away from that snake, as the mule bucked, but I missed the branch, and met the mules hoof which hit me on my way back down. And that was after I got onto its back."

"So where is the mule now? And it is not like Indians to swear."

"Who cares, I'm going to bed. You might want to ask the police though, it was last seen inside one of their police cars after it crashed through the windscreen. And upside down."

Which if true, accounted for 1 more of the 5 loose snakes. But getting an upside down mule out of a police car probably not covered in a US Police training manual, or a sub-paragraph, of which the US Coastguard loved in their books, having a sub-paragraph relating to upside down mules and a confused snake somewhere underneath.

But then, their regulations regards Grey Humpback Whales off the coast of California, not covering the fact that Whales don't show navigation lights at night, or at all, nor can they measure distance in yards of how close they can swim towards a ship as. Seeing as every ship in the world, except The US Navy, measure everything according to the metric system.

Going to bed did seem to be most pertinent. Trying to decipher any more English/Hindi taxing enough for anyone's lifetime.

Later though, and with no Police in sight, one particular crew member arrived back, as the master thought of bed.

"Got it captain! 10 pounds of powdered aluminium. Would have gotten back sooner, because aluminium in The US is spelt 'aloominum.' Why can't these buggers speak proper English?"

"Something my friend, I wish I knew the answer to. Well done though. Now I can make thermite."

"What is thermite captain?"

"It is a way of how you weld steel in near silence."

"Can I watch?" his curiosity now well and truly awake.

"Off course you can, you can even help, but don't let on to anyone else, as in the morning I have to go through the honest channels first."

"So captain, what are you going to weld?"

"The Department of Agriculture's Cutter, now astern of us, because the day after tomorrow, when we fire up the ship's main engine on trials having now replaced the crankshaft, if they don't move it will suffer from our prop wash, so I'm going to weld their wee boat in place, just to make sure it doesn't get, shall we say damaged. Well............. much,..................or maybe, just a wee bit."

The smile said it all, as he bid the captain good-night. This secret was not going to be short of volunteers, and as for not telling others within his crew taking about less than an hour before they all knew.

Next morning.

"Anyone seen the captain?" as they filed through from breakfast and into the ships offices."

"Well, the car keys are gone, and I haven't seen Christine this morning either. Her car is still at the bottom of the accommodation ladder. I checked his cabin as I came down, and his door was open and he wasn't in his bunk," from Mike, The Ship's Chief Engineer.

The mystery compounding as who but Christine came through the door.

"Anyone seen Doug?" from a beautiful German blonde, her appearance not suggesting anything other than a solid night's sleep and a refreshing early morning shower. "Sorry I can't stay, I'm already late for work," she collecting the necessary documents in her passing.

"Well that confirms one theory," from The Chief Officer, Blackie, "they didn't sleep together last night," as Celia walked in.

"Looking for something Celia?" looking rather ruffled, and a little dazed.

"Is the captain here?" already knowing the answer, as she looked around, left with a degree of bewilderment and set off for work also.

"Well, he didn't share his bunk with her either," being the general consensus of opinion, "so where the hell is he?"

"If you are looking for the captain," said the steward coming in to collect the empty cups, saucers and waste paper bins, he has gone to see The US Coast Guard, and doesn't expect to be back until after lunch."

Well, that solved the initial issue.

"He could have left a note. Right then, he's not here, let's just finish off getting that main engine fixed, and if we can get it finished today, we can then start filling it up with water, and put the heaters on, and then start getting the lub oil heated up as well. The Chockfast should have gone off by now."

The 'phone rang in the masters office. It was a query on how the ships main engine re-build was proceeding from the ships managers and taken by the Chief Engineer.

"Is the captain there" asked innocently enough.

"No, he's gone to see The US Coast Guard, but he'll be back in a couple of hours."

"Okay, ask him to give us a call, we have the charterers asking a few questions, such as when it will be possible for the ship to sail."

"Oh, I can answer that, "said Mike, "all being well, we should be okay later today to start warming the main engine up, with a view of firing it up in the morning. Class, if happy should all being well tomorrow giving us clearance to sail. The captain will up-date you later in his daily report."

"Ask him to give us a call anyway, and we do know how busy you have all been anyway."

The politics of ship management being the general consensus of opinion as this was relayed on. The underlying question though of why their master had to go to The US Coast Guard, again?

This not being anything other than an expert Master Mariner would know off. But explained later, as he arrived back in a somewhat subdued tone, if not disappointed.

"Blackie, I need 10 pounds of iron oxide," as the master re-sought his office.

"Where I am going to get that from? And where have you been?"

"You could try the grit blasting packs we inherited from the previous owners, and when you are at it, bring those, 2 three quarter rounds of flat steel with the hole in them, that we hadn't a clue as to what they were from the fo'c'sle?"

"Why"

"Because I've found a use for them. Just do it quietly."

"Care to tell us where you have been, and the long face?"

"Well I am not flavour of the month with The Department of Agriculture just now, so when I asked them to move their Cutter out of our proposed prop wash, was met with a flat no!"

"Well that is hardly unsurprising," a response as others joined in, listening carefully as this could go anywhere.

"So I went to the US Coast Guard and obtained permission to fire up our main engine on test mode tomorrow, before we actually get around to sailing out of this port under our own power. Which is why I went to see them."

"Was it refused?" asked a concerned few.

"Oh goodness no, it was granted, I have the document here, but in this convoluted port they have a rule, somewhere, that says that any craft in the vincinity, who suffer from any prop wash, such as tugs, the ship is liable for damages to any seaworthy craft which incur damage to their seaworthiness."

"I think I'm with you so far captain, but what has this to do with iron oxide?"

"Well, when we mix it with aluminium powder, and set it off with solid magnesium, currently underwater, we go thermite welding. In the UK, they use this mix to weld railway lines together, and it is virtually silent. So we are going to fuse these 2, three quarter round bits of steel around a piling beside The Department of Agriculture's Cutters berth, ease down their stern ropes, and weld their anchor on the starboard side to the piling to this ring, and then make their Cutter unseaworthy. Easy if you know really. We might need a bit of that 2 inch square steel bar that we can't find a use for as well."

"How?" as many concerned heads focused on one.

"To understand the term 'seaworthy,' you have to understand the 3 parameters of 'unseaworthy,' I won't go into this at length, but if it can be rendered 'unseaworthy,' then it cannot be classed as 'seaworthy.'

Confused heads sought out encouragement from others, none of which apparently forthcoming.

"So where does the thermite welding come in?"

"Well, we may have to put the ring underneath the anchor, but we'll also weld the anchor to its own cutter at the same time. See, if it can't drop its anchor, it is technically unseaworthy. Or put another way, it will become glued to the dock."

"And what excuse do we have to come up with?"

"It was struck by lightning. Awfully difficult to disprove is it not?"

The looks on the assembled faces conveying only one opinion, the smiles getting broader.

"WHEN DO WE START?" from an excited throng, itching to try this.

"Guys we have had a great time together, but our immediate priority is to get this gas tanker back into service, and that is today, or during the night, as the owners are losing $23 000 per day as it is. Leave the insurance claim to me, I'm on top of it. Now get busy doing it."

Later as an excited crew hell bent of getting this engine room up and running wondering just what might prevail, as there did not seem to be anything looking like a thunderstorm in sight. Far less a few clouds. Well, to be frank, nothing but pure blue sky.

Later.

"This evening, when they only have a skeleton crew are on board, which is an awful lot more than we have here, skeleton being about 4, as a few are still in prison, awaiting trial. They don't after all know when we are going to fire up our main engine, but in the meantime, we need to tie the ship down, and as we are only going to use ahead thrust, we can't afford to overload the astern thrust bearings, only one headline, everything we can find as forward springs, one back spring, and again, as much as we can find for stern lines. Even doubling up if we have to. I'll be on the bridge and will set the rudder. Which when their wee boat is welded in place will be about 10 degrees of port helm."

"Captain, they have put their mooring ropes over our ropes, without dipping their own eyes through ours, how do we get them to loosen their mooring ropes?"

"We don't, because lightning, apart from coming down as lightning, can also come down, and set off candles, via a few of you with cigarette lighters."

"Candles?" asked many, although a few not just quite as quick, still puzzled but preferring not to say anything.

"One per rope, about 1 inch or so and in position with a bit of sail-twine, so that when then the rope burns out quietly, and fails, it takes what is left of the candle with it."

"Then what?"

"We swim around and with a few ropes, quietly move their cutter into position, and then weld their cutters anchor to the pilings on their berth, the 2 rings we found in the fo'c'sle supporting the bits doing the welding. They should fall off taking the welding mix with them, as the heat generated is about 2 200 degrees Celsius, and literally fuses anything together. Hopefully, Abner, the 3rd mate will be back soon with a few bricks, some powdered cement and we've already got the sand. Ah, here he comes now."

"Sorry captain, I could only get 12 bricks and one bag of cement before the burglar alarm went off," from a rather tired 3rd mate, gratefully accepting the can of Gatorade offered by the master, at the same time steering him towards a chair. "Unfortunately sir, I lost the mule."

Going to be interesting how the explanation as to how he lost a mule, as when he started out, didn't actually have one. The explanation would no doubt come out later. Just exactly which burglar alarm went off useful as police cars were seen heading away from the ship. But one thing was certain, the ship was now missing a mule. Getting that into a rather complex insurance claim might need a tad more imagination. As in, from the captain, "I might need a wee bit of help."

To which he had, of the female variety.

"Right boys, you know how to make cement boxes, and where they are to go, the rest of us will start getting lightning to hit."

"Only one question captain, what is the mix to make this thermite work."

"Well, you know the old seafaring term, more is not always better, 50/50 to start with, and then if it doesn't look like white hot, chuck in what you think, and then chuck in a bit more, just don't take the magnesium out from under the fresh water, until you set it off, and then if you see the next cement boxes, chuck it all in. Just wait until we have it all lined up."

"Not overly scientific," thought Celia and Christine agreed treading water later, as the first mooring ropes melted, and the cutter started to move on the little breeze pushing it towards the intended final place to become welded permanently. Well, until some bright spark worked out a way of getting it un-welded, which by the standards experienced so far, could be quite a while. Months in fact.

"Christine," asked Celia, holding onto the bow, "do you and Doug have any sort of relationship?"

"Only if you keep it between us," replied Christine. "I have fallen in love with him, and he with me, but when his ship sails, will probably never see him again. He treats me as a lady, which is more than my husband does, although I rather like how he spends his leave in Scotland."

"So you know that I've become engaged to him?" Celia responded.

A sympathetic smile from one delightful German blonde to another female hinting that she had been conned, and with slow realisation shaping her mouth.

"Doug explained it to me as I lay in his arms, and between us, I've spent a lot of my time with him, and which my husband doesn't know about. I've been into some parts of this ship that most people didn't know existed. When you and he were on your little boat, and got as far as that small island, he put your little sailboat into the shade, carefully picked you up and laid you down in the shade and covered you with palm leaves to stop you from getting sunburnt. He knew from one of your father's friends, that you were working very hard, with long hours and at the same time he was also. It was all done to get you to stop taxing yourself, and you weren't asleep for 4 hours, you were actually asleep for 14 hours. He really cares about people you know. Look at how he cares for his crew, and all the time you were asleep, he was still working as these big insurance claims take an awful lot of explaining, and a colossal amount of paperwork."

"But why the engagement ring?" asked Celia.

"Well it took me a long time working that one out Celia, but when it was explained to me, is really rather clever. It was done to interrupt your daily routine, letting your curiousity over-riding your work routine. In effect, getting you to think or remember or something that you couldn't understand, which in turn made you leave your office and take a stroll to make you take a break."

This taking a little time to sink in, as Christine revealed to Celia, "he fished me out of the harbour a few weeks ago, only I didn't have a swimsuit on at the time. In fact, I didn't have anything on. But it must also have worked for you, as we are now both in the harbour, and what we are doing is something that neither of us would ever have thought off. Or are likely to do again. A change seemingly, as good as a rest."

A few paddles of the breast stroke legs slowly pushing this little cutter into position, and very quietly, Celia said, "I envy you Christine, my partner would never let me do anything as exciting as this."

"Nor my Australian husband Celia." whispered Christine.

"Are you going to leave your husband Christine?"

The reply conveyed in a way that only females could do, leaving one in a quandary and the other jealous.

"Celia, I'm a Jehovah's Witness. If I was to leave my faith, then I would be excommunicated, and all of my family and friends would dump me."

"Well if you don't love your husband, and have fallen in love with someone else, who can take you away from your present lifestyle, then go for it, especially if you could end up living in Scotland, I've been there once, it is an amazingly beautiful country, and which is one hellava lot better than living in Texas. But for now, let's see if we can get this boat into position."

The lightest touch confirming that they had arrived, quietly.

To which they did.

"We could stay and help you know," as they arrived dockside.

The look of disdain and the fleeting upwards eyes suggesting otherwise.

"I need to keep everyone safe. You two most of all, because when we leave port, my boys will be with me, and you two, I cannot afford to being the one's taking the blame, for the odd bit of how we are going to sail."

It was Celia, who first suggested it.

"Doug, as you know, I work for myself so can I sail with you? I've got a few weeks to spare, or maybe even a couple of months, if you will let me use your Inmarsat Satellite 'phone/fax."

Daggers from an adjacent Christine shaped face with very focussed eyes, making it clear that Celia would not be sailing with this ship, as the master came to the rescue, "I would love to have you both, sailing with us, but unfortunately, without proper clearance and notification from our P & I Club, we cannot get Insurance for you. And this being The United States, where anyone can sue anyone else for ridiculous sums, I know that I will not get clearance for."

"What's a P & I Club?" asked both in unison.

"Find out tomorrow, now for the present, we have a little welding job to do."

Two highly and adrenalin attuned females, not quite in agreement.

"If you think that we are going to get wet, and fobbed off like this, then you are very much mistaken. So we are going on-board this cutter and tell all of them on board just what you are planning," said Celia, and almost in unison with Christine. The threat however having no bearing whatsoever.

"Okay. Francis, The Radio Officer has a case of beer, although it is not all beer, as beer you told me in one of our more intimate moments, makes you sleepy Christine. He also has a chocolate cake, but whatever you do, do not eat any of it."

Picked up immediately by Celia. Oh ho! A married Jehovah's Witness from Germany having an affair with a Scottish Shipmaster, on a Norwegian gas tanker in Texas, USA, and her husband coming from The Antipodes, or as most would know it as Australia.

"Okay, I give in, what do I have to do?" from one Christine, her secret love affair of only a few weeks now truly exposed."

"You Christine, and you Celia, take this case of beer and chocolate cake aboard the Dept. of Agriculture's Cutter, introduce yourselves to the crew, and then get them talking. Oh and by the way, the tops marked green are water, but the rest are beer. Just play on their good nature, ply them with beer and make as much noise as you can. You know what I mean, appear to be a bit tipsy, but only for show. Give us just under an hour and we should have welded their bloody nuisance boat to the dockside by then."

"Okay sir, we are on to it." From an excited Celia, and a less excited Christine, noticing the look from her American counterpart.

Now boys, "Just keep your voices down, and this has to look like a lightning strike, the girls hopefully are our distraction and they know what to do."

Those from his crew involved in this nicely in position, the others not involved had to remain on board involved in powering this ship up. The 2nd and 3rd mate powering up the ships bridge, which to those not in the know is actually a complex operation trying to get everything balanced. Especially having been shut down and overhauled, since that last time it was running. Sort off.

"Okay bosun, that's a pretty good looking cement box," encompassing the Cutters starboard anchor, propped up on bricks on the old, now found out to be the funnel signs of the previous owners, and including one of the jetty piers.

"You got the second one ready to go yet?" asked the master.

"Just mixing up the sand and cement captain, we ran out of bricks so had to improvise. Mullah's idea really but it might just work."

"On your head be it bosun," replied the captain, but to be fair, might just actually work upon reflection.

"Captain," asked the ships' bosun, "have you ever tried thermite welding before?"

"Ages ago, but not on this scale."

The reply not believed by anyone, given what they had all been up to in the preceding few weeks.

"Where is all that laughter coming from captain?" as most drew back into the shadows."

"The girls are treating the skeleton crew with a cake and a few beers."

"Do we not get any cake captain," asked the bosun with a consensus of opinion suggested from those around.

"My friend, no, trust me, you do not want to go anywhere near that chocolate cake, as there is an extra ingredient in the mix."

Curiosity which could have killed the cat, only prompting even more curiosity. "Because there are 50 ground up laxative tablets in it, which after only one slice will see, after about 20 minutes, these hungry Americans spending most of the night in, in American parlance, 'the heads,' while we get on with welding their Cutter to the dock."

"Remind me," came a voice from the background, "never to get on the wrong side of this captain." This seemingly being heard before.

Twenty minutes being overly optimistic, as after 18 minutes the gaiety died down, and 5 minutes later the girls re-appeared, grinning from ear to ear.

"What are you doing here?" asked Doug, the master.

"We've come to help you with the welding," said Celia.

"But you don't know anything about thermite welding," promptly followed with by the bosun, "neither do you captain."

"Well at least I've read the book about it."

Not convincing at all, but replying. "Thanks for the vote of confidence mate, in my job you have to lie a lot."

"Lie a lot? More like most of the time."

"Do you think that you can do any better?"

"Captain, I, and the crew rather like it, we just wish we had the confidence to do it, so what do we have to do?" from the bosun.

"Right, we'll do the bottom one first, 5lbs of aluminium powder and 5 lbs of iron oxide, pour them into together so they get nicely mixed up," which was fine until Christine popped in with, "can I put in the magnesium Doug, seeing the lengths I had to go to get it?"

Celia looking a bit lost, not knowing about this.

"Okay, but you need to be quick, cut a chunk of it out, say about a pound and underwater, and when I say go, throw it onto the top of the powder mix. Just wait though until we get well out of the way."

"Is it dangerous?" from a now more concerned Christine.

"Don't know yet Christine, probably, but then but you volunteered."

Celia coming in with, "is it Doug?"

"Just about to find out. Okay Christine, go for it and as fast as you can, and then get back here." To which with a now realised apprehension duly did.

Not a lot was said by anyone for the next few seconds, or it may have been longer, time possibly stopping, but a general view expressed by everyone later, on average, amounted into 'fucking hell!' as Christine fell backwards into her current lovers arms.

"I think that we might need a wee bit more research here," ventured Doug, as the blinding light eventually subsided. Talking to himself, the others nowhere in sight. Even Christine. Gone. How she vanished from his arms no doubt would surface later. After his eyesight regained its' normal focus.

But had it worked?

Perfectly, well if you ignore a bit of burnt paint, and few scorch areas, the barnacles most probably not in agreement though.

Still no-one in sight, as the captain prepared to set off the next one, to weld the anchor cable to the cutter.

Still hadn't got it quite right though, too much magnesium probably, but it had worked, if you ignored the hole in the Cutters bow. The remainder of the magnesium, still in its box, and still in fresh water, suitably ensconced on a shelf under the jetty, which the next hurricane that came along would see it dispersed, safely or not. Probably not, but who cares, the ship would be long gone.

"Captain," ventured the bosun, "how are you going to explain this?"

"We aren't my friend, the crew on the cutter are, if one of them can actually get off the toilet seat, or head. Because that was one hell of a bolt of lightning that came down, melted the mooring ropes and welded their cutter to the dock. Our ship now in the middle of powering up also hit and for the next few hours we are going to be changing fuses. Well not actually changing them, but making enough noise as though we were. Which is why the 3rd mate has switched off all the floodlights. He'll switch them on in pairs over the next 15 minutes to make it look as though the bridge has been struck by lightning."

It didn't take long before all looked as reality, as the engine room started to come to life. And presenting another problem.

"Captain," and in his office enduring the un-ending paperwork, Einar and Mike arrived, but before they could speak, Doug raised his hand and said, "I've already heard the bang, it sounded like a lub oil purifier exploding. Am I right?"

Two bemused heads somewhat lost as they exchanged glances.

"How did you know?" from one.

"Let's just get it fixed, the other 2 will have to cope in the meantime let me know how badly damaged it is."

"Can you call in Pierre to take the old oil away?"

"Nope. Stick it a fuel tank, we'll burn it up on when we eventually get on passage. We'll use this delay of getting the water side of the main engine up to a higher temperature, before we fire it up in the morning. In the meantime, give me all the details of that purifier, and I'll get a new one flown in if need be. You are never going to find one of these in Texas, or anywhere in The US. Might as well as we seem to be getting other things flown in as well. I'll just add it to the Insurance Claim."

This taking a little time to sink in, but followed with, "we could actually fire the main engine now, if you're not too tired. It's up to heat."

"Okay, do it, but only if we have enough crew on board, let me check first."

A little look in the dayroom, confirming that all of his crew were on-board, before "Gentlemen, tonight we are going to go through the test procedures with our new main engine crankshaft in situ. You know what to do with the mooring ropes. Let's do it. And after that, split into 2 groups, one group getting some sleep, and if when we get up to full power testing, if you hear any alarms, then we will have broken our mooring ropes, and I'll have shut her down on the Emergency Stop button on the bridge."

He was very nearly run down in the rush, but managing, "we need the accommodation ladder up first."

The crew apparently just as keen as to getting back to sea as their master.

"Okay Mike, fire her up, I'll transfer main engine control to the engine room, as soon as I get to the bridge. Except the Emergency Stop button, we'll share that one."

Unfortunately, just as the accommodation ladder lifted from the dock, the Department of Agriculture arrived, or at least some of their numpties, those few not with bowel problems, and not having to cross their legs while walking. A pretty fair representation from those who may just have put something into their mouth without checking it first, such as an oyster. The old Scottish saying off, if it doesn't look right, don't eat it.

The gesticulations of putting the accommodation ladder back down falling upon deaf ears, at least from the ships bridge wings, and running into language problems to those within earshot.

It not coming out later just who started the fire pump, or just how that fire hose just happened to be pointing in their direction, but it did serve its' purpose of putting a damper on their protests. Getting wet, seemingly becoming a norm. But not for what came next, as the ship's main engine fired, albeit on only minimum power, but when the turbocharger kicked in, clearing a full months of soot and goodness knows what else, a lot of which changed into being very sticky, and caught on the cross wind, did unfortunately land on those who shouldn't have been there in the first place. Oh dear! ACC 9 cleaning the turbine blades most satisfactorily, including rather a lot of water which accumulated due to the high humidity, condensing in the funnel. Water being unable to be compressed, very useful in cleaning out funnels.

The ships main engine, settling into a pleasing rhythm, not appreciated by those on the dockside from The Department of Agriculture, but who cares. They could puzzle out a way of getting clean again.

"Okay boys," from the captain on his radio, "balance her up on our mooring ropes." To which was done rather effectively, considering that they had not actually handled any mooring ropes in over a month.

The 'phone from the engine room rang. "We'll shut her down when you are ready captain."

"Give me a few minutes."

"Right guys" from the master, "headline as tight as you can get it, and aft, back spring as tight as you can get it, and leave the ropes on the drum ends."

A minute later, "Okay Mike, from the bridge on the 'phone, shut her down, and let me know when we can re-start."

The steady rhythm dying away, as the main engine stopped.

The VHF didn't stop though with the poor little Dept. of Agriculture's Cutters person in charge astern on overdrive demanding all sorts of things, including such as, "I demand that you stop what you are doing," and answered with from the ship's captain, "Well we are preparing to go to sea, are you? You seem to have a little problem getting your bow free from the dock, but not to worry, when we've checked our crankcase, then we'll be starting up again, and after a few hours, will ramp up to full power testing. You've had enough warning, so stay off the VHF."

No-one noticing that Celia was hovering in the background, but thinking as females tended to do, and wondering that if it was wise to ask him quietly, so she could at least go with the ship down to the pilot station?

It might be worth a try, as she would like to see how they operated a ships' bridge at night. Celia becoming even more curious by the minute.

The master 'phoned the engine room, "Anytime you are ready Mike, we've got her as tight as she will go."

"Just finishing checking the crankcase Doug. It is all looking good so far."

Francis, the Radio Officer arrived, "I've got a telex for you captain."

"I thought we were on Inmarsat A, Francis, we only installed it last week! After getting the height of the mast sorted out with Coastal Iron. I didn't know that we still had telex. Mind you, I haven't read the Instruction Manual yet. By the way, where is it Francis?"

"Sorry sir, but this is important."

Reading the telex, which could not have come at a worse time, indicating that the ship had a change of orders, and needed a prompt response.

"Have we not got enough to do?" forehead raised upwards in disbelief.

The bridge 'phone rang, "Doug, we're all set to go for the long test, ramping up to full power testing, okay to begin?"

"Good to go Mike, but as soon as you are able, I need a full check as to our current bunkers on board, including lube oils, we're not going to Mexico, then NW Europe, we're going to Houston first, then Coatzacoalcos and Bahia Blanca in Argentina. And we are not initially going to load ethylene."

There was a distinct pause as this news settled in.

"Do you want us to start on minimum?"

"No, ramp her up as to our plan, I need to make a few calls after it starts."

The main engine started and the ship never moved.

"Francis, stay here until I get back, if the ship breaks out from her moorings, just hit this button. I'll be as quick as I can."

"Okay captain, this red one?"

"That's the one, and hold it down until the engine stops."

Arriving in his office, Doug picked up the 'phone and dialled, to be met with the voice of Christine, "you've just caught me, I was just leaving to come down to you."

"Christine, don't ask, but do as I say, get onto SAYBOLT, get them to appoint a chemist and get he or she to come down to this ship and test the dew point of our cargo tanks. Don't ask why, but this is important, and not tomorrow, but now. In the meantime, organise a pilot and two tugs for us sailing this time tomorrow at 1700 local time, we are going to Houston, before we go to Mexico. Make sure the pilots are aware, that when we leave the berth, we will not be using anything like full power, and if that means having 2 pilots then that is okay. And ask Richard to prepare for outward clearance. And get the 'phone companies to disconnect the 2 'phone lines and prepare their bills. I also need a compass adjuster. I've got most of the other bills paid, but can't afford to miss any, just do a check for me please. Now I can't stay, I'll be on the bridge for the next 3 hours. Bye."

Christine's heart dropped, but she did as she was required to do. This could mean only one thing, that this time tomorrow, her new very close friend and lover was leaving port, and all that was left for her were a few private hours if possible and the rest of the night spent with her husband. It did however giving her the excuse to her husband that she would be late back that night or maybe in the morning. The abrupt "Bye" suggesting that he would like to be more loving, but others were listening in.

This conveyed to the other office staff, including Romero and carried out.

Apart from one thing, "Christine," as she prepared to leave, said from her boss, "I've already cleared this with the captain, but I need you to fill out an Overtime Report, and I need his signature and ships stamp on it, can you see to it before the ship sails tomorrow?"

That's going to be tricky, she thought before it occurring to her that this could take up much of the night. Being a Jehovah's Witness though did if not done carefully, left her with 2 dilemmas.

Either tell the truth, that her private time spent with her new love would not require claiming overtime, but it had to be explained anyway by claiming payment for something that she had not actually done. Her resolution? Better ask Doug about this. Nothing like 'passing the buck' so to speak, something she learnt from Doug, and slowly realising that this could last all night.

Not much later, well if you do not consider an hour as not much later, the captain arrived back on the ship's bridge.

"Okay Francis, thank-you, have the engine room been back on?"

To which the 'phone rang, "if she's tight can we ramp up?" asked the ships master.

"She's tight, ramp her up and you are clear to go to 100% full manoeuvring power in your own time."

"What about that cutter astern of us?"

"Mike, leave that thing to me, if it does break off, then it is going to take a good bit of the jetty with it. Better still, if you can ramp up in the next two hours as The US Coast Guard have just come on board."

The mood of the bridge officers with their captain, cautious but excited at the same time. The third mate venturing with, "sir, what happens if that cutter breaks loose?"

"Who cares, we have permission to run up to full manoeuvring power on a static test, and they put it there in the first place. Not our fault, partly that some of their mooring ropes weren't quite up to scratch after that lightning bolt struck. Anyway, they know we are having main engine trials."

The mood on the ships bridge becoming more relaxed as the platter arrived, with the tipples being of the prawn and seafood variety. "Enjoy it now boys as we are sailing tomorrow night, hopefully."

The 'phone rang. "Doug, we'll keep our seafood platter for later, we've checked everything, can we run up to full manoeuvring power?"

"Just let me tell my boys," at the same time thinking, 'thought that he'd already told him that.

There was a few moments of delay.

"Mike, wind her up, full manoeuvring power in your own time."

It could be told that later in this ships life that nobody had actually run this ship on full power, and had been lying as to what she was capable of. And for the previous 5 years.

Not judging by the wash though, as the dock bottom was seriously changed, and one Dept. of Agriculture's Cutter finding itself in a position, no doubt awkward to explain welded to the dock and now aground at the same time. Well, sort of surrounded with mud, and a few other things, the odd crab or six, making getting that boat operational, just a wee tad awkward, although not quite aground, more so, stuck in the mud, as in, lots of it. One of whom in rather a hurry trying to close a door on the fore deck, the sheer thrust of displaced water, and mud, with a few other things, plastic mostly, being aimed for a place to a place that it wasn't actually meant to go to.

Oops, not an intended place for it, but one stuck at both ends.

Slightly, if so considered, easier to careen though. If anyone in this backwater port, just knew just what careening actually meant?

The office 'phone rang, picked up Francis and found himself talking to Christine, "Doug, the SAYBOLT surveyor is on her way down, I'm bringing her, how can we get aboard?"

"Christine, this is Francis, the captain is on the bridge, can I take a message?"

Duly done and conveyed with.

"Not by our usual ways, the water ways, we'll put the accommodation ladder down for you. But it won't be down for long, so hightail it when you are both ready."

"Romero, the 2nd mate, "get one of the crew to put down the accommodation ladder, and you supervise, and as soon as they are on board, lift it up again."

"Onto it captain."

Shortly afterwards, by VHF, "Blackie, I'm sending the third mate up to relieve you, get a hold of Erling and join me on the bridge, as soon as you can please."

These things always happen when you are busy as he waited for both to arrive.

As they did though, both were shown the telex, which did not go down overly well.

"We need gentlemen to split the gas plant, 2000 tonnes of Butene 1, to tanks 1 and 3, and 2000 tonnes of ethylene to tanks 2 and 4. The ethylene we load in Coatzacoalcos, but we are going to Houston first. Obviously, when we get the Butene 1 on board first, then we can leave it dormant, and use all of the re-liquefaction for the ethylene vapour of passage. So start right now, getting it ready, as we haven't got much time. I've just organised a surveyor to come on board to check our cargo tank dew point levels and if they are the same, we'll start to load the Butene 1 under 50% vacuum, and keep that transferred dry nitrogen for the ethylene. That should keep the Butene 1 dormant."

"Do we start tonight?"

"You are both experienced gas officers, shouldn't take much more than an hour, because tomorrow and before we sail, every single safety system has to be checked, and you know how many systems there are."

"But the main cargo gas deck breakers aren't in." The askance look conveying that propping up the bar that might just be a distant dream.

"Well, the engineers are in the engine room, you can either start right now at getting the breakers in, or tomorrow morning when they, who you need, are still asleep. I'd start with changing the gas plant, and after we shut down the main engine for tonight in about 3 hours' time, get everything lined up for about, shall we say 1200?"

A German and a Norwegian looked at each other, neither wishing to disclose that both had a date with a lady for that particular evening. Just how you define a lady open to question, as a few of the female variety of a somewhat rougher origin had already found their way on board, and a few behind the captain's back had to be carried off again.

"Let's get on with it then Blackie, it won't take us long," they not knowing that their captain had full knowledge of just where to split the ship, but also of their girlfriends, one of whom woke up with an enormous hangover, a few days back in a rather unusual place, encompassed in a rather wet car, it being a Pontiac 836. With a rather unusual roof, and a police officer beaming from ear to ear.

The intrigue of how this car got there and this not so beautiful woman inside, did as later transpire that she knew how to operate a ships crane, with a little help from the master, and a few others landed this somewhat unusual piece of junk onto the dockside. It taking a little time for draining the water out, although the roof now was no longer flat, more like a bit pointy upwards, due to the snotter. Great ventilation though as the windscreen had also suffered and doors only closing if a bit of rope was involved. Well, she was getting it for free after all.

As a final offering, "take care and drive it only in reverse."

"Why?"

"Because its brakes don't work overly well." An understatement and translated into modern English, as into 'they don't work at all.'

The policeman, one of those who had visited the ship with his family a few days back, and nearly driven up the wall by his kids almost constant pestering wanting to see the ship again, on his way to ask, witnessing this with his partner, who had not been there before, but also intrigued.

Francis asked, "Captain where, did that come from?"

It being rather difficult to tell with the shape of the face that most Filipinos had, as to eyes agog, actually were.

"I'm buggered if I know, but these short-sighted Texans can be talked into anything. As far as I know, it started off life as one in The Corpus Christi Mayor's office. Could be the one that got hot wired when we went rattlesnake racing."

In the interim, with the accommodation ladder lowered and 6 scampered up, it being raised almost immediately, as the main engine was now on almost full power, and the poor Department of Agriculture's cutter almost covered in mud, so who of the six were the first to arrive on the bridge, the relief master standing in for the one in prison, and now about to experience a similar fate.

Clearly, they not appreciating that they now had in port, a deep water berth, not a very big one, but if the ship was small, should fit into nicely. Providing of course that it wasn't too high for getting under the Corpus Christi Bridge.

The conversation didn't actually last that long after he started swearing at the captain, spitting him in the face and with threats asunder as to how he was demanding that he stopped his main engine immediately, or else!

Just as well, as the chief engineer had shut the main engine down, just before this threatening and arrogant Texan found out that being thrown overboard from the poop deck was an infinitely better way of getting wet, than he was now experiencing having just been thrown overboard from the port bridge wing, four and a half decks further up.

He who had accompanied him, preferring not to go the same way, preferring the stairs on HIS way back down. And then hide until he could get back onto dry land.

"Hello Christine," as she arrived on the bridge with a SAYBOLT surveyor, and it was quite apparent from the off, that she was not going to be short of male company later, as this was a rather stunning and slim young woman, who strangely enough also happened to be of German descent. This seemingly being a popular trait in Texas.

And introduced with a short shake of hands, "I'm sorry, I don't have much time just now, but this is Blackie, my chief officer and he will show you where the sampling points are. I need to know the dew point of all of our cargo tanks, and of the main liquid lines to tanks 2 and 4."

"No problem captain, I have everything I need, so I'll just get on with it then." She not as yet knowing that after this ship sailed that Blackie would not be sailing with it, he having caused the crew to 'lose face,' again! Hopefully one day, he would learn how to work with others, and that his Teutonic and arrogant attitude if maintained, was never going to work.

Meaning that the captain had his job to do as well.

"Hello John," as he shook hands with the first cop, "I didn't expect to see you again, family all well I trust?"

"They are Doug and this is Andre, my partner," as they shook hands, "my kids are driving me demented, as they want to come and see your ship again."

"Well John, they are going to have to be quick, as we plan to sail tomorrow at 1700. That's 5 in the evening in metric time."

"So they could come tonight? And they might have a few of their pals with them."

"And how many is a, 'few'?"

"Most of their school actually."

A so called pregnant pause, resulted in, "It would have to be between 9 tomorrow morning and 12, as we now have the deck breakers in, so no photographs, and limited access only for the main deck, except on the bridge or from the dockside, and as for food, sorry, as we are storing for South America."

"Engine room?" venturing just a little.

"We'll see, as my engineers will be spending most of tonight and tomorrow powering it all up, and that is one place that kid's inquisitive fingers are not wise to go into. Probably limit it to the flat above the main engine, and make sure they all have enough cotton wool for their ears"

"Could I get in touch Doug?"

"Off course, but our 'phone lines are being disconnected at 11 o'clock in the morning. Now, I don't mean to be rude, by my Chief Engineer has just arrived. See you tomorrow perhaps?"

"Doug, you will always be welcome in Corpus Christi, especially for what you said as we opened the new Seaman's Centre."

"Don't remind me, as I still haven't found out just who broadcast that on TV. I didn't expect to sign autographs when I took command of this ship."

Smilingly, both left. Andre curious as to what might happen next morning as his kids were also included. "John, what is so curious that school children are interested in?"

"Well I don't think that the captain would mind, if I was to show you round this ship, just don't press any buttons."

Christine sliding gracefully from the chartroom and just about to be gathered up in Doug's arms interrupted with "captain, we've got a problem," from Abner, 3rd mate, "we can't find Martin."

"Good!" Was the captain's response, until, "the hire car has gone as well?"

"What?"

Just as Mike arrived, somewhat perspiring on overdrive, and asking just "what" was "what?"

"It appears Mike, that Martin, who could drive, but not legally, has for some reason, who for now will say, has 'borrowed' the hire car and the reasoning will have to come out later. Anyway, how is the main engine?"

"About as good as we are going to get it, but are really struggling with the lub oil purifiers, when does our new one arrive?"

"Tonight actually, at least as far as into Austin, Texas, but I've told the agents to charter a plane and get it here overnight so with a bit of luck it should be here about 0600. I suppose that there is nothing else we can do until then, so why not get your head down?"

"But what about Martin?"

"Mike, just leave him to me, as I rather think as to where he has gone. You ever met a gambling Scottish AB before? Only this one is DHU."

"What's a DHU?" Many eyes focussed on the master.

"It stands for Deck Hand Uncertificated, and the only thing I could think off when I talked the Sheriff into getting him sent to us."

"So who is paying for his return flight to the UK?"

"I am, providing that he doesn't go DBS in South America, which I am rather counting on."

"What is DBS?"

"Distressed British Seaman."

"Which is?"

"Someone who has missed the ship on sailing, and doesn't have his passport with him. I'll explain this later."

To which one rather confused Mike accepted as he sought out the engine room.

Meanwhile, Christine arrived, looking a little bit worried.

"Come up Christine, I need a break from all of these questions."

"Doug," as they both arrived in his dayroom, "much as I would like to jump into bed with you, I need a bit of help with this overtime paper, that Richard needs in the morning with your signature and ships stamp on it. Could you help me please?"

Not being one noted as being slow on the up-take, asked. "Does this mean that your company are going to pay you for all of the hours that we have spent together, either in the restaurant or in my cabin, or even when we met for lunch, and also for the time your husband spent on board, plus the underwater bits?"

"Eh, yes."

"Including the time when you lost your clothes and were swimming around the harbour at night?"

"I'd rather forget about that," from an increasingly red face that wished to be somewhere else.

"Doesn't say much about your religious faith, does it? Having to lie?" The face withdrawing and getting ever redder, whispering in response to which an answer being very faint.

"Christine, much that I have fallen in love with you, and for the present, both of us cannot be together, we, as far as I see it, need to concoct something that your husband will get a copy off, and appreciate where all of these extra dollars came from, which will also appease Richard, your boss."

Christine sighing slightly, but not overly optimistic.

"Look, it will eventually find its way back into this Insurance Claim, and chicken feed to what the final bill will be. Now relax while I get the daily log book. Then we will put it together. But first, I need to go and find Martin. I may be an hour or so, so can I borrow your car?"

Concurring did so, with a hint of sadness, eating into more of the remaining hours that they could be together.

"Christine, kick your shoes off, relax and get a shower or would you prefer a bath? I won't be that long."

She, as he left in the meantime, undressed and went to his shower, forgetting about the invitation of having a bath, using the fine spray to alleviate most of her concerns, but deeply sad that after tomorrow, she may never see him again, and privately washing her tears away.

The captain knew where he was going, albeit in Christine's car, and entering a house of ill repute grabbed one Martin by the throat and dragging him outside. "You my friend, I talked a Sheriff into getting you away from Scotland, so that you didn't get sent back to prison, now we are sailing tomorrow, so get yourself back on board tonight, and leave the keys to the hire car on my desk. Savvy?"

"Yes Doug, it is probably the best thing that could happen just now," as he regained control of his feet, heading to the hire car, jumping in, and screaming off. The ship's master taking a similar route in Christine's car, with rather a lot of angry Texans shouting all sorts of things which could be described as, somewhat dangerous.

"Just exactly what were you thinking off?" as both met up in the master's office, "do you not know the terms and conditions, just as to why you are here. Even the American Police don't know. Now how lucrative has your picking the pockets of Americans, actually netted you?"

"I'm glad you came in when you did Captain, I just got caught."

"How much Martin? And don't lie to me."

"Do you want the full run-down?"

The daggers eyes conveying that this was not a good time to lie, resulting in, "217 credit cards, 129 banker's cards, 405 identity cards, and............... about 10 pounds of leather, of the type that holds it together, which, we.........call, wallets."

"Go on, how much in US Dollars?"

"Oh, it's not all in US Dollars, there were other notes as well."

"Now don't muck me about, I haven't got time, "how much in USD?"

"You promise not to tell?"

"HOW MUCH?"

"Will you tell the Sheriff?

"HOW MUCH Martin?"

Meekly answering, about $ 10.

"Do you think that I came up the Clyde on a banana boat? How much?"

"Can I keep it?"

"Last chance, or you are going back on the next 'plane to Scotland, and before you get there, The Sheriff, will know why."

"Just over twenty thousand dollars, and quite a bit of drugs."

There was as later described as, a pregnant pause.

"Right, this is what you are going to do. Gather all of it up into little bundles, sealed in plastic, cling film even and take the lids carefully off 25 litre paint drums and slip in just enough not to overflow them, then put the lids back on. Just remember which ones are where, as no sniffer dog can smell anything under wet paint. We'll sort it out after we sail. And from tonight and until we sail, get a case of beer, and hide somewhere under the jetty, just don't make any noise. Only leave me with the last 5 credit cards that you obtained, I know how to throw a spanner in the works."

He left in something of a hurry.

The captain arriving back in his cabin sighted Christine wrapped in a large towel, as he closed the door.

"I'm not taking you out to dinner dressed like that."

"But I've only got what I was wearing before, and I've been in them all day." Also puzzled as to what he was wearing. A suit, the collar though might just need a bit of adjustment.

"Do you remember the first time we made love, and I hung your blouse up in my wardrobe? Well go and see what I have for you in there, but carefully as the perfume is also on one of the hangers."

"I only came down to get my overtime sheet filled in." she said, a little lost.

"Already done and dusted, signed and stamped. Here it is. Now get dressed, we are going out for dinner. Taxi tonight as someone has, shall we say, found another use for our hire car. Don't worry, these things crop up just before we sail, no matter where we are. I'll just let Mike know where we are going. Don't worry, your husband has been told by Richard that you are working late tonight, so relax."

With a slight air of trepidation, as her husband had never bought any clothes for her as a surprise, she gently opened the wardrobe door.

Taking off the thin plastic covers, with the rather expensive Jaeger pattern, found a white airy halter neck dress made from silk, thick in layers around the neck, beautifully flowing covering her breasts and to her waist neatly fitting and then flowing full to the hem just above her knee. A sky blue bolero jacket in satin, all in her size, even the tights, knickers and shoes in her size. Not that a bra was necessary with this style of dress but there anyway. Even the lightweight purse in white satin, hung on a gold chain thought out by its contents. The usual female accoutrements also catered for, of the personal female things.

Stunned! as she slowly dressed, the light silk slipping gently over her body, the blue bolero jacket just amazing to her as her hair dried, and as to the perfume, after a slight sniff, keeping the rest for just before she met Doug.

Who in the meantime with his officers explaining what to do with the most recently acquired stolen credit cards, courtesy of a one certain Martin, who unknowingly had 'acquired' cards from those giving the captain the most hassle rather than help, and could certainly afford what they were going to find when the next credit card bill came in. All being corporate credit cards. Might not be overly chuffed though. As in, not in the least.

"Good evening," on one of the two landlines, "do you deliver?"

The answer being in the affirmative, followed with "right, I need 20 Margaritas pizzas, eh, the 18 inch ones, with extra toppings, and 5 cases of root beer. And 40 Calzone pizzas. Can you manage that?"

"Off course sir, but it might take a little time."

"That's not a problem, the boss will be here all night, so if you are ready, here are my credit card details, eh, I trust that you take credit cards."

"Fire away sir, I'm ready."

"And the 3 digit number on the back sir, is?"

A few long seconds passed, before, "that is approved sir. Thank-you, we should have it ready in about 40 minutes. What is the address sir, for delivery?" To which he was informed.

The others looking at him in awe. "Just what have you done?"

"Much the same as what you are about to do."

"So who is getting 20 huge pizzas with extra toppings? And the rest of it, Calzone pizzas are pretty big aren't they? Do they fit in boxes?"

"Let's say that the desk sergeant of the Corpus Christi Police Department, might in about 40 minutes or so, have one hell of a problem."

"And who is paying for all of this?"

"Strangely enough, the Mayor. Rather generous of him don't you think!"

Now here are another 4 cards, buy anything you like, get it sent to anywhere, but not to this ship, and let your imagination run wild, the more expensive the better, as you will appreciate after reading the names on these other cards. Just one thing, don't buy a car."

The heads listening to this, slowly smiling with minds on overdrive as each looked at the other.

"You look stunning," from all, as she nervously ventured into the ships offices."

Doug coming from his office with a gentle smile on his face, opened a little box and hung a luckenbooth on a fine gold chain around her neck.

"I think Christine, our taxi awaits."

"When can we expect you back captain?" asked Mike.

"Not later than midnight, but if anything crops up, you'll know where to find me."

After leaving, those present fell into a huddle, "she didn't come aboard dressed like that, and she didn't even carry anything with her, where did she get dressed like that! She was stunningly beautiful."

"If you have not as yet worked out just how our captain goes about things, then I think that we can leave just one of us here tonight, ready for main engine start tomorrow morning, while the rest of us go and spy on them. As long as were are back before midnight." Said Mike. "Now you know where he disappeared to yesterday, and before you ask, he parted company with just over $5000 for that dress and accessories. I think that you might say that he is in love with her."

Thankfully, no one was trampled in the rush, before remembering that they still had a few 'phone calls to make first.

"What are you ordering Mike?"

Another saying, "can I use the captain's phone, would he mind if I sat at his desk?" He of Filipino descent.

Over the next 15 minutes, it was not only pizzas that were ordered in abundance as one had found the 'phone book for Houston, and 250 MacDonald quarter pounders and 250 portions of fries, 500 portions of McFlurry ice cream, also were on their way to the local hospital. As ice cream is the best thing to take to patients in hospital, as the air is so dry, the girl training as a nurse supporting herself by working in MacDonald's, only too happy to empty the ice cream machine, and with a huge smile on her face, as she was let into the secret.

This being disclosed just upped the imagination of the others who were a bit more inventive, "hello, hello, is that the Loch Fyne salmon farm in Scotland? It is, good, can you air freight salmon to Texas, USA?"

"Ochht, that we can sir, how much do you want? Fresh or smoked?" The accent or brogue initially confusing.

"Which is cheaper? I need 100 pounds."

"Is that pounds weight sir, or pounds sterling?"

"Better make it weight, but in five weekly orders, here are my credit card details."

A rather stunned Scotsman carefully noting the details, and the reverse 3 digit number, before asking, "Will this be a repeat order?"

"That depends upon how well my chefs prepare it, but I would imagine that it will be." Lying his head off most competently.

"And the mailing address, carefully noted down. "It should be with you tomorrow night sir. We only use British Airways, they are the best. Thank-you for your order, we'll put in some extra as a token of our goodwill. This hasn't found its way onto the market yet, we are still experimenting with it."

The 'phone replaced.

"So who's getting all of this smoked salmon?" asked a few intent on knowing just what might come next.

"A certain up-market hotel, who else!"

"And who is paying for it?" the question narrowing down to The Chief Engineer.

"The Chief Harbourmaster."

Most satisfying. As a few remembered just what he had promised at the very start as the captain limped the ship in.

From the Filipino sitting at the captain's desk, "Is that you Mario? Great, Jesus (pronounced Yeysoos) Orlando here, remember me?" He should, they were cousins, "I'm in Corpus Christi, in Texas, USA, are you still in the ship chandlery business?" The reply confirming this, "what do you need?"

"Can you get 150 lobsters, and airfreight them to us in Corpus Christi?"

"I, would imagine so, might take a day or two to round them up, how are you paying for this, it might be expensive."

"My captain is having to throw rather a big party, and he knows that you, when he was previously in Lisbon, could get things that others couldn't."

"Would this captain, Jesus, be coming from Scotland?"

Mario smiled, as he had lost touch with who he had suspected.

"Okay, pass across the credit card details and the delivery address in Corpus Christi, and I'll get onto it." He Mario, knowing this shipmaster and always up for having a good old practical joke going on somewhere.

"Well done Jesus, that sounds very expensive, who is paying for it?"

"The Chief Harbourmaster's sidekick, The Port Manager."

"He really annoyed our captain and has been a thorn in our captain's side since we arrived here."

Mario just laughing on the 'phone before saying, "Tell Doug, that I wish I was sailing with him, and I'll make sure that The Wyndum Hotel gets these lobsters."

The hotel manager in for a forthcoming additional surprise.

"Well you could, if you could arrange flights for Houston in 2 days' time. Just use the same credit card number, and he needs a new chief officer. Know anything about gas tankers?"

"Absolutely everything."

Liar, but to sail with Doug well worth the risk of lying.

"I'll see what I can do, thanks Jesus."

The expensive mood only ramping up another gear.

"Only one card to go now chaps, let's put our heads together?"

Various ideas emerged, but dismissed as not being expensive enough.

"Anyone like oysters?"

"We, if you, haven't caught on yet, are buying things for other people," and have you ever eaten an oyster? Or tried to get in through its shell?

"Well, no."

"Okay, we can forget about that idea then." As squirmed faces rather objected to this.

"I was actually thinking of ordering in about 10 000, bound to get into the odd one or two shells, even if we need to smash them open."

Beers raised, dismissing this idea.

"How about 120 000 condoms, or as Americans call them, rubbers? There is this place in town, selling them cheap."

"Why?" From 4 puzzled faces.

"Send them to a catholic priest?"

"I think we can safely dispense with that idea. Good though, keep thinking. We're bound to come up with something even more dopey yet."

"A pity we can't get anything sent to the ship, or buy a car."

"Does anyone know if there is an orphanage or children's home in this port?"

"We could ask, what are you thinking off?"

"Does a minibus count as being a car?"

"Keep thinking, but we'll take this last card with us, time we went spying on our master and his stunningly beautiful girlfriend. Anyway, I'm getting thirsty."

Most concurring.

With his TV celebrity status meant going anywhere for a quiet dinner together impossible, so they went to The Wyndham Hotel anyway.

"I 'phoned in earlier and asked for quiet table in a corner."

That was a waste of time, as, as soon as Christine entered the dining room, the gentle hubbub fell almost silent.

"Doug, I don't like people looking at me," as they were shown to their table, as nonetheless her grace carried the occasion, accepting the napkin and menu."

"What am I going to tell my husband? I can't go home dressed like this."

"Christine, this is our last night together, so how about when we get back to the ship, you change back into what you were wearing earlier, then we parcel it all up, and send it to your mother in Mannheim? If it doesn't then work out with your husband, you can get it back later."

"Okay, that's what I will do."

"Good, then let's give up this despondency, and order dinner and eat."

"Doug, just what is a luckenbooth?"

"It is something peculiar to Scotland, and something for you to remember me by when we leave. Keep it in your desk drawer in your office. It is 2 entwined hearts belonging to 2 people in love. I had it made by this Jeweller I know in Scotland, and the diamond is a quarter of a carat. Do you like it?"

Her heart on the point of breaking, as she rather knew what was going to happen.

Their chosen dishes arrived. Champagne not appropriate, as this was no time to celebrate, so both settled for water.

Spying from the bar not exactly what the group had in mind, and they still hadn't worked out what to do with the 5th credit card.

"Can we get cash on it?" The older of the Filipinos asked.

"Nah, we don't have the pin number. Keep thinking."

"How about the fire brigade, they're usually hungry?"

"Chinese?"

"Did we not see a menu as we came in, Mullah, have you got that in your pocket?"

Indeed as he sampling the freebies, most known as salted peanuts. The odd handful though being saved for later in his pockets. Well, to be fair, pockets bulging. He not as yet understanding that salted peanuts don't actually fully digest in the gut, but making their own way outwards in a rather painful way attached to stools of the non-sitting on variety. And something which started, rather difficult to stop. Roughly 2 days after the last peanut entered the throat, and remember, this guy had no teeth, apart from one old molar and a very strong tongue.

Duly recovered, the menu though, and read through.

"My goodness, there is some selection here. I've never even heard of some of these dishes.

Anyone got a pen and a piece of paper," to which both materialised. The bosun, now on over-drive.

"Only Texans could come up with this, a set meal for 60!" said one in amazement. "As a doggy bag?" known to most Europeans as, a carry out.

"Hold on, they do a rystaffel."

"What's that?"

"Hardly Chinese, more Indonesian. It's a collection of individual dishes, anything up to 84 where you only get a nibble of all sorts of different flavours. It takes ages to get through them all, but possible if you take your time, after you get the hang of chopsticks. Last time I saw one of these was in Rotterdam.

Right, how much does it cost?"

It took a few seconds to sink in.

"Wow! That much!"

It now having been found that this was going to be rather expensive, as one of the group took charge. And not the bosun.

"I like ordering dishes by numbers, ever so easy to get tongue tied, which occasionally gets translated into more than you actually order."

The telephone connection being established and one unfortunate individual on the other end wrote down this incoming order.

"Right we'll have, 10 # 26, 40 #35, 15 #42, 20 # 56, 68 # 86, 10 # 110, 35 # 156, and we are going to need quite a bit of rice to go with that lot, so, let's say, 90 # 180, and 30 # 185, and rystaffel's, well, it's early yet, what do you reckon, 6?"

"Nah round it up to a decent number, say 10." Soy sauce, they might need a lot to wash that down with, a case of 24 bottles."

"Drinks?"

"A case of Chinese white wine?"

"Can you get such a thing?"

The answer not forthcoming, but probably.

"Nan bread?" asked one, "didn't think of that," replied another.

"We are supposed to be ordering Chinese, not Indian."

"Okay," said Mike, seeking inspiration, "let's count the window panes in this restaurant, and whatever number we agree on, and get the same number of portions of 3 tier rice, whatever that is."

Nobody thinking up anything more stupid, as they all got to counting.

"You know this counting bit is thirsty work," as more beer arrived. "Right how many panes of glass are there?"

"Well, I got 56," said one, "Nah, I counted 145," said another, "you're both wrong," said a third, "96."

Seeing that this was never being to be resolved, "let's settle for a nice round 114. Okay?" Well, logic has no place in this order.

Quite a few more minutes passed.

"How'd you get on?"

"A large order certainly, but I got the impression that they have in the past, probably had bigger orders, and for some peculiar reason, I rather think that he has gotten some of the order numbers mixed up with quantity numbers. Should be interesting. Anyway that's it done, let's get back to the ship."

"Who is paying for it?"

"I never looked that closely. Oh dear. The name looks familiar."

"Let's see. It should look familiar, it's The Head Coach of the local American Football Team. By jove, Martin certainly gets around."

Only one rather unforeseen, problem, so far kept quiet about, but with the size of their order qualified them for a new and fitted Conservatory, in American parlance, a greenhouse that you could sit in, attached to the side of a house, or thereabouts. And to which required an immediate answer. Who to send it to? So much for special offers. After a bit of head scratching came up with No 10 Downing Street, Manchester.

Americans in general having no clue as to Geography in their own country, and for overseas, even less. Even although there was a Manchester in the USA. Someone was in for one hell of a surprise.

However in the meantime, their master, Doug, had already spotted them, and sent over a bottle of Tequila, they not knowing that he had a 6th credit card.

Unfortunately, as the head waiter approached, "Excuse me Captain Harvey, but there is a telephone call for you, if you would mind coming with me, I'm told that it is urgent."

"Excuse me Christine," as he left.

Picking up the receiver, to be informed by his Second Engineer that the new lub oil purifier had arrived.

"Good, so why are you 'phoning me?"

"They won't let it out of the box, until either you or Mike sign for it."

"Okay, I'll be there as soon as I can, just make sure that you have all of the tools ready. We'll fit it tonight, and with a bit of luck, we'll be sailing sooner than we thought."

"Thank-you sir," as he replaced the receiver, "can you call me a cab, I have to leave, but your bill would be appreciated ASAP."

The shifty eye "as soon as possible." In response.

"Sorry darling, I need to leave, the part that we were waiting for has just arrived, and with a bit of luck, we can fit it tonight."

"Ah thank you" as the bill arrived, and over the cost of $135 was added a most generous tip, the previous owner of this credit card probably sometime in the future giving serious consideration as to his signature. Or as to how he lost it in the first place. The $1000 tip though being appreciated by the restaurant staff, although the hotel manager may having a bit of a headache, and deciding just what to do with the 20 lbs off Scottish Smoked Salmon arriving next day. And the other 80 lbs arriving for the next four days, and no-one having a clue as to where it came from.

The arriving lobsters though, more than filling the restaurants sea water fish tank, presenting another headache.

"Doug, when we get back on board, what are you going to do?"

"Change into a boiler suit, grab a few tools and if we can find anyone, fit this thing, test it, and all being well, we can get away by noon. I'm under a lot of pressure to get this gas tanker up and running."

"Can I help?" asked Christine.

"Not the way you are currently dressed. No."

To which they both arrived back at his ship, the taxi driver given a $100 dollar bill, and told to keep the change, as he ran back on board and shouting, "Martin, get your arse up here, I need you," heading for his office, and signing the delivery note.

"Right sec, fit it, I'll be down as soon as I change."

It not being noticed until about 20 minutes later, that one formerly attired beautiful woman was now in the engine room bilges, covered in oil and holding onto a ring spanner as the new lub oil purifier was secured in place, the impact spanners noise distracting all fitting it.

"Right, sec, test it."

"Eh, captain, before we do, do you think we could get Christine out of the bilge first."

The transformation from beautifully clad to now being downright dirty, not covered in The English Language as an adjective, as this gutsy German woman slithered out, pulled by 2 gracious Filipino's. The oil certainly assisting as she came through the narrow parts, but breathing out also helping.

Back in the ships office, and somewhat cleaner, as the rest of the ship's crew arrived back. At just before midnight.

"Christine, you are welcome to stay on board tonight, but I need you up and early, as I want to re-schedule our departure time to 1200."

"Okay everyone, head to bed, those of you not on watches. We sail tomorrow at 1200. And one of you, or maybe two, go and get Martin, and if there is any beer left, drink it between you, if needs be it to sober him up, then kick him into the dock, that much gas in this beer should keep him afloat."

Somehow, Christine had disappeared. So had Doug, a little later, well not completely as he took a little private time checking out his ship's bridge, which absolutely had to work perfectly, and as far as he could tell, was. The quiet whine of the radars not something that he had heard for nearly 5 weeks, but to an experienced master, sweet to the ears.

With the bridge in darkness, the floodlights giving an eerie glow was all about to change later as engine testing was one thing, but they were now going to take her out to sea, and start loading cargo, in of all places, Houston.

Sitting on the pilot chair, and enjoying the peace and quiet for almost an hour, mind lost in private thoughts, the bridge door opened quietly behind him, and just as quietly, closed. "Thought I'd lost you. Are you coming to bed?"

"Does your husband know that you are here Christine?"

"He does, and that you and I and the rest of the ships' officers are working through the night to get clearance for your ship."

"Well, a few hours rest might just help."

Not quite what Christine had in mind, as after leaving the duty 2nd mate, to pass on that the captain required a call at 0700, and he falling fast asleep as soon as his head met the pillow. Christine, now cuddling up to the one who she wanted to spend the rest of her life with.

Her beautiful clothes, not being sent to Mannheim, but stored away under her/his bunk. He just not knowing about this yet.

Time flies when you are both tired and asleep, but that damn telephone ringing, pulled Doug into the shower and 10 minutes later into his office, the steward having already poured his coffee.

"Right, first things first," to his officers, "Is everyone on board?"

"They are sir."

"Any hangovers?"

"None sir. When can we sail? We are all itching to go."

"Wind her up to go at 1200. We haven't used the mooring rope winches much, so start them at 1000, to let the oil warm up. In the meantime, do a stowaway search, make sure that all of the watertight doors are shut by 1130. We've got a load of kids coming for a look around, keep them out of the engine room, and make sure that they all leave. Okay?"

"Get to it then. Let's take this ship to the place where it belongs."

Christine arrived.

"All I need from you, as agents, is an outward clearance document."

"Romero is already on his way down with it," as she quietly closed the office door.

"Take this with you Doug," handing him a Jehovah's Witness Tract. "Read it, and you will always know that you are always in my heart." Kissing him lightly, with one finger over her lips, and leaving very quietly, but with a very dreadfully heavy heart.

It was not long before the door opened, and Mike came in, quietly. "She's gone Doug. Want to talk about it?"

"No Mike, let's just get this boat out to sea."

"The kids aren't coming, the harbour master put the kybosh on it."

"About the only useful thing he has done, since we came in here. Goodness knows how he is going to explain away his credit card account."

"Right Mike, I'll go up to the bridge, and bring forward again, our sailing time. You okay for main engine start."

"Any time you are."

"Ah good, Romero, I don't think that we missed anything."

"No Doug, nothing missed, here is your outward clearance. We're going to miss you, it has been one hellava lot of hard work with your ship, but at the same time, damn good fun. Have a safe voyage. I think I hear your tugs arriving."

"Thank-you my friend. Until we meet again."

Romero knowing that they would and not wishing to hurt Christine.

"Okay Mike, we go to stations, let's take this ship to sea."

"Good morning pilot, I trust that you have been informed as to why we need to take a few precautions after we come off the berth."

"That captain, I know all about, you don't look as tall as you do on TV."

The sly grin with up-turned eyes met with a similar response from the pilot, with a broad smile, as two seasoned mariners knew exactly what to do.

"Our main engine does not have a clutch, so if we can use the tugs to hold her alongside, while we get all of our mooring ropes in, then we can fire up the main engine, and after we turn around, then we'll be on Dead Slow for the first hour, and then increase according to this plan. Okay?"

"Perfectly captain."

"Right then, let's do it."

"Fore and aft," on his radio, "single up to springs."

The tugs in the meantime connected.

A few minutes passed as ropes were drawn aboard.

"Singled up captain," from both ends almost simultaneously.

"Let go everything, confirm when the propeller is clear."

Two minutes later.

"All clear aft captain."

"Blackie, start main engine. Pilot as soon as it fires we can go."

The ship, for the first time in nearly 5 weeks started to move and with tugs assistance was changed round to face the out of port way. Her main engine starting to make way, and when able to control her head, taking over from the tugs.

"Looking good captain, we'll let the tugs go I think."

"Certainly pilot."

"Fore and aft, let go the tugs."

Calling the engine room, "How does it look Mike?"

"All good so far, just ramp her up carefully. The load indicator lower than I expected, so try slow ahead now."

"Pilot, we are going to power her up now, ready?"

"I am sir." The telegraph indicating slow power, and the increase in vibration, initially as more fuel and air fed in, slowly reducing as the propeller caught up."

"We'll go to full ahead manoeuvring, when my Chief gives the word pilot."

"Captain this ship is a delight to handle. I've checked your compass, it is one degree low. Any help?"

Perfectly pilot.

As the 'phone went.

"Doug, everything is in balance, load indicator still low, take her up to full power manoeuvring when you are ready."

Confirmed with the pilot as 1000 horsepower more was gently fed in.

The little shudder slowly dying as the propeller caught up.

"Captain, we are showing 13 knots, at this speed we will need to slow down in 30 minutes for me to get off."

"Just long enough pilot, for you to sample the delights of my brilliant chef. Prawns, only how he does them in 7-UP and a secret sauce."

Only one was enough for the pilot to suggest Dead Slow Ahead, but told that there were enough for not only he, but the pilot boat crew as well. Along with the complimentary bottle of Scotch. Not many masters still doing this, but then this master was not usual.

A final wave as the pilot safely left, and "power her up boys, let's go to Houston."

"Francis, I'll send the ETA telexes after I've had a shower. I'll phone the managers after that."

"Mike, how is the main engine looking?" on the 'phone.

"Just coming up to full power now, but everything is in balance. I think that we are good to go.

"Okay, FAOP at 1530."

Which was fine until it got dark, when the ships main engine was shut down, in a hurry. The captain in his office not bothering going 4 flights up to the bridge, taking 1 down to the ME Control room, and told what was wrong, then legging it to the bridge, throwing Blackie a radio, and told, starboard anchor, 4 on deck, as Doug threw the auto-pilot over, taking the ship out of its lane as the main engine died underneath them.

"It never rains before it pours!" said drainfully to the 3rd mate.

"What the hell has gone wrong now?"

It didn't take long before the bridge 'phone rang.

"Captain, we've bent the push rods on number 4 cylinder. They were in the wrong way round."

"Do we have any spares?"

"We do sir."

"Then fit them, and start up that main engine ASAP."

"Blackie, forget about anchoring, head back aft."

On passage again, 30 minutes later, it only took from Mike to Doug, a look, suggesting that this was something to forget about.

"You'd think that the engine builders would know just what holes they were meant to go in, any damage to the camshaft?"

"No."

Being the only bit of good news.

"Houston is the last port that I would have wanted to load in, but the sooner we get 2000 tonnes of Butene 1 in, the sooner we can get away to Mexico."

"Are you expecting any problems Doug?"

"Many, and hopefully, for as long as no-one recognises me."

Twenty four hours later, no-one had as the ship slipped its ropes, and headed out to sea via Galveston, the general air on the bridge being mostly of relief, that they were leaving The US of A. Never a happy country to be in for a gas tanker master.

And a rather arrogant pilot leaving with just more than one of a problem. American pilots in the same groove as some European Pilots, in particular River Forth Pilots in Scotland, as not actually having a clue as to what they were doing. Many of whom had no experience in ship handling, but still called themselves captain.

"Right Blackie, he's away, wind her up, and let's go to Mexico."

"Mike," as the captain 'phoned the engine room, "pilots just gone, we are loading her up, FAOP about 1800."

"Roger that, I'll be up shortly, but it is all looking good so far."

"See you for a beer then after I send the sailing telexes."

A few little surprises awaited the captain though. He now had 3 more crew than he had when he arrived with in Houston, and didn't know it yet.

This is going to be rather difficult explaining away. Mostly as one came by the name of Christine, who he found sitting on his bunk as he went for a shower.

But the other 2 presenting an even bigger problem, as their Christian names just happened to be Celia, and Mario. That he wasn't going to even find out about till next morning.

Christine leaping off his bunk and falling into a tight embrace, kissing him very passionately.

Breaking her tight hug was met with a question, "Does your husband know that you are here Christine?"

Lips trembling and a small tear coming from one eye, replying with, "I told him that my mother was ill, and that I had to go back to Germany to look after her."

"Did he believe you?"

The failure of looking into his eyes, confirming not.

Gathering in this un-happy head to his chest, and kissing her hair, before saying, "so you have left not only your husband, but you have left your church as well. No going back now then is there?" The words being rhetorical, as the tears started to flow.

A few minutes passed as he gently wiped the tears away. "Only one thing for it then darling Christine, and I hope that you like ships, but you will be here with me for the next 4 months, and then, when we get back to Scotland, we can think about getting married, if you'll have me."

The gorgeous green eyes becoming radiant, and the voice replying with, "only if I get a better engagement ring than the one that you gave to Celia."

The broad smile confirmed it all, but still hiding a few important secrets that she had not told her future husband about. She wasn't actually married in the first place to her Australian husband. In fact, she wasn't married to at all, to anyone! Neither wonder that she had left The Jehovah's Witnesses' before they found out! Nothing worse.

But she was hiding something very important from her new future husband, and hoping like hell that he wouldn't find out about, which on a ship totally impossible, before the galley radio kicked in.

It only lasted till the next morning, before, "Captain", asked Julius, the cabin steward, "which cabins do you want me to put our new guests in?"

Having just emerged from a refreshing shower, and still not fully awake, although fully dressed on his way to the ships bridge, caught a little off guard by this question.

"Julius, Christine has already moved into my cabin. Can you not see the female touches that she has already brought?"

"Oh, captain, so you don't know about the other two yet?"

"Other two what, Julius? And don't piss me about, it has been a long and trying 3 days."

"We've got captain, two more stowaways."

"Did I not give an order that this ship was to be searched for stowaways before we left Houston?"

"Yes captain, you did, but somehow, these two were missed."

"Well where are they now?"

"Eh, sir, just outside your cabin door, shall I ask them to come in?"

"Just give me a minute to cool down, Julius do you know just how much hassle is involved with getting rid of stowaways? I suppose by now that we are too far offshore to chuck them overboard, so that they could swim ashore."

"Captain, will all due respect, I think that you already know who just one of them are."

The pair outside somewhat trembling and beginning to wonder if this was the right idea from the start. "It'll be okay, just relax, as it takes a hell of a lot to get Doug angry," said the male one, trying to placate the other.

The door curtain thrown aside by the master, in a slight bit of a temper, to be met with, "Hi Doug, remember me?"

You could have heard a pin drop.

"Mario?"

The smile broadening as two old pals met up again after some years. A handshake not enough as both embraced. "But Mario, where is Francesca?"

"Doug, she died, about 10 months ago. Breast cancer."

The sympathy between two old friends not requiring words, the empathy conveying enough sorrow.

The brief pause confirming that.

"No doubt you will tell me just why you have chosen to stowaway on a Norwegian Gas Tanker, while I get us both a coffee."

"Oh, I'm not a stowaway, think of me as more of a delivery boy coming for a change of scenery. Anyway, I was invited, by one of your crew, who also happens to be one of my cousins."

"Go on...........just what tell me what are you delivering?"

"Didn't he tell you, I even got an open return airline ticket on his credit card, well, maybe not his, but someone else's and which paid for the purchase and freight costs of what he asked me for."

"Go on Mario." With an air of wonder, not knowing what was coming next.

"Couldn't actually get all 150, had to settle for only 135, but they were a decent size and still alive. Or were when I delivered them."

"Which was?"

"The Wyndham Hotel in Corpus Christi, although the manager was, as you say in Scotland, 'a wee bitty slow.'"

"Julius, where is the second stowaway?"

"I'll just get her captain." Which was going to take a little time, seeing as she had vanished.

Christine now awake and in a dressing gown rather taken aback not expecting to be introduced to a Filipino male, and having to confess to him, that she was a stowaway as well. Only a more up-market stowaway, having stowed away in the ships' masters cabin.

"Well Doug, nothing seems to have changed much since we last met in Lisbon, you still have an eye for the girls. Just what do they find attractive in you?"

"I'd quit while you are still ahead Mario," as there came a gentle knock on the door.

"Come in," said a little too quickly.

The curtain tentatively drawn aside.

"Celia! What the hell are you doing here?"

"Now don't take this the wrong way Doug, but after your ship left Corpus Christi, I was at a loss for what to do, and my dad said that I needed a vacation, and I rather thought that if I could get on board your ship in Houston, that 3 weeks to Argentina, might just be what I needed."

The reply from the ship's master took a little time in coming, in much the same way as the one voicing it hoping that she did come over as, convincing.

"One stowaway, I could get away with, two, pushing it a bit, but three! And from **THREE** different countries! You are all going to have to become 'persona non grata' but with a little variation, as there is absolutely no way that I can tell the ship managers about this. Far less the P & I Club."

The delay as he thought about this.

"Celia, if you were to get off in Argentina, can you make your own travel arrangements back to The United States?"

"Off course, but I'd need an Argentinian entry visa first, so I could get out of Argentina."

"You just leave that to me Celia." An idea already formulating in his head.

"Mario, how long do you want to extend your free cruise for?"

"Well no pressing need for me to hurry back to Lisbon, and I'm willing to work my passage for as long as it takes."

"My friend you are going to be working your passage anyway, as will you Celia."

A strange look passed between Celia and Mario, before one offered "Will Christine also be working her passage?"

And answered with, "She will, as when she and I eventually leave will fly home to Scotland, whereupon she will become my wife."

"Julius," he hovering around in the background, told "Pilots cabin for Celia, Owners cabin for Mario, and you do not look after their cabins, they will do that themselves."

"When you've settled in Mario and Celia, join us for a beer or two, just before lunch."

"Now excuse me, I need to be on the bridge."

"Mario," said Celia, "what does he mean by 'working your passage?'" as the two left on their way to their designated cabins.

"It means Celia that we are going to have to do the same thing as his crew do, and I can assure you, it does not include lying on a sunbed in the sun, apart from mid-day, or a Sunday afternoon. I think you might say that we are both going to get rather dirty, and probably, very sweaty. But he is also, rather generous, when it comes to free beer, and hospitality."

Celia thinking, as she settled into her cabin, that this might just work out for her, a change as good as a rest.

A knock on her cabin door.

"The complements of the captain miss, a half case of beer and a half case of soft drinks."

Just a pity, that she didn't really like beer. Now Scotch perhaps?

"Alcohol of the bottled variety, after we sail from Coatzacoalcos, just be careful though, the captain got it cheap from a ship chandler in Houston, and I've sailed with this captain before, and when he gets something 'cheap', believe me, the word 'rot-gut' is pretty much how it starts off, until well watered down. He even used it to get rid of pirates once."

Celia, wondering at the mention of 'pirates' if stowawaying might not be such a good idea after all.

"How does he use it to get rid of pirates?" asked a concerned Celia.

"Its' a variation of a Molotov cocktail, only you want to be well out of the way when he makes them, but when one hits, usually destroys their boats. End of pirates see," and attempting to leave, but caught by the arm.

"What do you mean, a variation of a Molotov cocktail?"

"Well, I suppose you will find out anyway, just don't let on that I told you, okay Celia?"

Intrigue just heightened Celia's curiousity.

"The captain buys the cheapest alcohol, not to get the alcohol, but because it comes in the cheapest of bottles, which when he adds in his secret ingredient, makes them highly unstable."

"Okay Julius, just what is this 'secret ingredient'?

"Well if I told you it wouldn't be a secret would it?" Julius trying to get out through the door, but blocked by one rather curious Texan female, with the look that conveyed, 'either you tell me, or you are not going anywhere.'

As he gulped, and in a very quiet voice, "he uses liquid gas, which is why we have a few extra freezers lying around. You don't have to light them as you would with a normal Molotov cocktail. The engines on the pirate's boats do that. You should have seen the last one.........but realising that he had already said too much. Excuse me miss." Thankfully escaping.

Celia, now privately thinking that stowawaying may not have been such a bad idea after all.

A worrying hour passed for all 3 un-invited guests before assembling in the master's dayroom along with 3 senior officers, two of who had licentious thoughts towards one called Celia. And one crew member, unusually for a ship crewed by Filipino's and the odd Indian, well, odd being a sum total of four.

"Right, okay everyone," addressed Doug, "fun time on this voyage to Argentina will be after we sail from Coatzacoalcos, because when we arrive there tomorrow, will take us 2-3 days cooling the cargo tanks down. And officially, you 3 do not exist, so you are going to make me 6 more crew, quietly, and this will involve getting wet. The smug smile, not revealing anything,.....perhaps?

Lightning Source UK Ltd.
Milton Keynes UK
UKOW04f2017111214

242960UK00001B/62/P